Loot the Moon

Loot the Moon

Mark Arsenault

Minotaur Books ♏ New York

A THOMAS DUNNE BOOK FOR MINOTAUR BOOKS.
An imprint of St. Martin's Publishing Group.

LOOT THE MOON. Copyright © 2009 by Mark Arsenault. All rights reserved. For information, address St. Martin's Press, 175 Fifth Avenue, New York, N.Y. 10010.

www.thomasdunnebooks.com
www.minotaurbooks.com

Library of Congress Cataloging-in-Publication Data

Arsenault, Mark.
   Loot the moon / Mark Arsenault. — 1st ed.
        p. cm.
   "A Thomas Dunne book for Minotaur Books"—T.p. verso.
   ISBN 978-0-312-55576-4
   1. Judges—Crimes against—Fiction.   2. Murder—Investigation—
Fiction.   I. Title.
   PS3601.R75L66 2009
   813'.6—dc22

                                                        2009012736

First Edition: October 2009

10   9   8   7   6   5   4   3   2   1

For Patricia Arsenault,
my mother

Loot the Moon

one

Tobacco smoke and moonlight filled the car. Outside, the head-lamps painted a blur of green and tan onto whatever they touched in the forest as the old Lincoln raced through the gray night. From the backseat, Stu listened to the big V-8 gargling under the hood. He saw the slick of sweat on the driver's face as the young man hunched over the wheel, gasped and wheezed, and willed the lumbering car through the twists of an old country road. *The driver's as goddamn scared as me*, Stu thought. And the driver didn't have the gun at his head. Stu flinched at the casual tap, tap of the carjacker's pistol on the bump of bone at the base of Stu's skull. The dashboard clock said 1:30 a.m. The road through the woods followed the curves of a river. The trees were almost on the road. Stu would never forget those trees. White oak, six feet through their middles, older than the Constitution, stiffer than the hurricane of '38, unbending and unforgiving.

Stu's hands quivered in his lap. His palms stung with road burn, from falling when the gunman had dragged him out of the car. *Why did I stop? Never stop for strangers.* Even two strangers around his own age, midtwenties, hitching along a darkened road. They had looked in Stu's headlights like a pair of graduate students desperate for a ride to the university. They were desperate all right, each for a different reason. Stu tried to understand what was going on here. A kidnapping, maybe? The gunman had taken the other man hostage. He sighed; the breath left him in a shiver. *I've been carjacked.* Still hardly seemed real. He swallowed hard. Stu thought back ten minutes. What could he have done differently? He had not seen the gun until his transmission was in park and his window powered down. The pistol jammed into his face had touched Stu's upper lip. His legs had turned to liquid at the smell of black powder and gun oil under his nose. He could not have run if he'd tried. Still couldn't. The scent lingered.

In the backseat with Stu, the carjacker pulled the gun from Stu's skull for a moment, flicked a lighter, and fired up another cigarette. Stu chanced a glance at him. The lighter was turned down low, to make a flame no bigger than a kernel of glowing golden corn. He saw sharp features, a long pointed nose with a bump at the bridge, no more than a day's worth of whiskers. Wet eyes unblinking, big round pupils that shrank from the light. A dark smear of blood on his cheek, though he had no cut. *Not his blood?* Stu lost his nerve and looked away before the gunman met his gaze.

"A little faster," the gunman urged. He was calm. The gun returned to Stu's head. Tap, tap.

"I don't dare," the driver said, eyes never leaving the road. "This thing's a sled."

The driver had a thin voice, shaky. Stu was vaguely angry with him for just standing there by the side of the road and letting Stu stop for this madman. *He could have sent a warning*, Stu thought. Even with a pistol pressing against his ribs, he could have shouted. *Villain with a gun!* His sacrifice would have allowed Stu to escape—he'd be remembered as a hero. But instead he'd let Stu get stuffed into the backseat, allowed himself to be pushed into the front to drive. Now he complained about the goddamn car. From the middle of the backseat, the gunman on his right, Stu could see only a slice of the driver's face, skin and shadows in the moonlight, shining with terror. Stu suddenly felt a scrape of pity in his throat for the young man at the wheel, and then toxic guilt for blaming him—two more emotions to stir with disbelief and raw fright. He made a silent apology in his head to the driver. *My final thoughts must not be petty,* Stu decided. He surprised himself with this reasoning. Stu was a freelance musician for hire—brass mostly, the guitar in a pinch, drums in an emergency; he never thought himself a deep thinker. He concluded that all men are philosophers at their last breaths, and surprised himself again.

The night was clear, cold for the season. Stu stared through the untinted sunroof, to the stars. So many stars were visible from the woods of South County, far from the lights of Providence. He imagined the pinpricks were a handful of salt scattered across black velvet. There was no helicopter trailing them up there, no help anywhere. The car swept down a steep dip and Stu felt a cold whoosh in his belly. The driver worked the brake as the road turned hard right. Stu's trumpet case in the trunk tumbled over noisily. He resisted the force of the curve pushing him toward the carjacker. The driver worked the gas again, the V-8 snarled under the hood, and Stu let himself be gently pushed to the seat back. His window was cracked a half inch and the wind hissed though it. Stu leaned toward the door, felt the fall air.

"Where the hell are we going?" the driver asked.

The red dot at the end of the butt glowed brighter when the carjacker sucked the cigarette. He blew the smoke straight up toward the stars. He yawned. "Stay on this road a while yet," he said, speaking out of half his mouth while the other half clenched the butt. He gripped his chin and gazed out the back window to nothingness. As an afterthought, he added, "You're both free to go when I get where I need to be."

Stu's eyes widened. *Free to go?* He had dared not even dream it. He wiped the sweat off his forehead and eyebrows. The salt stung the bloody scrape on his hand. His face steamed hot, his body shook with chills.

The driver muttered, "You're a goddamn liar."

The carjacker said nothing, but he withdrew the gun from behind Stu's head and aimed it generally toward the front seat.

"You can't kill the *driver*," Stu croaked, shocked at hearing his own thoughts, not in his mind but with his ears. *Was that out loud?*

"Oh, fuck that," the driver said in disgust. His fists flexed on the steering wheel for a few seconds, clenching and unclenching. He spat into the dark space where a front passenger would sit. Rage rose in his voice. "You can't let me live. Not after what I seen."

"Drive the car," the carjacker said sharply. He shifted in his seat, cracked his window an inch, and stuffed the cigarette butt out.

"You can't," the driver said again, more to himself than to anyone else. "You couldn't take that chance." He pressed harder on the gas. The car revved to attention and sped faster into the night.

"Easy now," Stu said. His mouth was dry. He gripped the seat in front of him with one hand and felt for the seat belt with the other.

The old Lincoln barreled around a curve. The tires whimpered. With the road ahead straightening, the driver pounded the gas. The engine gorged on superpremium; the car's chunky chug-chug noise smoothed into a heavy purr. The big V-8 liked the speed. Trees zipped by on either side. The tires rumbled over bumps. *Where is that goddamn seat belt?*

"That's enough!" the carjacker shouted.

"Can't shoot me now," the driver called back.

"He said he'll let us go!" Stu yelled.

The carjacker leveled the gun at the driver's head. Sounding calm again, he said: "I will blow your skull open."

"Fuck you, you will," the driver said. "Kill me, kill yourself." He grimaced and tugged the wheel left and right, working the play out of it. "Throw the goddamn pistol in the front seat!"

The road suddenly bent left; the driver gasped, let off the gas, and yanked the wheel. Stu's body hit the door. The trumpet thudded back across the trunk. The engine took a breath. Then the driver punched the pedal again and the car roared. "The gun! Throw it in the front!"

The gunman barked, "Count of three—you're dead."

"No!" Stu cried.

"One!"

Hairpin turn to the right, out of the blackness. The driver cursed and banged the brake. The pads ground into the rotors. The hood dove down and the tires yelped. A white oak scraped alongside the car and plucked off the mirror.

"Jesus!" Stu heard himself shriek.

The Lincoln bounced off the road and careened over a hill. Dark shapes rushed at the car. The headlights bore down on the final white oak. The light played within the grooves of the bark and electrified the tree with flickering shadows. Stu instinctively reached over the seat for the wheel and added his wet scream to the chaos of voices in the car. The oak forgave them nothing, probably didn't drop a leaf. With a tremendous crunch, the car crumpled into the tree and spun off. The windshield shattered with a muffled pop and the forest twirled. The gunman rolled onto Stu, then Stu rolled on the gunman. The car tumbled with a deafening boom into a boulder and bounced off the earth. The lights went black. For a second there was silence, like a gasp between screams, and then the head-splitting noise of the Lincoln rolling over and over and ravaging itself against the ground.

two

The man who surprised Billy Povich at the dog track smelled like vegan bath oils—not tested on animals, probably not even tested at all—and a ripened human armpit. He was a modern-day hippie, who wore a linen business suit the color of wheat, and fake-leather shoes that reflected light in a melting rainbow, like in a petroleum spill. His gray ponytail had been lassoed by a strip of cotton shoelace; the whiskers of his white Santa Claus beard were kinked and stiff. He did not bother with a necktie. His shirt was open two buttons, to reveal a smooth shard of blue beach glass on a braided silver chain peeking through the whiskers.

He collapsed into the chair next to Billy as the handlers were leading the dogs out for the third race. "You won't return my calls," the man said, speaking up over the bleeps of electronic slot machines that sounded like a laser gun battle. Though a lawyer who defended the most violent and vicious and impoverished people in Rhode Island, he had been cursed with a flighty voice, like a nervous speaker in front of a crowd.

"You won't take a hint, Martin," Billy answered. He looked Martin over. "I see that your wife is still dressing you."

"I do not argue with the Keeper of the Nookie. How's your pop?"

Billy recoiled at the question. "Fine," he lied. He pressed his lips together, looked up from the racing form marked in yellow Hi-Liter in his lap, and subconsciously scanned for the most direct route to escape: down the rows of stadium seats that angled sharply to a two-story wall of glass, to the dirt dog track outside, the color of a clay pot, past the infield lawn dotted with regal concrete statues of anonymous greyhounds and sickly shrubs that never seemed to grow, to the hand-lettered tote board beyond the far straightaway. Beyond the tote board, in a wasteland of parking lot ten times bigger than it needed to be, Billy's white van waited like a lone houseboat on an asphalt lake.

Just looking around calmed Billy. He felt comfortable in his regular seat at the indoor grandstands, one chair in from the aisle, with unbroken views to twenty television screens showing simulcast races that brought out-of-state action to Rhode Island gamblers. He even found familiar comfort in the stench of the place: like a used ashtray moistened with glass cleaner. He hated only the noise, still new and unsettling—the electronic giggles of digital slot machines, a recent addition to Billy's beloved dog track.

"I'm here to talk to you," Martin said. He pulled a manila envelope from his inside coat pocket. "I need help."

Billy said nothing. He watched seven muzzled dogs, in numbered bibs, and their human handlers parade down the near straightaway, toward the gates. Dog number 3, a brindled male, pulled against his leash.

"Oh, Christ, look at that," Billy moaned.

"What?" said Martin. He squinted down to the track. "Holy shit, don't they feed them skinny pups?"

"That dog, number three—look how he's fighting to get to the gate."

"Maybe he has to pee," Martin offered. He crossed his legs.

"That dog's name is Runnin' for Bob," Billy said, a quick glance to his racing form. "He's going off at thirteen-to-one." Billy scraped fingernails over his chin stubble. "I remember that dog. Good on a muddy track, not much heart on a fast surface like today. But he looks like he came to run."

"Not your dog, I assume?"

Billy glanced to the nearest cashier—ten people in line. Too busy to lay a wager before the next race. He sighed. "You ever have a hunch arrive too late?" He tapped his Hi-Liter on the paper. "My dog in this race is Move Over Rover, at five-to-two odds."

"Which one? The one that looks like he needs a nap?"

"Rest now, run later," Billy said. He was never so sure he was about to lose. "I saw you on TV last week, during your big trial. Must have been the day of the verdict, because your client was being led off in handcuffs. You were trying to look suave. Your client looked put out."

"Put out? He drank a quart of Canadian whiskey and ran down a teenager—on the sidewalk! What did he expect would happen at trial?"

"Probably expected you to get him off."

Martin grumbled, "I went to law school, not magic school. There are no guarantees in my business. Sentencing is coming up. I'll be glad to be rid of that case." He uncrossed his legs and then recrossed them with the other leg on top. "What's with the goddamn racket in here?" he snapped. He frowned and looked over his shoulder at the rows of digital slot machines in formation like an invading robot army behind the grandstands. "Sounds like a Pac-Man tournament."

"Computers collect money faster than the greyhounds," Billy

said. "It's like a tax on people who don't understand statistical probabilities."

"You don't play the slots? I thought you played everything."

"A circuit board is pure randomness—immune to my hunches."

He turned to Martin. The lawyer's eyes had a dull sheen over them, squiggling red veins beneath it. This was not quite the Martin Smothers whom Billy had come to know. *Where's the righteous twinkle?* Martin was a slave to justice and the law, in that order. He was the kind of lawyer always ready to hike up his pants and pick a fistfight to defend some constitutional ideal that had fallen from favor. Billy knew of no other man who once had his ass kicked in an allnight diner after an argument over the Fourth Amendment.

He's wounded, Billy realized.

Two old men nearby began to holler at a televised race. They were retirees, both in tweed cabbie caps, buttoned-up sweaters measled with pills of yarn, and polyester slacks that draped at the crotch. They looked like most of the men at the track on a weekday afternoon. Billy watched them. Near the end of the televised race, both crumpled into their chairs, gutshot with the despair of losing. A lame puppy that didn't want to run at a track in upstate New York had destroyed their afternoon. Billy never liked betting on the televised races; he preferred the local dogs. Some gamblers thought nothing of watching the daily local races on TV too, rather than turning their heads to watch the dogs race live on the oval outside the windows.

The handlers on the track loaded the dogs into a row of concrete bunkers at the end of a straightaway. Billy always wondered what the dogs thought about inside the gates, in the dark minute before the race began. Were they nervous? Did they ever question why they ran themselves to exhaustion in chase of a rabbit on a rail that none of them had ever caught? Did they wonder how a rabbit could run so fast with no legs? Did they find their lives futile? Or were dogs just optimistic?

Martin snatched away Billy's racing program and glanced at it. "I like Sassy Lassie," he said. "At twenty-to-one." He offered his right hand.

Billy shook it. "You're on. One buck."

The bell rang, the gates flew open, the rabbit whirred ahead. Dogs shot from the gates, flinging a wake of dirt as they sprinted down the front straight.

"That's a rabbit?" Martin said disapprovingly. "Looks like a dog bone made of sheepskin."

Billy's dog, Move Over Rover, started slowly, and then tapered off.

Billy sighed and tore apart his betting slip before the race was half over. He let the pieces flutter to the floor. The dogs circled the track, then dashed one-half turn around again to the finish. Sassy Lassie pressed for the lead right to the end, and finished second to Runnin' for Bob.

"I knew it," Billy muttered. "As sure as my own name, I *knew* Runnin' for Bob could not lose that race. Goddamn late hunch." He pulled out his wallet.

"You really don't have to pay me," Martin said. He snickered and hiccuped at the same time.

Billy handed him a single. "Can't afford another legbreaker on my ass."

Martin took the dollar, sniffed it, smiled, and tucked the bill into his shirt pocket. He let the grin fade, gazed to the empty track, and said flatly, "You know that a friend of mine is dead." He stroked his beard, discovered crumbs in the whiskers, frowned and brushed them away. "Judge Harmony was my first law partner, back when I passed the bar."

"I thought Abe Lincoln was your first law partner." He gave Martin a sad smile.

"He came later," Martin said, grimly going along with the joke. "My original mentor was Gil Harmony."

"I wrote his obituary for the paper," Billy said.

"It was beautiful, so I figured it was you who did it. Did you do the obit for the kid who slaughtered him?"

"Murderers don't get obits when they're killed during the getaway."

"A quick death was too good for him," Martin growled. "We should have shut him in a concrete box for the rest of his life, with no hope, no contact with anyone, nothing except the very best medical care to make his sentence as long as possible."

Billy smiled and tried to lighten the mood. "I always thought you opposed the death penalty because you're a flower child."

"I oppose it for premeditated murderers because I've *seen* inside the prisons, an hour or two at a time, with my clients. It's like being locked in a gas station restroom, forever. States who poison their worst killers—or hang them, or shock them—are doing them a favor." Martin laid a hand on his shiny bare forehead, as if checking himself for a fever. The hand holding the envelope dropped slowly to his side, as if he were overacting a death scene on daytime television. Was he acting? The anger seemed real. Martin swallowed hard. His Adam's apple bounced in his throat.

"Martin," Billy began, "I don't know what you think you need from me—"

"The judge was shot just once," Martin said, interrupting. "Lawyers used to say Judge Harmony had an eye for when they were full of shit. Well, he was shot once through the eye." He paused a few seconds, and then added a stray thought. "His wife's name is June."

"I remember from the obituary."

"She's an old friend of mine too. I have a vague recollection of their wedding, but I used to like tequila back then, so that decade is hazy."

"Marty—"

"What I remember best is Gil's advice when I split our partnership. 'Marty,' he told me, 'you're a goddamn fool for leaving this firm.'" Martin laughed; a twinkle of life stirred in his eyes. He imitated his former partner in a lockjawed aristocrat's voice: "'Don't make the same mistakes I made—make *different* mistakes.'" Martin chuckled, gazed away, looked backward in time. "And though Gil was a crusty New England Yankee, as emotional as the average Vulcan, I could tell on the day I quit to join the public defender's office that he respected what I had done."

"So you're a vegan *and* a Trekkie," Billy said. "I'd guess you didn't date much."

"I'm a closet carnivore—don't ever tell my wife. And I prefer *Battlestar Galactica*."

"You certainly made your own mistakes."

Martin smiled. "My mistakes," he said, "are why Gil Harmony drove a custom BMW, and I drive a Ford Escort with two hundred thousand miles on it."

A gambler ten rows behind them barked profanity at televised dogs. Two crumpled betting slips sailed in high arcs, five seconds apart, far over Billy's head, as if the angry bettor were shelling the front of the room with mortar fire.

Billy inhaled deeply and meted the air out slowly. Lawyers around Rhode Island sarcastically referred to Martin Smothers as "the Saint." Now in private practice, he was the patron saint of hopeless causes, the Saint Jude of legal services. A few rare attorneys devoted their practices to people stuck on America's bottom rung; Martin's clients were lower than that—they were the ones under the heel of the ladder. Martin had helped Billy once, and few things bothered Billy as much as an IOU. Unpaid debts had led him into many face-to-fist confrontations with bookmakers. His nose itched. He traced a finger over the bump where his sniffer had been broken on three occasions by collectors.

Billy folded his arms. He knew he could not refuse Martin, but he tried to put up a fight: "Have I mentioned this isn't a great time for me to take another case with you?"

"I can't investigate this myself," Martin said. "I'm too close to it. Plus, I'm representing Gil's wife"—he paused, grimaced, smacked the envelope on his knee—"I mean his *widow*, in probate court, as a favor. Her son is still battered from the car crash. June needs my help. I want to be ready when they open Gil's will later this week."

"What's left to investigate?" Billy asked, still hoping to get out of the job. "The killer died in the crash."

"Naw, that's bullshit," Martin said, not angrily, merely as a point of information. From the envelope he pulled a five-by-seven photograph—a police mug shot enlarged to the point it had just started to become fuzzy.

The young guy in the picture looked lean and rugged. He was shirtless; the characters of a dark tattoo on his shoulder were too blurred to be legible. His triangular-shaped head pointed down through a sharp chin, to which clung a tuft of black goatee. His dark hair was long, unwashed, and stringy. He had obviously taken a beating: his nose and lip were swollen; the smear of a shiner glowered like a thumbprint under one eye.

"They say that the night this picture was taken, he had resisted arrest," Martin said.

The man's expression was grim and hollow in the picture, as if he had just witnessed something he'd prefer never to see again. Like maybe an extreme close-up of a police nightstick. Billy flipped over the picture. The name printed on the back read:

RACKERS, Adam A.

"The guy who shot the judge?" Billy asked.

Martin nodded, as if he didn't want to acknowledge the fact out loud. "That police mug was taken five years ago, after the cops grabbed Rackers in an electronics store, several hours after closing time. He was helping himself to a crate of iPods, and apparently never noticed that this store also sold silent alarms."

"So he was no genius."

"He pled out to robbery, did twenty months in medium security."

"Hmm—stiff time. Not a first offense, I assume."

Martin snorted with an ironic laugh. "His police record is longer than 'Freebird.'"

"The news reports on the shooting were sketchy. Do the cops know what happened to Judge Harmony?"

Martin looked away for a moment, as if organizing the narrative in his mind. He explained, "The judge and his son, Brock, were spending the weekend at the family beach house, a big clapboard McMansion on a salt pond in South County." He grinned. "I got invited there once, Gil barbecued two rabbits he and Brock had shot, and I thought my wife was going to divorce me—that woman won't eat animal *crackers*."

A crumpled betting slip bounced off Martin's scalp. He watched it land in the aisle, then continued as if nothing had happened.

"Two weeks before the shooting, Rackers had cased the place," Martin said. "A local cop ran his ID and warned him about loitering."

"This cop remembers Rackers? After that much time?"

"An ex-con with six B&Es on his record? Hanging around the pricey beach houses? Yeah, they remembered him. Rackers got into Gil's house through an unlocked window in the garage—his fingerprints were all over it. From there, he forced his way into a crawl space above the ceiling that led into the main house, between the rafters, above a little mudroom. The space he wiggled through is rough, unfinished, nails sticking out everywhere. He left a tiny wedge of his skin and a few hairs on the point of a tar-paper tack where he scraped over it."

"What was this supposed to be?" Billy asked. "A robbery?"

"If you agree with the police investigation."

"Would we be talking if you did?"

Martin ignored the question. He said, "The judge owned two dozen firearms, but they're all accounted for, so Rackers must have brought his own gun, a forty-caliber semi. Cops found it near the wrecked car in the woods, one shot discharged."

"Where was June Harmony?" Billy asked.

"Home—their condo on the East Side in Providence, a five-minute walk from superior court, where Gil sat on the bench. She had left the boys alone for a father-son weekend." He sighed and hunted for a bright side. "Though it's probably better that she wasn't there." He gave Billy a sad smile, not needing to explain any more. Then he rubbed the back of his own neck and seemed to lose energy, like a wind-up toy at the end of its spring. He closed his eyes and slumped. "I have an image in my head," he said, a hand waving lazily before his face, where this image might have hovered. "It's Gil. He's surprised in his study by a punk with a gun. I can see him slowly rise from behind his mahogany desk, like a thin column of steam. He sets a bookmark carefully into whatever law text he was studying for the classes he teaches, then tugs down the bottom of his suit vest, and thrusts his big chin toward the gunman. Gil would have called him a ruffian or maybe a scoundrel. In my vision, Gil knows he's about to die, yet *demands* to know at once, in the name of God and the Constitution, what is the meaning of *this*." Martin smiled, opened his eyes, looked off to the track. Billy said nothing. Martin turned to him and shrugged. "How do you fuckin' shoot a man like Gil Harmony in cold blood?"

Billy sat silently and felt the slow osmosis of hurt spreading from Martin's heart into his own. He could see why Martin loved the judge. Gil Harmony was a father figure to Martin; in his memory a flawless giant with brains, wisdom, and guts. Billy's thoughts drifted to his own father, sick and shrunken, betrayed by his kidneys, being poisoned by his own blood. *Rancid on the inside.* He shook the image from his head and brought his mind back to the moment.

"Here's another oddity for you," Martin said. "Three days before the police spotted Rackers casing the judge's beach house, somebody broke into the Harmony family's condo in Providence. A real Spiderman, came in through the balcony around two o'clock in the morning. Brock Harmony was staying there alone that night. According to the police report, Brock heard a noise, grabbed one of his old man's pistols from the gun locker, and ran into the hall. The intruder fled empty-handed."

"Good."

"But Brock couldn't identify him. He only saw his shadow."

"Do you think this break-in was a failed attempt to kill the judge?"

"Or a recon mission, to gather information for a strike in the future. It's a hell of a coincidence, ain't it?"

"Have you seen Brock?" Billy asked.

Martin pinched the bridge of his nose for a moment and grimaced as if the spot were tender. "Can't bear it yet," he said. "What would I say?" His eyes widened with dread. "The cops interviewed Brock in the emergency room after the crash. I saw their report. The night of the shooting, Brock was asleep upstairs. The bang of the gun woke him. He thought his old man might have fired the shot by accident, and he rushed down to see if Gil was all right. He ran into Rackers in the hall. That punk mumbled something about a wall safe, which I'm reliably told the beach house doesn't have. The Gil Harmony I knew kept his valuables in a bank. Except for June Harmony's diamond earrings, which were in plain sight in a jewelry dish in the dining room. Four carats total. Insured for a hundred and fifty thousand, and Rackers left them right where they were."

"Jesus, did Rackers take *anything*?"

"Just Brock," Martin said. "He marched the kid out at the point of a gun, through the woods, to the road. Rackers carjacked the first Good Samaritan to drive along, a kid named Stu Tracy, some small-time musician—a philosopher-poet, the type who writes lyrics so obscure nobody gets them. Brock doesn't remember the crash. The car rolled over nine times, all three were ejected. Rackers got the worst of it; he was pronounced dead at the scene.

"Stu Tracy is still in the hospital," Martin continued. "He's out of intensive care, and expected to make it. But he's rebuilt in stainless steel and needs three or four more surgeries to walk properly, as he gets stronger. This crash could cost him two years of his life, to heal and rehabilitate."

"And Brock?"

"Thrown clear of the wreck. Grade-two concussion, lost consciousness. Somewhere around sixty stitches all over. Nothing broken. He's lucky." Martin paused, then corrected himself. "Lucky that he lived, though now he has to bury his father."

The dogs blew out of the gates for the next race, heads bobbing in high-speed unison. "Ooo," Billy said, pointing. "I got half a nickel on this race. It's my lock of the day."

Billy watched his dog fight to break out from a box-in on the first turn. But his pup tangled legs with another dog and went down in a rolling heap as the pack ran on after the rabbit. Martin gasped. Billy stared, mouth open, saying nothing. His dog righted itself, paused, violently shook the dust from its speckled white coat, and then trotted, unhurried, the wrong way around the track. "That probably just cost me a year of my life," Billy said, finally.

Martin chuckled and stroked his beard. "How much is half a nickel?"

"Two hundred fifty." Billy said absentmindedly. His attention was on the picture of Rackers. The photo was no longer accurate, of course; Rackers was in the morgue. His hard-scrubbed, wind-burned face would have been blue in the freezer.

"I still don't see the point," Billy said. "It's a tragedy that the judge is gone, and a crime that Stu Tracy got mangled. But the killer is dead. Not much else we can do to him."

Martin leaned in close. The intensity in his eyes pushed Billy backward as surely as a hand against his chest. "The break-in at the judge's place was not a robbery that got out of hand," Martin said in a low voice. "This was an *execution*."

Billy looked away. "You got proof?"

Martin took the photo of Rackers and shook it gently in Billy's face. "This cretin left behind June's jewelry, the family silverware, the hundred bucks in Gil's wallet—all he did was shoot my friend. And think about Rackers's police record—no prior gun charges, not one! This guy didn't go from unarmed burglar to point-blank assassin by chance. Somebody *hired* him for the job, to exterminate the judge." He let the point sink in. Then he said, "Which means the killer, the one who really made it happen, is still free."

Yellow dots reflected from the ceiling lights swirled in Martin's eyes. Billy messaged his temples. *A theory built of one part conjecture and ten parts faith*. Reluctantly, he said, "It's a decent hunch, but, like I said, Marty, do you have any proof?"

The patron saint of hopeless causes broke into a wide smile. "More proof than you had that Runnin' for Bob would win that race."

Billy grinned. He had walked into that line. He said, "I'll fish around and see what I can find out. I'll do my best, but no guarantees."

"That's the line I give my clients."

three

The hospital smelled like disintegrating people and the chemicals invented to clean up after them. These were two odors, really, the primitive pong of unhealthy gases and flakes shed by bodies being cremated alive by disease, and the high-tech tang of cleaning compounds and lethal drugs prescribed to kill infection before the medicine poisoned the patient to death.

"I hate this place," the old man grumbled.

"It's keeping you alive," Billy replied.

"As I said . . ." The old man trailed off into mumbles. He melted, dejected, deeper into his wheelchair.

They passed a humming red Coke machine, the only color along a long bone white hallway lit by fluorescent ceiling tubes. Bo pointed and said, "I want a Sprite."

"Let's get Grandpa to his appointment first," said Billy. "Do you want me to push?"

"I'm driving," Bo said. He clutched harder on the pistol-gripped handles at the back of the wheelchair and pushed a little faster. He could barely see over the back of his grandfather's head. "Who's got Albert?"

The old man held up the kid's Albert Einstein action figure, a soft doll about fifteen inches long, in a tiny white lab coat, with a shock of white hair and a bushy mustache. "Al's riding up front with me," the old man said.

"He wants me to hold him," Bo said.

"What's that, Mr. Einstein?" The old man pressed the doll's face to his wrinkled ear. "He says it's all relative to him."

"Hardy-har," said Billy.

"Get the boy a Sprite," the old man said. "We got time."

"Once you're hooked up," Billy said.

No detours until you're hooked up.

The old man huffed. "You got time," he said. He touched a quivering hand to his temple. Then he turned his time-ravaged face to Billy. The old man's skin had a yellow tint, dotted with tiny blue bruises. He had not shaved in ten days and dry white whiskers lay flat along his cheeks like wheat stalks felled by a wind. His shoulders heaved and he said, "I'm tired."

"You'll nap in the chair," Billy said. He absentmindedly picked a cat hair off the old man's sweater and flicked it away. Then he met the old man's eyes; they were the same bright living blue as Bo's peepers. Billy wondered, *How could the old man and the boy, so near the opposite ends of life, have the same eyes?*

"You don't understand—I'm *tired*," the old man repeated.

Billy understood. He looked away and retreated to humor. "Push him a little faster, Bo, but don't crash him. There's a five-hundred-dollar deductible on the wheelchair."

"That's five hundred Sprites!" the boy cried.

Billy massaged his chest over his heart, rubbing a spot of soreness he imagined was there. Though William Povich Sr. had never said it aloud, Billy had come to understand that his father wanted to stop dialysis.

The old man was tired of being old.

A grotesque, involuntary smile spread over Billy's face.

Goddamn it . . .

He could not suppress the grin. The smile was a lifelong curse, he had come to think, which hijacked his lips whenever death made a near pass. Self-defense from deep within his psyche, he thought, a smile to ward off the cloaked figure of death should it come too close to Billy Povich. It first appeared after high school, when the girl voted most likely to succeed shot herself through the forehead three months into their college freshman year. He had poisoned the smile with vodka that night, in a cold autumn drizzle, around a smoky campfire made with gasoline and wet pine, with ten other teenagers feeling death for the first time. He had fought the smile again when his mother, who never smoked or touched a drink, silently handed Billy an X-ray with an egg-shaped shadow over the lung. She had not removed her necklace for the X-ray; the silver crucifix had glowed white over her heart. The smile appeared again last year, when the police sergeant had rung his bell, and Billy had padded downstairs in moth-bitten boxers and bare feet to find the man in a crisp blue uniform holding Bo's hand and speaking nonsense about a crash and a motherless little boy who would be moving in with his divorced father.

His fingers pulled the smile from his lips and pressed it out of existence.

They wheeled into a waiting room recently renovated to look like an insurance office, with beige floors and walls and a receptionist penned within a single office cube. Unlike the rest of the hospital, the waiting room smelled like new carpet.

Billy gave Bo a dollar for the soda machine. The kid grabbed Einstein and sprinted off for sugar.

A door opened and a young tech in a sea green hospital smock appeared, holding a clipboard and a tiny pencil that looked like he had taken it from a golf course. The tech was midtwenties, tall, with a five o'clock shadow over his shaved scalp, and an ear pierced with a big brass hoop, like a pirate. He brightened when he saw Billy and the old man. "Perfect timing, Mr. Povich," he gushed. "I'm Matthew. Do you remember me?"

Billy watched the old man's face sour. "Why wouldn't I remember?" the old man said. "I got bad blood—I wasn't hit on the head."

Checking his clipboard, the tech asked, "On a scale of one to five, with five being the best, how are you feeling today?"

"Shitty."

The tech didn't flinch. "Call it a one," he said merrily, scratching a note. "And again, on a scale of one to five, how have you been sleeping?"

"Shittily."

He frowned in sympathy. "A one—well, that's no good." He sighed dramatically and said to Billy, "Maybe the doctor will want to increase him to three treatments a week."

"I'm down here," the old man said. "Why are you talking to him? Did you get hit on the head or something?"

The tech took a half step backward. "Oh, Mr. Povich, it's just that—"

"Would you *like* to get hit on the head?"

"Pa," Billy said, cutting off the old man before he took on a six-footer one-third his age. To the tech, Billy nodded and mouthed, *We'll talk later.*

The contraption that cleaned the old man's blood reminded Billy of a robot from a 1950s science-fiction movie. The dialysis machine was boxy but roughly human-shaped, with a flat-screen monitor for a head, which showed statistics that meant something to the doctors, but nothing to Billy or the old man. Plastic tubes snaked through the robot's chest, and when these tubes surged with blood the machine took on a lifelike quality.

The old man had moved from the wheelchair to a medical lounge made of squishy memory foam; even Billy's father had to admit the chair was comfortable. The old man's left forearm, brown and spotted like an overdone chicken, lay flat on the armrest. The first needle, angling through his skin about midway on his forearm, took the blood out. The dirty blood passed through a skinny tube that lay across the old man's lap, and then flowed into the machine. There, it squeezed through the filters. The cleaned blood flowed the other way through another tube across his lap, and reentered his system through a second needle set just six inches from the first.

The room held six dialysis machines. They were all busy—always were. Billy noted that kidney disease did not discriminate, neither by class nor by race nor even by age; young people waited here, too, for their blood to be scrubbed. The patients read magazines, watched TV on screens at each station, napped, whispered into cell phones, stared at the sprinkler heads in the ceiling.

"I got two movies," Billy said, fanning the DVDs in his fingers like two-fifths of a poker hand. "The library was a little low on variety, but I found *Terminator 2: Judgment Day.*"

The old man squinted, as if into a bright light. His heavy black-framed eyeglasses magnified the disgust in his eyes. "Say who?" His bottom lip puffed out. "I wanted a relationship movie, like from the olden days."

"And that's exactly what this is. It's about the *relationship* between a boy and his mom and the robot sent backward in time to kill them." Billy frowned at the disc. "But I think this is the Spanish version."

"I don't know Spanish!" the old man cried.

"Okay—the dialogue is English," Billy said. "Only the subtitles are Spanish."

"I said I don't know Spanish!"

Bo chugged Sprite and then pulled the can away with an exaggerated, *Ahhhh!* "Let's watch the robot movie!" The boy had not been allowed to see sci-fi when his mother was alive; now he wanted to watch nothing else. For an instant Billy tried to recall the moment when his eight-year-old had graduated from love of dinosaurs to this obsession with robots and Albert Einstein, the world's greatest scientist; it seemed like some kind of boyhood milestone. Soldiers would be next, probably. *G.I. Joe with the kung fu grip.* Then the kid would fall for Marcia Brady.

"Any soft core?" the old man deadpanned.

"I got these at the library, Pa."

"That's why I asked for *soft.*" He dropped his head back and sighed hard at the ceiling, his thoughts someplace else.

"I also got *The Third Man*, an Orson Welles movie. He's from your era, Pa. It's about a guy who might be dead, might be alive. Seen it?"

The old man's blue eyes, the part of him that seemed the most alive, shot for a moment to the boy, then back to Billy. "I'm in that movie right now, Billy," he said. "I'm like the star, but I don't like the script." He grinned. Old age had inserted stripes of darkness between his teeth and turned a once perfect smile into a mockery of itself.

He wants to quit. He wants to die.

A bulge of fear squeezed down Billy's throat. He casually pinched his Adam's apple.

Bo held the soda can to his lips but did not drink. He watched them. It seemed the boy had caught the scent of some grown-up thoughts passing overhead.

Billy wanted to protect the boy. He would speak in code. Holding up the two movies but staring at his father, Billy said, "You have a decision to make. Not one you ought to make on impulse, or when you're feeling low. We should talk it out."

"Albert and I say the robot movie," Bo offered tentatively. He rubbed a hand through the jungle of golden cowlicks on his head, and then brushed Einstein's hair with a finger.

"Will you support what I choose?" the old man said. He glanced to Bo with a pained look—the old man wanted to protect the kid, too. "Or will you force me to . . . ah, ah . . . watch the movie that *you* want me to watch?"

Billy licked his dry lips. "This isn't something I can force, Pa."

"You can." The old man tilted his head slightly, almost imperceptibly, toward Bo. "By guilt and by pity."

They stared at each other.

The old man's right, Billy thought. He could force his father to stay on dialysis by using the old man's grandson against him. Just tell Bo: *Grandpa will die without his treatment*. The old man would suffer anything to stop the child's tears. By guilt and by pity, Billy could force his father to live.

"I can count to eight in Spanish," Bo said. He no longer sounded tentative. The adult conversation had grown too abstract for him, and he had given up on learning its meaning.

Billy glanced from his father to his son, noticing how alike they looked. Mostly in the striking blue eyes, serious and sad and with a mythical quality, like the eyes of a wizened old leprechaun.

"Okay, Bo, it's the robot movie." Billy poked the buttons of the DVD machine, slid the disc inside, and started the film on the twelve-inch screen.

The subtitle said: *Terminator 2: Día del Juicio.*

"I can't read Spanish!" the old man cried.

"Don't read it," Billy said. "Just listen to the dialogue in English."

"But the words will keep popping up when somebody says something! How do I not read them?"

"You can't read Spanish," Billy reminded him.

There was no answer to that. The old man wrinkled his brow and shoved his thick-framed glasses higher up his nose. The corners of his mouth drooped in defeat.

"I gotta run an errand on the other side of the building," Billy said. "You two keep an eye on each other, okay?"

The old man gathered himself and huffed. Billy expected a wise-crack. But William R. Povich Sr. just said in a hollow voice, "I'm tired, Billy."

"He hardly looks like our son," the woman said in a gasp. Her shoulders heaved and she cried into her hands, outside a hospital room. Billy looked her up and down. He noticed the cheap tin cross around her neck, her unpainted fingernails, the frayed laces of her white tennis shoes. She did not notice Billy, who was in plain sight but in something of a disguise. "Will he ever *see* again?" the woman cried. "Oh, goodness, Michael, will he ever *walk*?"

"Easy now," the man told her gently. "We can't *ever* let him see us this way. We need to keep his attitude positive. Don't scare him." The elevator button was already lit, but he jammed his thumb violently against it, as if to show the machine how urgently they needed to leave the trauma wing.

"He barely knew who we are," she said.

The man took her in his arms. "He's drugged," he told her, "for the pain." His voice was matter-of-fact, but Billy saw him press his eye to her shoulder for an instant, to crush his tear into her cotton shirt. "We'll know more when the swelling goes down, but the X-rays told them a lot, and they wouldn't have moved him from intensive care if he were in danger of . . ." He paused a moment to edit a grave thought, then said: "If he were in danger."

They were in their late forties, Billy guessed, judging by the lines in her face and the gray whiskers on his, though they could have been younger people who had not slept well in a long time. The elevator yawned open, then gobbled them up after they stepped inside. Their desperation for their son to survive clashed in Billy's mind with his old man's desire to die. He pushed the thoughts from his head and slipped into the room the couple had exited. The name on the door tag said: *Tracy, Stuart M.*

The room was dark but for a bleak white light, above a lump on the bed.

Jesus Christ, look at him!

four

Before he heard the door click shut, Stu had sensed he was not alone. He marveled at how quickly his other senses had sharpened to compensate for what he could not see. Just one week since the crash, five days since Stu had woken up. Could his senses have grown more acute so quickly? *The ability of my other senses must have always been there*, he thought. *I just didn't notice them.* Perhaps the subtler signals from his ears and his skin had for decades been squeezed to the edge of his bandwidth by the flood of information from the eyes. But now, as he lay blind, the weaker signals had a clear path to the processor. In his time of need, his ears and his skin were doggedly serving him, despite all those years he had failed to appreciate them. Such loyalty! He felt a warm column of pride in his chest for body parts that were so faithful.

Wow, I am so stoned!

"Mom? That you? Pop?" Stu's mouth would open just half an inch and made him sound like he was a hundred years old.

"Excuse me, Stu . . . uh," said a voice from the other side of the bandage over Stu's face.

"You a doctor?"

"No, no. I'm—are you okay to talk?"

"It only hurts when I exist." Stu smiled at his best line. That joke had cracked up the nurse with the cool, dry hands—Angela—the second-shift angel who smelled of Calvin Klein's Obsession. *Mmmmm.* Stu slid out of the moment, and smiled at the recollection of her scent . . . that time she had leaned over him. *She must rub the perfume on her neck. . . .*

"Stu? Stu?" The voice rang with agitation. Or was it worry?

"Sorry," Stu said, not really sorry at all. "I drifted."

"Not a problem, I understand," said the voice; it was a man's voice, low and a little nasally. A pleasant voice—clean, with no scratchiness or crackling. Stu had auditioned dozens of men for his band and could identify a great singer by the way he said hello. This voice speaking to him couldn't sing "Yankee Doodle." But this was a voice for fine speechmaking. The words came at Stu from a low angle, just above the bed. Was this man four feet tall?

"My name is Povich," the man said. "And I am, well, I guess I'm an investigator, for lack of a better term, working for the lawyer that represents Judge Harmony's estate, and I want to ask you a few questions."

A barrage of yellow fireworks exploded on the inside of Stu's eyelids. "They told me this was a private floor," Stu said. "Only family is allowed in here." His fingers felt for the call button that would bring the nurse.

The man who called himself Povich paused for a second. Stu heard his shirt ruffle and the cartilage click in his shoulders. *Amazing. I can hear a shrug!*

Povich said, "Sure the room's private, it just ain't impenetrable."

"You snuck here? How?"

"I'm using my old man's wheelchair right now. He had a stroke some years ago, and doesn't walk more than a few steps at a time. He's downstairs getting dialysis, so I borrowed his ride. Comfortable. Low miles. Handles like a dream. And I borrowed a white smock from the laundry room." He made a long sniffing noise. "Smells unwashed, so I hope whoever wore this last was here for something like a broken ankle, not the Ebola virus."

Stu laughed. He felt a stabbing in his ribs. He groaned, stiffened against the pain until it passed, and then chuckled. Not so bad. The laugh was worth it.

"You're an honest dude, Povich," Stu said.

"It's Billy."

"I think you're the first honest person that's come see me, Billy."

What had been worrying Stu was not the pain that raked him from the inside, like a trapped animal trying to bite its way out; it was the awkward distance he sensed from his parents and the hospital staff—an odd formality, as if nobody dared get too close, because Stu might not be here much longer. He sensed it in the pauses between his questions and his parents' answers. When he asked about his prognosis, he got encouragement in response. When he demanded answers, they gave him drugs. He could not *see* his parents exchanging glances but he could *feel* it. Their secrecy terrified him. *What is wrong with me?*

Stu said, "I know I've been hurt bad, but nobody will tell me how bad."

Povich paused a moment. "They don't want to worry you."

"Everybody says I'm gonna be fine, and they can't wait for when I get home and we play touch football in the snow this Thanksgiving, and all this happy horseshit. Nobody will tell me the truth."

He heard Povich smack his lips, then a light scrape as Povich passed a hand over the stubble on his chin. *So he's unshaven but doesn't wear a full beard.* Stu tried to picture him, but his imagination produced only a silhouette.

"What do you look like, Billy?" Stu asked.

"Huh? Me?"

"I can sorta tell when the lights are on or off in the room, but that's all I can see at the moment. My world is opaque, dirt-colored. I've been burned, battered. I hope to recover my sight, but who knows? How will my eyes work once the swelling goes down? For now, I have nothing to see but my imagination. Tell me—what do you look like?"

"Like a bodybuilding anchorman," Povich said, "but with a better tan." He chuckled. Stu grinned, as wide as his swollen lips would stretch. Povich confessed: "Actually, I'm a tall, skinny Polack, with a face full of triangles—nose, chin, the hairline around my cowlick." He laughed. "My teeth are real straight—too straight, maybe—because they aren't real."

"What happened to the real ones?"

"Punched down one storm drain or another, a tooth or two at a time, by the impatient men who collect overdue bills in this town."

"So you know hospitals."

"I got a bump on the bridge of my nose, right where it always breaks—there's another triangle for you, though more like a pyramid with round edges."

Stu moaned happily. He could *see* him, floating in front of Stu like a character projected onto a dark screen. There was no wheelchair in the image. As Stu stared at the man his imagination helped create, Povich's head sprouted a tall, pointed magician's hat, blue and covered with yellow stars. "Man, I don't like being so wasted," Stu said, more to himself than to Povich.

"It's for the pain," Povich said. "You must have a lot of it."

"Billy, you have to help me. Tell me, how do *I* look?"

A pause. "Well, shitty."

Stu laughed until the pain shocked him like two hundred volts, seizing his body for a few seconds of torture, and then dropping him limp. *Okay, that time the laugh wasn't quite worth it.*

"Your face is bandaged with white gauze, stained pink a couple places," Povich said. "The skin that I can see is swollen, raked with scabs and scratches. Your arm is hooked to an IV hanging on a silver hook. It's dripping a liquid the color of chamomile tea into you."

"Is that decaf?"

"Probably would be, if it was actually tea. Jeez, you *are* wasted." Povich chuckled. "Both your legs are encased in soft casts; the left cast is more complicated and rugged than the right. Makes sense—the police report I've read said you nearly lost your left leg. It broke a couple places, apparently, when you got thrown from the wreck."

Povich paused, breathed deep, and Stu thought he could also hear the wet click of his eyeballs turning in their sockets, but that *had* to be the drugs. Povich said, "There's a sheet over your midsection that I don't dare lift, with some tubes coming out from under there. And there's, ah—hmm, a bag of urine hanging from under the bed."

"Got it," Stu interrupted. He couldn't believe nobody had told him he'd nearly lost a leg.

"I know you had internal injuries, spent nearly a week in critical," Billy continued. "I heard you're going to need a few more operations on that left leg. You're supposed to make it. But when you fly, the metal detector at the airport will ring like a slot machine."

Stu glimpsed his near future—first a wheelchair, then crutches, then a cane, then just a limp. Sorrow poured over him, but then poured off just as quickly, like a bucket of water over some rainproof fabric. He was too doped to be morbid, and he embraced the feeling of well-being the drugs created. Fake, but useful. He took a silent minute to shove the thoughts about his future into a heap in some back corner of his mind. He would sort through that pile later. "Thank you," he croaked, "for the truth."

"The truth sucks," Povich said, in what sounded like an apology.

"Truth is a relief," Stu said. "Sometimes when I can't decide if I'm asleep or awake, I wonder if I'm already dead."

"What happened in that car?"

Stu told him about the gunman and his prisoner at the side of the road, about the pistol in his face, the slalom down the old country road at seventy miles per hour in a car built for Sunday drives and backseat necking at the drive-in.

"Do you remember the crash?"

"I can't know if this is a memory or a dream," Stu admitted, "but I'll tell you."

Stu listened to the voices. Were they real? He struggled against sleep and opened his eyes. Through a blur, like through a smear of grease on glass, he saw tree trunks, looking like gray scratches on the black night. A trickle of cold water ran over his left arm. He was on his back. His whole left side was soaked. He wondered, embarrassed: *Have I pissed myself?* He listened to the gurgle of a tiny spring and realized he was on the ground. The earth beneath him was soft and smelled mossy. He was on a bed of pine needles. *This would be a good place to camp,* he thought. He listened for the voices. Somebody moaned. Footsteps shuffled through the underbrush. Stu's breathing was shallow. He balled his hands into loose fists and wiggled his right foot. The left foot ignored him. What he felt was not pain, exactly, but a stunned detachment from the broken parts of himself. He understood that his mind had erected a dam to delay the flood of pain that would drown him if he felt it all at once. He was hurt deep inside his belly—that much, he knew. He was hurt in places only a doctor could reach. He tried to lift his head, but it weighed too much. He could not save himself; he would have to wait for help.

He inhaled deeply and smelled the car. His nose wrinkled at the stench of gasoline, burnt rubber, and the sickening fumes of smoldering vinyl and foam. There was a spicy metallic odor, too, he could not place at first, until he felt the hot rivulet down the side of his nose and realized he could smell his own blood.

He thought about his parents and felt a pressing sadness. They had decided twenty-five years ago to invest all their love in just one child, and now were too old to have another.

Someone moaned again. Stu thought about calling out but decided to save his strength. The moan had come from atop a steep embankment that began at Stu's feet. He could make out the dark scrape on the hillside where his sliding body had gouged the forest floor. The underbrush crackled. Stu's field of vision steadily narrowed as the flesh near his eyes swelled around his injuries.

With a hollow roar, a sudden explosion upon the hill flung yellow light against the trees. A fireball spun skyward in the shape of an unraveling question mark, and then burned out, leaving a thousand tiny orange fireflies where the flame had singed the pine trees. Stu waited to feel the heat of the explosion on his face. He felt just the coolness of the air beneath the hill, and was disappointed. He watched the fireflies die out to black. He listened to the fire excitedly explore the innards of his old Lincoln. The car had been his grandfather's. His grandfather had been a spiteful eccentric, and Stu had not cried when he had died. He cried for the old bastard now.

five

The men hitting Kit were not sexists. No, they beat her as hard as they would any man. Kit saw the blow coming and clenched her stomach muscles. *Whump!* The fist popped off her flat abdomen. She ground her teeth and tried to stay silent to deny them the satisfaction of her pain, but she could not help releasing a low grunt and a puff of air.

Just a bruise, she thought. *Nothing more.* The two men holding her arms snickered.

Anonymous dance music vibrated through the walls and filled the narrow hallway where the three goons had caught her trying to sneak into the nightclub. They could have had her arrested for breaking and entering. The law citation flashed into Kit's mind.

Title 11, Chapter 8-5.1. Unlawful breaking and entering of a business place.

The monetary fine for B and E was three hundred dollars, which seemed light compared to the possible jail time—three years. Had they called the cops after they had grabbed her, Kit would have argued she didn't *break*, she had just *entered* through an unlocked back door.

Maybe she could have pleaded down to trespassing. Not that it mattered; her captors had decided that the police, the lawyers, the judge, jury, and the media would only get in the way of punching her.

"Hey, Robbie," said the hulk holding Kit's left arm. "That's your best?" He laughed. He had sharp fingernails for a guy, and they bit into her bicep. His long goatee, dyed pure white, brushed her shoulder. "I'd let her go, but I'm afraid she'd kick your ass." He squeezed her arm. "She's been in the gym."

The hulk on her other arm leaned close to Kit. His eyes were dazzling green, the eyes of a movie star or a fairy-tale prince. He smelled like cigars and Old Spice. "You got any skirts our friend Robbie can borrow?" he deadpanned.

"What are you, Rob?" the first hulk asked. "About a size eight?"

The guy throwing the punches was Kit's height, five foot five, and by far the smallest of the three thugs. He dressed in a black turtleneck and a Charlie Chaplin derby hat made of shiny felt, with a rolled brim and a red silk band. He wore sunglasses, indoors, despite the late hour and the dim light of the hallway. The glasses looked like something a poker player would wear to hide his eyes: two round, shimmering, rainbow-colored discs in an invisible nylon frame. Though slim in the waist, his shoulders were mushy and he seemed pitiably out of shape—after just three punches his colorless skin, peppered with freckles, glistened wet, and he pretended not to pant.

He had confined his blows to her midsection. Probably to avoid making marks a prosecutor could examine, she figured. *They won't kill me, not tonight.* They intended only to knock her about. The revelation gave her new confidence, which burned in her chest like a hot shot of whiskey. *I can handle this.* She stared at Robbie, the little man in the silly derby, who looked more exhausted for hitting her than Kit did for taking it.

Kit sucked a deep breath and said in a hard whisper, "He's no bigger than a size six."

The two hulks shook with giggles. Robbie's lip peeled up in a snaggletoothed sneer. He drew back his arm as if to slap her face. She flinched and turned away. He did not slap her. Instead, he suddenly rocked back and plunged another uppercut into Kit's stomach. *Whump!* She had not had time to fully tighten her muscles, and the punch wobbled her. She gasped, and was thankful for the hulks holding her arms; if not for them, she would have gone down. She'd rather have taken five ounces of speeding lead behind her ear than let Robbie see her go down.

It's just pain, she reminded herself as she grimaced against the void in her lungs and waited for the air to return. She remembered the runner's proverb, the code for her life etched with a knife into her headboard: *Pain is weakness leaving your body.* She spoke the code out loud every night before she slept. The code had helped her, now at age thirty-three, through twenty marathons and six triathlons. Robbie's jab could inflict no pain worse than what Kit regularly inflicted on herself, in training. She thought about the interval workout she had run two weeks before: up a one-mile dry ski slope in New Hampshire, a double black diamond cluttered with boulders, downed trees, and winter wheat. She had run until her legs could no longer support her weight. After she had collapsed on the mountain, she dry-heaved until she thought she might squeeze out her spleen or gallbladder, or maybe something important she might need in a race.

For a runner, Kit's legs were a little short of ideal, her hips a little wider than Olympic proportions. Slightly bowlegged, with high arches and a choppy running gait that no film study had ever fixed, she had never beaten a professional marathoner. That was all right with her; she could not control genetics, and was content to condition herself to within a whisker of her theoretical maximum. She had never lost a race to another amateur.

She wheezed a half breath.

Whump!

Pain is weakness leaving my body.

For a shrimp, this guy was whacking a lot of weakness out of her.

The dance club racket bled continuously through the walls of buckling plaster. One song blended into another, mixed by a skilled DJ who knew how to keep a crowd of ravers on their feet. The walls of the hallway were covered with a high-gloss cream paint. The floor had long ago been painted red, though thousands of footsteps had worn a path down the middle to the tan floorboards. At the far end of the hall, the outside door was closed, to not invite attention to Robbie's Tae Bo workout. One screw-in fluorescent bulb, curled like a pig's tail, hung from the ceiling. The exit sign above the door was dark. Hmm, a burned-out bulb in the exit sign. *That's a fire code violation*, Kit thought. *Section 23-28.* Somebody needed to write these guys up.

Kit coughed, spat on the floor, and stole a deep breath. One hulk held up his hand to freeze Robbie in place. "Let's see if that was enough," he said. To Kit, he asked: "Want to tell us why you were snooping around back here?" He chuckled. "Don't want to pay the cover charge?"

"I told you . . . gentlemen," she said, her voice sounding scratchy in her own ears, "I'm here . . . to speak to Mr. Glanz."

Robbie suddenly stuck a finger in her face and blurted, "People make appointments to see Mr. Glanz!"

These were the first words she had heard him speak. The outburst, and the thin voice, as colorless as the lines of sweat running down his face, surprised her. The two hulks smiled at each other, sharing some inside joke at Robbie's expense. Kit didn't know which thug to address. "I tried making an appointment," she said. "He won't return my calls."

"That," one hulk said, "would be known as a hint." He nodded to Robbie.

The little man reared back and aimed a punch at Kit's abdominals. She tightened in time. The blow bounced off with little more force than a slap. Robbie was too tired to put much behind it. He shook his hand at the wrist. Her breath had quickly returned.

"So what's so important," said the second hulk, "that you gotta interrupt Mr. Glanz while he's ignoring you?"

Robbie pointed at her again and shouted, "What you wanna see him for?"

"I'm here to talk about Judge Harmony."

Robbie reared back to hit her again, but the first hulk, the talkative one, waved him off. He stroked his silky blond beard in silence for a few seconds. Their grip on her arms slackened, and it was clear the beating was over. "So who are you?" he asked. "You're too young to be the wife."

"Maybe the judge's *comatta*?" the other hulk said.

Kit wrenched her arms and they let her go. "I'm not his mistress," she growled, with a moment's glare for each of them. "I was his law clerk."

Robbie's lips slowly rolled in on each other, until his mouth was just a colorless slice across his face. He cried suddenly, "That judge put my brother away for life!"

"Easy, Rob," said hulk number one.

His brother? Kit could hardly believe it. So this *pipsqueak* was the younger son of David "Rhubarb" Glanz?

This was nepotism at its worst—she had been pummeled by the runt son of a mobbed-up nightclub owner who obviously wasn't *qualified* to be a backstage hooligan. Robbie clutched his sore wrist and panted like a racehorse. If this were a state job, he'd probably file for disability. No wonder the two hulks, the real muscle, despised him. Kit clenched her right fist and fantasized about driving Robbie's teeth down his throat. Her breathing was still shallow and her abdomen was sore. There wouldn't be much power in the blow, and it would be a shame to be stomped or killed over one mush punch.

Someday, Robbie, she swore.

The four of them stood there in the hall for an uncomfortable moment. There seemed nothing more to say. They were all aware of the criminal conviction of David Glanz Jr., Robbie's brother, on two counts of manslaughter, and of Judge Harmony's harsh sentence. Nobody had expected the judge to hand down the maximum—thirty years for each count, to be served *consecutively*—but, as the judge had told Kit, he had seen enough of the son that reminded him of the father, and he put junior away.

They were all aware, too, of Rhubarb's threat to get even with the law, and with Gil Harmony.

"A shame what happened to the judge," said the second hulk, his voice flat. "Killed by a trespasser. That happens sometimes." He stepped closer to Kit, almost touching. She held her ground. He looked straight down at her. Softly, he warned, "Most of the time, it's the trespasser who gets killed."

His gentle smile mocked her. The beauty in his green eyes unnerved Kit. Those were the devil's eyes, she thought, the perfect eyes of a fallen angel. She was suddenly frightened by what the beauty had hidden from her—for the first time that evening, she realized she had blundered close to her own funeral in trying to force her way to see Rhubarb Glanz.

Fear attacked her body with electrified jaws; its low-voltage bite shocked her all over.

six

The rattling of boots up a chain-link fence in the middle of the night was like white noise in this hardscrabble neighborhood of three- and four-decker apartment buildings. People scaled fences all night around here, and nobody with any street sense ever gave them trouble for it. Citizens minded their own business, out of fear or indifference.

He climbed the eight-foot fence where it met the wall of the apartment building, beneath the front porch. With a foot atop the fence, he could reach the porch roof.

The slanted roof looked like a raft pitched to starboard in a rolling sea of blackness. The shingles were dry and rough and they shed a tiny avalanche of grit into the tin gutter when he climbed onto the roof. The shades were down in the second-floor windows; not that it mattered much in such darkness, with no working streetlight for two hundred yards.

He lay on his back on the roof and rested. The night was clear. A few stars hung dimly over a cloud of light pollution from the city. A distant car alarm sounded. He watched the stars for a few minutes because he thought it especially important to appreciate whatever small beauty he might find on a night such as this.

Then he climbed the fire escape. The iron rails smeared rust on the palms of his tight rubber kitchen gloves. He stopped at the third-floor landing, a narrow metal grate cluttered with clay pots sprouting greens. He passed his nose over the pots and smelled rosemary, overpowering the other garden herbs. The landing was just below a window looking into a small bedroom. Deeper inside the apartment, a light had been left on. He could see the unmade twin-sized bed, and clothing strewn about. His putty knife wiggled easily in the crack above the jamb. The old-fashioned window, counterweighted on a rope and pulley system inside the wall, slid open almost by itself, and he slipped inside, onto the worn-out mattress that squeaked and sank under his weight. The room smelled of dirty laundry and cigarettes. Twisted butts filled a glass ashtray on a pine dresser, next to a digital clock that glowed red—1:07 a.m. The two dots between the one and the zero pulsed to tick off the seconds. He lost himself in the pulse, until the clock flashed 1:08 and knocked him from his trance.

The narrow closet had no door; that was no place to hide.

Instinctively, his hand went to his belt to feel the pick. The ice pick was a rounded steel shank, ten inches long, with a point on one end and a wooden handle on the other. The handle was grooved with four indentations for fingers, and he liked the shape of it in his hand. The antique tool came from an era before refrigeration, when the iceman sold blocks packed in sawdust from the back of a truck, and customers who forgot to empty the drip pan under the icebox had to mop their floors.

The tool's handle had not been oiled in a generation; the wood was dry and splintering, but the pick's hardened metal tip had recently been sharpened to a vicious needle.

The hallway to the kitchen was some ten feet wide, and it served as a living room in the efficiency apartment. A plaid fabric sofa had been pushed against the left-hand wall, next to a decorative wooden footlocker dressed up with black iron bands and lumpy round rivets to make it look like a treasure chest. Three pairs of jeans, a half dozen T-shirts, and a pair of sneakers had been neatly stacked on the footlocker. The light in the hall came from a compact bathroom on the right-hand side, opposite the sofa.

He walked past the bathroom, to the kitchen.

Jesus Christ!

Standing alone in the dark by the window, a man.

He grabbed for the pick, a flush of adrenaline momentarily blackening his vision. He fumbled for the weapon . . . it slipped from his hand and knocked on the floor. He dove after it.

Wait a second . . .

Why hasn't he yelled for help?

What the . . . ?

"Oh," he said aloud, then snorted in ironic laughter and pushed himself to his feet.

Just a department store mannequin, that's all. Not even realistic, either—a boyish waif with shiny sand-colored skin, a molded plastic hairdo, and a stiff pose, like a teenager with a bad back waiting for the bus. The figure had been dressed in tan chinos and a white polo shirt with the collar turned up and the price tag dangling from the sleeve. The right arm had apparently once broken off near the shoulder; it was crudely bandaged with blue painter's tape.

Feeling his heart slow, and as leftover adrenaline tickled his bowels, he looked around the rest of the kitchen. The room was small and crowded: a white refrigerator and electric range side by side; a giant first-generation microwave consuming most of the counter space; a deep porcelain sink half filled with gray water, dirty cereal bowls, and stainless tableware. A round butcher-block table and a single white farm chair had been shoved in the corner, in front of the only window, next to the mannequin. The apartment door was beside the refrigerator. His mind pictured the sweep of the door. No, he decided, there was not enough room to stand behind it when it opened.

He tried the bathroom.

What a tiny space! To the right, a cheap wood-grained vanity held a small oval sink. On the vanity, a toothbrush stood in a pint glass with crud in its bottom, next to a new cake of soap with the word *Ivory* still legible on it.

There was no medicine cabinet, just a mirror on the wall, about two feet wide and three high, speckled with toothpaste spatter, and streaked from where a hand had once wiped it clean of fog.

Opposite the mirror and sink, a night blue shower curtain decorated with twinkly gold stars stretched on a rod across a shower stall.

The toilet was tucked in the corner next to the shower, a stack of ten wrinkled magazines piled on the tank. The top one was *American Cycle*. The ceiling was barely seven feet; his head felt heat from the bright halogen light fixture, which must have been left on for hours.

He pushed past the shower curtain and stepped into the stall, letting the curtain close behind him. The bottom of the stall was wet. A clump of brown hair had settled with soap scum over the drain. Streaks from a drippy showerhead had stained the wall. The space was no bigger than a coffin. An uncomfortable pressure built inside his head, filling his sinuses with a sense of fear just short of tangible, like a heavy, odorless gas that was slowly suffocating him.

The shower was the best place to hide. He wiped his nose on the back of his rubber glove.

In an hour, he reminded himself, he would be done here.

But first, practice. He took a dry run in slow motion. The right hand drew the pick from his belt, left hand reached across his body to sweep the curtain aside. His weight shifted nimbly from back foot to front.

One quick upstroke . . .

He burst from the stall, saw himself in the mirror, and froze.

Such a familiar face, warped by tension that pulled his mouth into a grimace and bunched the flesh at the hinges of his jaw, as if he had the mumps. How odd to see that face, so ordinary to him, in this strange apartment. He felt like he was looking at something other than his own reflection. Like he was looking at a bad twin, an ugly copy of himself.

Time seemed to stretch, until the reflection seemed more like a snapshot from long ago, on some forgotten night when his ugly twin had done something terrible. His eyes went to the ice pick in the mirror, and he gasped. The sight of the pick attached to his hand—the tool meant to puncture another man's lung—knocked the breath from him. He stood there, as still as a picture, and watched shiny sweat gather on his forehead and the bumps of his cheekbones. Some odd compulsion drove him from the bathroom.

There must be another place to hide.

He leaned against the wall in the hall and pinched the bridge of his nose. With that goddamn mirror, he'd have to watch himself do it, like seeing real-time video of his darkest thoughts. He must not watch himself. Sticking a man between two ribs was something he would *do*, but it was not who he *was*.

Seeing the act would make it too real.

Of course he knew intellectually that the distinction was crazy— if murder you do, a murderer you are, and forever—but he had struck a mental barrier he could not cross.

He fought an irrational fear that his reflection would be able to identify him as the killer.

Or that *he* would identify *it*.

He stalked the apartment, the gleaming steel pick in his hand. Behind the sofa? Inside a closet with no door? No, there was no place else to hide. No goddamn place. The clock had raced to 1:23. There was not much time.

He ran to the kitchen, rummaged through the cabinets beneath the sink, and found a dark plastic grocery bag, the name of a super-market on the side. In a nearby drawer, he found scissors and clear plastic tape.

He cut one thin, horizontal rectangle from the bag for his eyes, then a single vertical slit for air. He pulled the bag over his head, wound the tape three times around his neck to secure the hood, and then left the kitchen as he had found it.

Back in the shower, he peeked from behind the curtain, saw some unknown killer in a mask, and was calm.

The fleet feet of the bartender everybody called Scratch had extra bounce that night. He felt like dancing down the streetscape like Gene Kelly in Adidas racing flats. He hummed "Singin' in the Rain." With seventy-two dollars of tax-free tips in his pocket, and carrying two bags of stolen treasure from the mall, the part-time bartender/part-time crook had enjoyed a profitable day. He felt like a superhero, except in reverse. Scratch's secret identity was his night job, as the mild-mannered mixer of watered-down highballs in a dive bar in the Jewelry District. During the day, he was Shoplifter Man, faster than a speeding mall cop, who could boost a seersucker suit right off your back and leave you nothing but the wrinkles. He tapped a few happy dance steps on the concrete, hummed louder, and added silent lyrics in his thoughts.

> *I'm singing in my brain*
> *Just singin' in my brain*
> *Da'doo da'doo da'doo-do*
> *Gonna buy me some champagne*

Scratch's apartment building was a wooden triple-decker in a renters' neighborhood that was noisy 24/7 with car alarms and police sirens, fireworks and occasional gunshots, roaring engines from un-sanctioned drag races, and heavy metal and rap music pounding from car stereos worth more than the cars.

The buildings were similar old Victorians, packed as tight as teeth. On either side of Scratch's place, vacant lots of knee-high weeds cut two gaps in the smile. For a hundred years, a twelve-room Victorian had occupied the space on the left, and it took twenty years of neglect from absentee landlords, and two weeks of attention from a grumbling bulldozer, to clear the lot.

A budding arsonist had flattened the house on the other side in barely half an hour. Beginner's luck, the insurance guy had said.

What you saw when you walked or drove the neighborhood depended on your perspective. If you were financially comfortable and *just selfish enough* to feel guilty around poverty, well, you'd see the gang graffiti and the broken windows and the greasy stray dogs trotting in packs and leaving shits on the sidewalks that would stay there until the next thunderstorm. Someone more like Scratch, a lover of cheap rent and anonymity who chose to live here, saw different touchstones around the neighborhood. He noticed the hopscotch boxes drawn in chalk. He saw the six-year-olds fluent in two languages, who translated effortlessly for parents who didn't know ten words of English. And he noticed the circular economy of immigrant markets selling food from the old country to homesick adventurers experimenting with the American dream. He would not steal from those kind of people . . . well, unless they were dumb enough to leave their doors unlocked. He was as sentimental as anybody, but a man's gotta eat, and if you left your cash drawer open or your payroll lying around willy-nilly, you got what you deserved.

The neighborhood ruthlessly punished fools.

He bounced up four concrete steps with tiny seashells embedded in them, and let himself into his building. The vestibule had four mail slots, though two of the building's apartments were empty. One of those empty places held several grand worth of Scratch's boosted loot.

With a small key, he opened the mailbox labeled Gary Gleason.

God, how he hated seeing his real name on so many credit card and utility bills. The building superintendent kept a small ash can in the vestibule for junk mail. Any envelope with the words "Open immediately" or "Do not discard" or "Check enclosed," or any other hoax the junk mailers had invented to get people to open their spam, went right in the can. One letter said, "Do not fold or mishandle." Scratch creased it down the middle before he slam-dunked it.

There were two credit card offers addressed to his former roommate in the mailbox. If only these card companies had known how crazy his roommate had been—crazier than Scratch had ever imagined.

Crazy, and now dead.

With a shudder, he pushed the letters back in the box, slammed and locked the door. Putting his old roommate out of his mind, he hummed some more on his way up two flights of stairs.

I'm singing in my brain . . .

Inside his apartment, Scratch flicked on the light, slapped his baseball cap over the head of his pet mannequin, then dumped the shopping bags on the table. He had scored six women's business suits, jackets and slacks. Each was navy blue, made from fine summer-weight wool. He had four suits of size 6 and two of size 4. Each had a security tag on it, of course. The tags were never much of a problem. He held a pair of slacks to the light and examined the device—a simple dye bomb, essentially a thin glass tube of permanent red dye, partially encased in plastic. The fragile glass was designed to break and ruin the garment with ink if anybody tried to remove it without a special machine. The dye bomb was pinned to the pant leg with a heavy needle embedded in a hard plastic disc. Scratch had defeated plenty of similar security devices, but none of this specific brand.

Let's try one.

He carried a pair of slacks down the hall, past the bathroom and the battered plaid sofa that had been his roommate's bed, which Scratch had unofficially inherited. The dresser clock in the bedroom said 1:37 a.m. He walked across his squishy bed to the window, eased it up, and climbed gracefully onto his balcony herb garden.

The match method of removing a dye bomb, his favorite tactic for this type of device, required lots of ventilation. He lit his cigarette lighter and held the bulbous side of the dye bomb in the heat. The plastic caught fire in a few seconds, and then burned with a low smear of flame that sent up a thread of deep black smoke, which gently waved in the still night air like the world's skinniest charmed snake. The gases were loaded with cancer-causing dioxins, and Scratch turned his head from the fire. He let it burn for thirty seconds or so. Then he blew out the flame and used a pottery shard to scrape away the softened plastic. That exposed the interior locking ring. A few jabs with a ballpoint pen dislodged a tiny BB under the ring, and the device fell apart, dye tube intact.

He laughed and tapped a few more dance steps, which sent happy vibrations down the fire escape. Freeing these garments from retail bondage would be easy.

Back in the kitchen, he made sure the slacks were undamaged, then left them on the table and went to the bathroom to scrub the soot from his hands.

He lost himself in the washing, thinking of profit. The retail tags on the suits said $575. Nobody ever paid retail; this kind of high-end garment was generally on sale for $499. He could unload them to a fence he knew, probably for no more than fifty bucks each. Or he could sell them himself, anonymously, over the Internet. Say he could get $250 each, plus shipping . . . *Shit, I can't do math*. No matter. He said aloud to the mirror, "Whatever price I get will be the square root of a great score—squared." He blasted his own smile in the mirror with double-barreled finger guns, then cranked the water shut and half listened for the echo drip from the shower stall, a quirk of his inferior plumbing.

What's that?

Huh.

He turned the water back on, then off, and heard an odd crackling again, an unnatural noise in an apartment he would know in the dark.

Scratch turned toward the shower as the curtain scraped open, gloved fingers sweeping it away.

Impossible.

Imfuckingpossible.

A chill paralysis spread through him like a voodoo drug.

I'm not seeing this. This is a movie I saw. I'm remembering this.

Then he saw a head encased in a plastic bag with just a slit for the eyes and a wrinkle of brow pressing heavily. The black pupils were swollen huge, encircled by a delicate gray ring of iris no thicker than a wedding band. *A man's eyes*, Scratch thought.

A water droplet raced down the plastic face, recoiled ever slightly at the chin, as if gathering itself for a leap, and then cast off.

The figure's right hand had been moving at him all this time, Scratch finally realized.

By instinct, Scratch's hips jerked to the side, to matador away from the clumsy thrust.

He would pretend the man was real, just until he figured out why he was seeing this.

As if in slow motion, he watched the stranger push a thin shank—*Holy Christ, an ice pick*—through the empty space Scratch had just abandoned. The man was out of the shower stall. He wore a black sweater, tight black pants. Momentum carried him across the tiny bathroom. He was growling.

This cannot be happening.

At the violent stab of the ice pick, the bottom half of the mirror shattered. For an instant as they dropped, each shard reflected a chaotic fragment of the scene in a tiny moving picture.

The crash of glass obliterated the hope this might be imagination. Scratch set his feet and drove his palm at the man's shoulder. A glancing blow.

He's real, all right. But why?

The attacker regrouped. Scratch turned his right side to him, to keep his heart as far from the shank as possible, as he had learned during a four-month bid in state prison. He had never been stabbed, but had once seen an inmate take a shank to the shoulder, wrestle it away, and jam it back from where it had come. His eyes locked on the pick, on the bright white point at the end of it, on which his twenty-six years of life, plus nine months in the womb, delicately balanced. His brain flooded his body with fight-or-flight chemicals, racing his heart, tightening his testicles, rerouting blood to the big muscles that could save him.

The figure swung the weapon in a wide arc. Scratch ducked, felt the drag of a forearm across his hair, and shot a frantic uppercut to the man's rib cage. Bang. Fist on ribs, but without much leverage. A grunt, nothing more. Scratch threw an off-balanced hand toward the bagged head, and missed.

The pick flashed up. Scratch shrank from it.

Suddenly from the left a fist crashed into Scratch's cheekbone. He knew instantly he was hurt, though he felt no pain, not yet. Just a high ringing in his ear.

With a guttural growl, like from a beast, the man lunged. Scratch leapt blindly aside. He had a vision of his body spiked on the metal and abandoned in the bathroom, undiscovered, until the super came to collect the rent.

The pick pierced the pale inside of Scratch's left forearm, driving effortlessly through skin and fat cells and capillaries and muscle meat, sliding between the radius and the ulna, pushing a channel through flesh and fat on the other side, exiting the skin on the backside of his arm between little brown hairs standing on end, before stabbing the wall and burying into the wood.

There was no pain, just a shocking sense of invasion; a rape. He gasped. The attacker's body carried into him and knocked his head against the wall.

Scratch smelled the man's salty sweat.

The scene seemed to slow down again, as the man in the plastic hood pulled at the pick, growling in frustration.

The shank had stuck fast in the wall, pinning Scratch's outstretched arm through a tiny bull's eye of blood. Scratch shrieked at the sight, high and shrill, like a child surprised by a spider.

I'm crucified.

For a second, the man seemed to transfer his wrath to the ice pick that refused to budge. He fought it with a staccato roar, like a growl and a sob together.

Scratch drove his right forearm up, catching the man just under the chin. His head snapped back, though he kept his grip on the pick, and gave the weapon a fierce yank.

The tool's old wooden handle splintered and came off in his hand; he tumbled backward against the vanity. His shoes skidded on chips of broken mirror and he went down.

With no handle, the tool was just a spike, a long nail with no head. Scratch tore his arm from it, felt a hollow whoosh in his gut, and warm blood racing free. He tried to stomp the man's leg as he thundered over him, out of the room. A hand slapped his shoe and Scratch staggered into the hall. He stumbled into the sofa, caught himself. The man was up, coming at him. Scratch lurched off toward the kitchen.

The door, the goddamn blessed door, so close.

A fist clubbed his shoulder. He crashed into the refrigerator, heard bottles of Bass ale tumbling inside. His wound spattered red on the door. An arm wrapped around his neck from behind, catching him under the Adam's apple. The attacker's body pressed tight against him. Scratch leaned forward and lifted the man's feet from the floor. The attacker rode his back as they slowly spun in the center of the room. The bagged head pushed on Scratch's right shoulder. Swampy panting breath pulsed against the plastic. Scratch's mannequin stood frozen, a witness to nothing, its eyes just shallow indentations.

Was this bagged assassin really trying to suffocate a man of equal size and strength? With just his arm? *Where'd this guy learn to fight? The movies?* The attacker had surrendered leverage, the most valuable advantage in unarmed fighting. Scratch bent at the knees, tightened his midsection, reached back to grab two handfuls of sweater, and violently yanked the man over his head like he was whipping off a shirt. Now it was *this clown's* turn to smash into the fridge. He slammed into it with a moan and rolled.

From his ankle-high boot, the man drew a steak knife serrated like piranha teeth.

Holy Jesus, gotta have a weapon. Anything!

Scratch yanked the loose arm off the mannequin. The crude club was surprisingly well balanced, like a fairway driver with a slight kink in the shaft at the elbow. He swung a mighty uppercut as the man tried to rise.

Fore!

The plastic arm whacked above the man's temple; he dropped like he had been shot. On the floor, he clutched his head and squirmed, still holding the knife.

For the slightest moment Scratch considered beating the man with the makeshift club. But the assassin was only stunned; Scratch was deeply wounded, and bleeding.

And the enemy was armed with a real weapon. Scratch was armed with an arm.

Instinct insisted: *Run away.*

He flung the arm, flew out the door, rumbled down the stairs, out into the night. He ran with one hand over the hole in his forearm. He didn't look back.

seven

The breakfast buffet began with stove-boiled Autocrat java, inky black and infused with coffee grounds in what the old man liked to call "chunky style." The chrome toaster on the table was forty years old, same age as Billy, but it delivered four perfect shingles at a time. Not one of the thirty flapjacks piled chaotically on a tin plate was round; despite Billy's best short-order cookery, the cakes had hardened into the shapes of Confederate states. On the table, arranged like a row of books, were four boxes of sugared cereal, a box of golden raisins, a half-gallon carton of skim milk, and a quart of orange juice. The bacon hardened on a greasy paper towel. The boy had arranged six triangles of seedy watermelon flat on a plate, like pizza slices. A butterscotch short-haired cat, with a potbelly and an overdeveloped sense of entitlement, relaxed sphinxlike on the table among the dishes with its front paws tucked invisibly beneath its bulk.

Surrounding this feast were three generations of males with the same name.

The eldest William R. Povich had parked his wheelchair at a short end of the rectangular table. In the late-morning sun, his startling blue eyes looked like those of an optimist, maybe a poet or an adventurer, or like the eyes of a young bridegroom. But sunken into the head of a living corpse, among the scars of old age, the jagged creases and pockmarks littered with white whiskers, the eyes shone like stolen goods.

Across the table, boosted on two copies of the Providence Yellow Pages, sat the youngest William Povich, a second-grader with little white legs leopard-spotted with brown bruises. Bo hurt himself often because he rarely moved at less than full speed, and had not yet developed the grown-up pessimism that made people hesitate before they jumped off a shed with a pillowcase for a parachute, or tried to pilot a bicycle down a flight of stairs.

The stuffed Mr. Albert Einstein, which had become some sort of security anchor for the boy, leaned against the orange juice, silently contemplating space-time, light speed, and the twin paradox. Billy didn't understand what the kid saw in the doll, which the old man had bought for him over the Internet. The Einstein action figure did not talk or move. It did not use batteries; it lacked the kung fu grip. Did the kid even know Einstein had been a real person?

Bo tore open a paper sugar pack saved from Dunkin' Donuts and sprinkled the excess energy over his Frankenberries.

"Ziggs put his tail in the butter," the boy said. He giggled.

"No one likes a tattletale," the old man told Bo. The kid laughed and slapped a hand over his mouth. The old man shooed away the cat's tail, then used a knife to scrape hair off the stick of soft butter.

Billy laid a folder of documents on the table. His eyes dutifully passed over Adam Rackers's arrest record, but the distractions prevented the words from actually entering his brain. He sighed and glanced around to clear his head. The giant white range had left the kitchen too warm. The ten-year-old cat sat pensively on the table, buttered tail silently slapping the cherry red laminate. Outside the window, cars lined the street for a service at Metts & Sons, the funeral parlor on the first floor of their old Victorian apartment house. Beyond the street, a parade field of green, broken up by paths and clumps of trees, stretched to the base of the old Cranston Street armory, a tremendous yellow-brick castle of gates and turrets.

"His tail would taste like popcorn," the boy said. He stroked the cat's soft back.

"Maybe that's why he licks it sometimes," said the old man.

"I'm working," Billy said.

"We're eating," sassed the old man. "This ain't the library."

"Can't even chew gum at the library," Bo said.

"Where's the horseradish?" the old man asked.

"Puts hair on your belly," Bo said, parroting what the old man had taught him to say whenever somebody mentioned horseradish.

Organ music from the funeral home downstairs percolated up through the red-flecked black linoleum and vibrated into Billy's bare feet.

"Who's dead down there?" the old man asked.

Billy consulted an index card on the kitchen counter. "According to the schedule Mr. Metts sent up, this would be Mr. Crespie, of Eden Park. He was a foreman at the brewery."

"You knew him?"

"I wrote the obituary."

The old man wheezed. He tapped a knife on his plate four times, sounding impatient. He said, "I want to go out and sit in the park."

"You know we can't use the stairs during a funeral. It's in the lease."

He moaned, "Are they gonna be long down there?"

"How should I know?" Billy said. The cat slapped its tail back into the butter. Billy brushed the tail away and slid the butter dish out of range.

"You wrote the obit," the old man grumbled. "What kind of life did this guy have? Was he worth mourning for the full hour? Did he do anything worth remembering?"

"He lived to ninety-two."

"Whoop-tee-damn-doo," the old man said. He reached a trembling knife to the soft butter, scraped off a smear, and spread it on toast. "The lucky fool walked between the falling pianos for ninety-two years before something finally crushed him. Maybe he was Mr. Magoo."

"There's cat hair on your toast," Billy said.

The old man took a huge, exaggerated bite. "Mmmmm," he moaned. "Tasty!"

Bo giggled. "I want some cat, too!"

"Puts hair *in* your belly," the old man said, mouth open, the toast circling inside a cage of tan teeth and blackened metal molars.

"This guy Crespie—his son flew fighter jets for the Air Force," Billy said. "Won some medals."

The old man swallowed with a little gag. He cleared his throat and then said, "Then I guess we're lucky it ain't the son's funeral, 'cause we'd be stuck in here *all day*." Some emotion that Billy could not identify had cut the old man's voice ragged. He went on, "What the goddamn does it matter what the *son* did? Any idiot can be a father. Even monkeys hump by instinct."

"Pa," Billy pleaded, weakly.

"Why do you only write about dead people?" Bo asked.

"Because he's good at it," the old man answered.

Billy's eyes widened at the compliment. When was the last time he had heard praise from the old man? "Because that's my job," Billy told his son. "I don't do the investigating reporting I used to do. I'm an obituary writer. I write a lot of them."

"Did you write Mom's?" Bo asked.

Billy felt a wave of internal heat, and an invisible hand around his throat. "Not that one," he said. He couldn't look at the kid.

"Why not?"

After a beat of silence, the old man rescued Billy. "Meow!" he cried. Then he gasped. "Ohmigod! I think I *did* eat cat hair." The boy laughed.

Billy seized the distraction. "I need to read these documents for the case I'm working for Martin."

"Whatchu got there?" asked the old man.

Billy counted the sheets of computer printout in his hand. "I got the five-page arrest record of the guy who shot Judge Harmony." He thumbed quickly through the pages. "Martin is right about this guy—Adam Rackers wasn't a regular street thug. He was a professional thief. Mostly B and E's in unoccupied homes. Some shoplifting."

He flipped the page, then another.

"*Lots* of shoplifting. But other than getting involved in a couple of bar fights—"

"Which can happen to anyone," the old man interrupted, with an evil smile.

"—there's no violence on his record. Not a single weapons charge, either."

Downstairs at the funeral, the gathering prayed aloud. Their muffled words bled through the floor in a mumble.

"Just because he was never *arrested* for shootin' somebody doesn't mean he never did it before," the old man said.

"Meow," said Bo. The cat answered him with a little whine. The boy laughed and crunched an open mouthful of cereal at Ziggs.

"Still feels odd that this guy would suddenly shoot a judge," Billy said. "Martin thinks he got paid to do it, and I'm beginning to think the same thing."

"Maybe it was personal," the old man said. Billy couldn't be sure if his father was trying to help, or just being argumentative. "Did this guy know the judge?"

"Never had a case in front of him."

"Did he meet him in a bar? Did he sit behind him one day at Mc-Coy Stadium? Did they have words over somebody's eyes on somebody else's wife? Did the judge threaten to have him arrested?"

The cat popped up from the table, stretched, then jumped to the floor. It walked away like a runway model, crossing its feet in front of each other over an invisible line down the middle of the hall.

This was an emergency for Bo. The kid slid off his seat, grabbed Einstein, and ran after the cat, calling urgently over his shoulder, "Ziggs wants to play!"

"Keep an eye on him," Billy ordered.

"Don't let him slip on that buttered tail," the old man added. To Billy, he said, "Maybe the judge was blackmailing this guy. Maybe they were in some crime ring together, and so he killed him."

Billy squinted at his father a moment, and tried to remember the path of their argument. How the hell had they gotten *here*? "The judge was rich," Billy said. "He made a fortune on the law books he wrote. If I had his money, I'd throw my money away."

"Or gamble it away," the old man cracked.

"And Gil Harmony was too honest . . ." Billy flipped papers in the folder. "Look at all these commentaries the judge wrote for the paper. Here's one on juvenile justice. And this, on gang prevention. Here's something on constitutional law . . . religion in politics. And he wrote about more than just the law. Judge Harmony rode the train twice a week for the past five years, to teach in Manhattan, and *this* essay is his plan to improve Amtrak service down the eastern seaboard. The guy was an expert on *everything*." Billy stared at the paper, at the byline that read *Gilbert D. Harmony*. He said aloud to himself, "Martin was right, Judge Harmony was Mr. Perfect. He wasn't part of a crime ring." Billy stopped, lightly slapped his own cheek, as if to wake himself. "Why am I even arguing something so ridiculous with you?"

The old man picked at the dangle of chicken skin under his chin.

He looked away. "When I croak pretty soon," he asked, "will you write my obituary?"

"Pop—"

"Because that rag you work for don't have anybody else who can write a good one." He looked at Billy. "You'll be honest, won't you?" The old man's stare sent a cold tickle down Billy's back, like a drip of ice water. "Because back in my youth, I walked around with lies stuffed in my pockets. Your mother could have told you that . . . Probably did." He looked at Billy for confirmation.

Billy did not flinch, did not even blink. He had accepted his father into his home after the old man's stroke, but Billy would not discuss his dead mother with the man who had abandoned her in Billy's youth.

The old man sounded guarded. "So when I go, I want to be carried out on the truth. The lies, the affairs, everything—put it all in there. Okay?"

He seemed to get older before Billy's eyes. Not exactly like he was aging; more like he was beginning to decompose. Billy wasn't sure if he could speak. "I'll write it," he heard himself say.

Organ music rumbled through the floor again. The song was supposed to be a hymn, but played painfully slow, it sounded like a death march. The old man dipped his head and flashed a canine tooth at Billy, like a little dagger in the devil's grin. "Long ago, people used to think that I was Mr. Perfect, too, just like your judge," he said. "They all died disappointed."

eight

Martin probably should have been listening to the testimony being offered to the court by the mother of the teenager who had died at the hands of Martin's client. But there was nothing else Martin could do for his client, who sat beside him, already convicted of motor vehicle homicide.

This was the gut-wrenching part of the sentencing hearing, the victim-impact statements, and Martin allowed himself to be distracted. He thought about June Harmony and her son, Brock. They would be on their way to Martin's office by now, so that the three of them could walk together to the opening of Gil Harmony's will. Martin had not seen Brock since the crash—actually, he realized, had not seen him since he was a teen. And though he knew Brock was now in his twenties, he dreaded having to look a fatherless little boy in the eye.

Thoughts of Brock reminded Martin of his client, who, at twenty-seven, was just a few years older. He was an incurious roofer named Stokely, who seemed incapable of a single empathetic thought. Martin looked at him. Stokely was a pudgy son of a bitch, deeply tanned, with a buzzed haircut and a sour expression that made him seem eternally put out. He had worn blue jeans to his own sentencing, which had nearly given Martin a heart attack. Was he *trying* to get the maximum?

They sat together at the defense table, a varnished maple rectangle as smooth as a mirror. At trial, the table had been cluttered with documents, transcripts, and notes. For sentencing, it was bare.

At a podium a few feet away, the mother of the young man Stokely had run down addressed the court. She spoke slowly, in a low voice, about her boy. In the sausage-making process of criminal justice, the court always gave victims or their families the chance to testify about how the crime had wrecked their lives, before the judge pronounced the sentence.

". . . and you never once during the trial showed remorse, Mr. Stokely, for what you've taken from my family," she said.

Stokely stared straight ahead, looking bored. Martin looked away.

She's right, Martin thought. In private conferences, Stokely had seemed contemptuous toward his seventeen-year-old victim, whom he vaguely seemed to blame for ruining Stokely's life by dying under the impact of an SUV doing forty miles per hour on a sidewalk.

". . . you have stolen sixty or seventy years of a young man's life and forever changed the course of our family history. . . ."

Martin dropped his hands in his lap and looked at the witness. She was trim, a little older than most moms of a teenager, maybe fifty-five. Her hair was cut in a perfect shoulder-length bob. She had worn no makeup to court and her eyes looked lifeless. Maybe she didn't want to take the chance she'd cry and smear mascara over herself, or maybe she just felt lifeless. She stood stiffly at the podium and spoke from notes handwritten on sheets of paper that were ragged down one edge where they had been ripped from a spiral binder. She spoke directly at the side of Stokely's head. He did not look at her.

The mother's grace awed Martin, and fed the disgust he held in his heart for his client. Martin had busted his ass for this guy, uncovering a crack in the chain of evidence with Stokely's blood test the night of the accident. A cop had left the test sample unguarded for three hours in an unlocked cruiser. With a ferocious argument, Martin had the blood test thrown out of evidence. Prosecutors could not prove by science that Stokely's blood had approximately the alcohol concentration of a Polynesian mai tai. Then Martin had negotiated a fair plea bargain with the prosecution. Some reasonable jail time for Stokely to think things over, but not so much that he couldn't salvage the best part of his own life.

The deal was just.

His client had rejected it.

"Don't want justice," Stokely had said. He had wanted Martin to get him off at trial.

". . . my son was an industrious young man who was studying education. Being a teacher, that was Clarke's high hope, not to conquer Wall Street or Mount Everest, just to teach children how to read. . . ."

The prosecutor didn't need a blood test to prove Stokely had been drinking all night. Not with the testimonies of bartenders and other patrons, and with Stokely's own credit card receipt for seventy-five dollars in liquor, signed by Stokely in handwriting that looked like a kindergarten doodle.

At trial, the prosecutor had pounded the facts. Martin could only pound the table. The Constitution provides that no matter how cold your heart and how terrible your crime, you deserve a competent and robust defense. If Martin could have won the case on some arcane technicality, he would have gone for the prosecutor's throat. He gave Stokely a tenacious fight, and lost.

Sometimes, despite the best efforts of everyone involved, justice prevails.

He thought about Gil Harmony, and of justice. Martin hoped that justice didn't consider that case closed, as the police did.

Stokely sighed in boredom and blatantly checked his wristwatch. Martin blanched. *What the fuck are you doing?* Was he really that obtuse? Or was this a message to the court and to the grieving mother that he just didn't care?

The mother paused a moment, then raised her voice. "Am I bothering you, Mr. Stokely?" she asked. She drummed her fingernails on the podium. "You know what bothers me? You ran down my son from behind, so you never saw what he looked like. Well, I want you to see him."

She left her notes on the podium and grabbed a shoe box from the front row of the gallery. With her lips sealed with determination, she marched toward the defense table. Martin glanced to the judge, a rookie on the bench, who seemed startled by this breach of courtroom procedure. The judge hesitated, silent, jaw open. He reached for the gavel but seemed unsure if he should pound it.

Stokely ignored the mother until she was beside him. He shot her an uninterested glance. "Not looking at your pictures, lady," he mumbled.

Calmly she said, "Meet my son, Clarke."

She flipped the lid off the shoe box and cast the contents over the table. Pale ash, as fine as talcum powder, flowed across the desk in a wave and poured into the laps of the two men. Particles swirled into the air, and seemed to come together as a ghost that brushed almost imperceptibly on bare skin.

"Jesus Christ!" Martin screamed. He bolted up. Ash clung to his suit. He tried to wipe away the stain, but his bare hands refused to touch it.

A few minutes before the opening of the will, Billy met the judge's brother.

He was everything Gil Harmony had been, except less.

Judge Lincoln G. Harmony, six years younger than his brother, sat on the bench of the traffic tribunal, a maligned fiefdom of the judiciary, despised by Rhode Islanders summoned there for motor vehicle violations. Traffic court was the sweatshop of justice, where people waited hours on pine benches under buzzing fluorescent lights in steamy rooms with fake paneling on the walls, before their cases were brusquely called and disposed of with the grace of an assembly-line production.

"So you work for Martin Smothers?" Lincoln Harmony said. He had a big shock of wavy gray hair, and a sweaty palm. Billy freed himself from their handshake and casually wiped his hand on his pants.

"I help him out from time to time," Billy replied.

Lincoln Harmony wasn't listening. "Because I never imagined that Martin Smothers *earned* enough to hire full-time help," he said. His skin was pink and rough, as if scrubbed by a hard brush. His oily face gleamed wet under the hot lights in the law office. He struck Billy as a small-minded man of immense self-importance. He was accustomed to having his butt kissed by lawyers and clerks and bad drivers, in the small pond of the traffic court.

"Sorry about your brother," Billy said, mostly to change the subject.

Lincoln Harmony waved a hand, as if to shoo some bug from around his head. "Tragic. Senseless. And beyond our power to change. What did the wise one say? 'The future, present, and the past. Fly on proud bird. You're free at last.' That was Confucius, I believe."

"I think that was the Charlie Daniels Band."

"Oh, whatever, Povich," he snapped. "The point is, Gil lived high and mighty, and now he's gone. If there is an afterlife, my brother has finally realized that money can't buy security, and accolades won't stop a bullet. He was mortal, like the rest of us. Imagine his shock."

He paused, smiled, showed teeth. Billy caught a whiff of alcohol, very faint, like the echo of an odor. Vodka, maybe?

"Don't look at me that way, Povich," he said in a low voice. "I *loved* my brother. Don't you think I know what I owe him?" He pointed to himself with a thumb. "I'm on the bench because I'm Gil Harmony's kid brother. I work four days a week, I got a pension coming my way in a few years that's worth more than most people will ever see. But I've known for a long time that Gil was going to get knocked off Mount Olympus. He'd been up there too long. It's a shame he had to be knocked so hard."

Lincoln Harmony suddenly clapped Billy on the shoulder, as if telling him to *buck up!* He excused himself and wandered away, clipping his elbow on the door frame on his way out of the conference room. He recovered without a sound, and disappeared around the corner into the receptionist's hallway, where the world's slowest elevator made its stops on this floor.

Billy pulled out a winged leather chair on wheels and sat at the head of a long table that would fit a dozen people, though there were just seven chairs.

This would have been Gil Harmony's chair, he figured.

Though the judge had left the firm when he had been appointed to the bench, the law offices of Harmony & Thybony still carried his name. Billy had expected chandeliers and marble tile in Gil Harmony's law office, and was surprised by creaky floors and wall-to-wall carpet. This was a utilitarian space, on the mid level of a three-story, brick-faced building, discreetly tucked among the office towers in Providence's financial district. Between the tall buildings, the sky was a strip of gray. Rain was on the way.

The conference room windows looked out to an intersection paved in cobblestone. Across the square, a stone sultan hung like a gargoyle above the arched entrance of the Turk's Head Building. The statue glowered at Billy and made him feel like he was being watched.

Billy closed one eye and pretended to aim a gun at the squinting stone statue, which had been chiseled nearly a century ago with angry features and a drooping mustache.

Lincoln Harmony had looked up to his brother all his life. Not that he had a choice.

When you drive past Respect, how far is Jealousy?

He turned when he heard the elevator *bing*. The steel doors crept open. Martin Smothers burst out as though he were shoved. He turned to a woman and a young man in the elevator and blurted, "Claustrophobia! It comes and goes." They followed him off the car. The woman sighed and pulled off a wide-brimmed safari hat. "I'll take that," Martin said, snatching it from her. He looked around for a table or a hat rack, or something, and saw Billy.

"Povich!" he shouted. He flung the hat, Frisbee style, in Billy's general direction. It sailed over the table and crashed into a set of Venetian blinds.

"Povich!" Martin shouted again. "You could have dived for it."

"Had this been a playoff game, I would have," Billy deadpanned. He stared at the woman, who watched him back, expressionless. She was very tall, close to six feet, with dark brown hair, nearly black, wound into a tight bun. Her cheekbones pressed sharply from beneath the skin; her mouth was an arch of red lipstick. Her light eyes hovered over blood-blue dark circles—the stains of stress or tears or insomnia. Her face looked tightened by emotion. Anger maybe? Even in anger, she was stunning. She looked to be chiseled by the same artist who had done the Turk's Head across the street.

June Harmony, of course.

The dark-haired young man at her side was in his early twenties, a few inches shorter than June, with similar bone structure, similar eyes—this was her son, naturally. Billy's eyes widened at the black slash up the young man's face—a row of surgical stitches like train tracks that began at the jawbone, climbed past his ear, and disappeared under a baseball cap. The brown remnants of a fading shiner lingered under his eye.

Judge Harmony's son, Brock, was still recovering from the car crash that had killed his kidnapper and sent Stu Tracy to intensive care. Brock kept his hands in his pants pockets. He glanced around the office without looking anyone in the eye.

The woman said to Martin, "Do we wait in here?"

Martin pressed his hands together, as if praying. "You know your way around this firm. Why don't you check in with Mr. Thybony, in his office, so he knows we're here." He chuckled, sounding nervous. "I'll get your hat."

"Is my bother-in-law here?" she asked crisply.

They both turned to Billy, who nodded.

"Don't let him touch my hat," she said, and then turned sharply and walked away, deeper into the office. Her feet thumped heavily on the carpet. Brock followed a step behind. He had a limp, as if favoring a gimpy right foot.

Martin closed the door behind them, then collapsed against it and sighed.

Billy picked up June Harmony's hat and flipped it onto the table. "At least you didn't throw it out the window," he said.

Martin pounded his temple with his palms. "Why does that woman make me so goddamn nervous? It's gotten worse since Gil died." He paced to the window, looked to the street, frowned, and then yanked the cord for the blinds. They fell with a clang on the sill. "Never take a friend's widow as a client."

"She doesn't like her bother-in-law," Billy said. "Why?"

"Did you meet Lincoln Harmony today?"

"He's drunk."

"Linc and June never got along. Some old feud there, goes back a long way."

"We don't pick our parents or our in-laws. How's the judge's kid?"

Martin stepped closer, rested one ass cheek on the table, and passed a hand over his scalp. He seemed pained. "Brock is morose. Polite. Wounded. In denial." He thought a few moments. "Sealed off from the world. Unreachable, at least by me."

"I'll try him."

"Gently," Martin commanded.

"I need to know what he remembers about that night. Something he might have overlooked when he gave his statement to the cops. Or something the cops didn't bother to include. Physically, he's getting better. Maybe he'll remember more details, too."

"Be discreet. June didn't want any more people here than necessary." He glanced to the door, and then lowered his voice, so Billy could barely hear him. "I told her that you were a clerk for me, to help with the paperwork."

Billy leaned close. He was about to needle Martin for lying, but then blurted, "What's this shit in your beard?"

Martin looked straight down. "I'm too farsighted. Can't see a thing from this close . . ."

"Some kind of gray dust? Are you flicking cigar ash into your own scruff?"

"What . . . ? Oh, Jesus Christ!" Martin yelped. "It's in my beard!"

Billy put his hands up. "Whoa! Easy now, Dusty."

Martin popped to his feet and ran around the conference table, furiously pretending to comb his fingers through his beard, without actually touching it. "Get it out! Get it out!"

"What's the matter with you?"

Martin turned to him. His eyes squeezed shut. "Get it out!"

What the hell is wrong with him?

Billy grabbed two handfuls of hair, just below Martin's chin, and shook furiously. The beard released a cloud of gray dust, and half an empty pistachio shell. "Look at this mess," Billy marveled. "You ought to do this at least once a year."

"Just shake it out!"

The door flew open. Billy and Martin froze in place, beard in hand, a cloud of dust settling around them.

"When you gentlemen are ready to begin," said Mr. Thybony, a wizened white-haired Yankee lawyer, who gave no hint that he was startled by the scene in his conference room, "I believe all the invitees are in attendance."

nine

As an employee of Martin Smothers, and not a party to the ritual opening of the will, Billy sat alone in a corner of the conference room. Fine with him; he could watch everyone at once, though he could feel the stone eyes of the Turk's Head poking the back of his head through the window.

People settled into seats, three on each side of the table, and the scene looked like a negotiation was about to break out.

Martin sat closest to Billy. He picked intently at his beard like a chimp inspecting itself for fleas.

Next to Martin sat June Harmony. She spun her chair sideways, placed her elbow on the table and her hand in the air with two fingers spread in a narrow V, as if she held a cigarette. She looked like a former smoker who had quit the habit but had unconsciously retained the mannerisms.

At his mother's side, Brock Harmony slumped, hands in his lap, eyes glazed, lips parted, and breathing through his mouth. He stared across the table to a blank wall. Occasionally he glanced to the grandfather clock in the corner and gave little sighs that seemed to beg, *When will this end?*

Another trio faced them from the other side of the table.

Lincoln Harmony pushed his chair an arm's length from the table. He slouched, feet planted far apart, and stared at June. She would not look at him, he refused to look away, and this seemed like some kind of contest.

Linc Harmony's lawyer sat next to his client. He was a doughy lump in a chalk line suit. His eyeglasses were as thick as coffee-table glass.

Next to the lawyer sat a compact woman, midthirties, who had arrived last, and whom Billy had not had the chance to meet. Her name was Kit Bass, according to Martin, and she had been Judge Harmony's law clerk. As the judge had cut back his trial schedule and eased into semiretirement, Kit had worked with other judges, too, unless Harmony was presiding over a trial. She had worn a simple cotton sundress, and Billy's gaze lingered on the stripe of freckles across her shoulder, which carried his eye to the cuts of her sharply developed biceps.

At the far end of the table, Mr. Thybony placed a flat-screen computer monitor to face his guests, with a sleek laptop computer and a single bookshelf speaker. He stood behind the computer screen and silently reviewed his audience.

"You'll forgive an old man for indulging himself with a few words," Thybony said. His voice had that particular hollowness that is caused only by age. "Bertrand Russell told us the trouble with the world is that the stupid are cocksure and the intelligent full of doubt." He smiled, looked away, gathered himself for a moment. "My friend Gil Harmony was the exception." He looked at Martin. "Don't you agree, Mr. Smothers?"

"You knew him well," Martin said.

For the benefit of the rest of the audience, Thybony explained. "I was the fortunate lawyer who replaced Mr. Smothers when he left this firm more than thirty years ago." He pinched his rubbery nose for a moment and seemed to force back some emotion. "I'm not ashamed to admit that my mentor in this business was a wee bit younger than I am." The words snagged on his grief, but he got them out. "Gil was stolen from us in a barbaric manner. I would have liked to see his killer come to trial, but the Lord decided that the perpetrator would not face a jury. A pity."

Billy looked out the window. He could feel Martin's eyes on him. They poked harder than the Turk's Head.

"Gil didn't believe that bad people somehow got whichever curse they deserved," Thybony continued. "For him, there was no justice outside of a courtroom. And though he left this firm years ago for the bench, he maintained an office here, did his research in our library, and prepared lessons for his students on this conference table around which we now gather. Gil traveled back and forth from New York twice a week to teach law because he thought sharing what he knew was an obligation to the next generation of great lawyers."

Lincoln Harmony burped a stream of air, and then tapped a fist on his chest. The distraction brought Mr. Thybony back to his duty.

"Let me now do," Thybony said, "what Gil had asked of me."

He loaded a disc into the laptop, explaining as he worked the computer mouse: "Gil's formal will is in document form, of course, and I've made copies for the attorneys here today. Throughout his life, Gil set up a multitude of charitable trusts, and his will contains several lengthy sections concerning the eternal maintenance of those trusts. What I'm to play for you today is the abbreviated version of the will, the part that concerns the people here in this room."

While the program loaded, Billy thought of his father's will. Did the old man even have one? What would it say?

To Bo, I leave my collection of World's Fair memorabilia, and my perfect blue eyes, which you have already received. . . . To my son, Billy, I leave an Autocrat coffee can with two hundred dollars stuffed inside, all the money I have in the world, plus I leave you my addictive personality, my lack of patience, the childhood scars from my serial philandering, and the eternal mystery of our fucked-up relationship. . . . I'm outta here, my boy! . . . Enjoy!

The computer screen flickered and then lit up with an image of Gil Harmony—square jawed, clean shaven, pure white hair swept across his forehead, wind-scrubbed complexion from sailing the bay, a regal look that reminded Billy of an eagle. He wore an open-collared polo shirt and a light cotton sports jacket.

"Good day," said the image, in a baritone sounding slightly robotic in digitized audio. Gil smiled on the screen.

Martin gasped. People around the table shot glances at each other. June Harmony instinctively grabbed Martin's arm. Lincoln Harmony muttered, "Self-indulgent son of a . . ." He seemed to suddenly realize his mouth was broadcasting his inner monologue, and he cut himself off.

"This is my last will and testament," the image intoned, "which I covertly rerecord each year with the help of my good friend Ken Thybony, my lawyer, my old partner, my videographer, and the keeper of my secrets."

Mr. Thybony responded with a sad smile. He dabbed the corner of his eye with a pinkie.

"You all recall my annual fishing trip with Ken every June? Well, before we hunt down the stripers each year, we also make a new video, and then I chuck the old one off the boat." Gil grinned on the screen.

Billy and Martin exchanged a glance. This recording was just four months old.

"Ken is my executor and he'll enforce my full last will in accordance to the documents, but I wanted to address the people watching this recording in a more personal way."

"Seems remarkably upbeat for a dead man," Lincoln Harmony observed.

Kit Bass shushed him.

"Whaaaat?" Linc persisted. His lawyer tapped his hand to shut him the hell up.

What an asshole, Billy thought. Though he couldn't argue . . . Gil Harmony did seem chipper for a corpse. But why not? He was a few minutes from chasing the bluefish on the bay. Saltwater fishing is so deeply carved into the history of Rhode Islanders, the right to use the bay is guaranteed to each resident in the state constitution. How many times had the judge rerecorded this video? Only to have to do it again the next year?

On the screen, Gil Harmony looked away for a moment, then stared hard into the camera. "To my wife, June, I fear the pain you must be suffering right now."

June Harmony lifted her chin toward the image, as if offering a dare. *Go ahead. Hit me. I can take it.*

"Please believe me, June, that I didn't intend for it to happen, all this hurt you're feeling. Some things are, well, just larger than ourselves. We can't control them. Marriage isn't always easy. Everybody knows that. But my love for you has never faded, and I suspect my last conscious thought was of your face."

His delivery is off, Billy thought. *Sounds more like a pickup line than an eternal good-bye.*

June did not flinch.

Across the table, Kit Bass, the judge's clerk, pressed a crumpled tissue to her eye.

Lincoln Harmony chewed air like a cow with its cud.

"Our home in Charlestown, with both our names on the deed, is already yours, as well as our liquid assets in the joint accounts," Gil Harmony said from the next world. "So I leave you, June, something of purely spiritual value. My gavel. The only one I've ever used. The varnish has worn off the handle but it's still a good piece of hickory." He smiled, sadly, as if it had finally dawned on him that the only way anyone would see the video was upon his death. "I've wielded that gavel to strike down the guilty, and to offer them mercy. Use it as you see fit, but I pray you choose mercy."

June suddenly realized she was still clutching Martin's arm. She released him as if he had been electrified, and then nodded some vague apology.

On the monitor, Gil Harmony paused for twenty seconds. For what? Applause? For the rest of the gathering to congratulate June? When he spoke again he addressed his brother.

"Lincoln . . ."

Linc Harmony leaned forward in his seat and answered the screen with a sarcastic, rolling "Yeassss?"

"There isn't much you need from me, my brother, that you haven't already received. I had high hopes that when I left the superior court bench you'd be ready to assume my place, but that's not the way things have worked out, have they?"

"Skip to the punch line," Linc Harmony murmured.

"To you, Linc, I leave my law texts, including the complete General Laws of Rhode Island, which I have studied nearly all my life."

"Those books are online now," Linc argued.

"I leave you my copy of the United States Constitution, a mere eighteen pages in which history's greatest nation was born."

"Defendants quote it all the time in traffic court," Linc replied bitterly.

"And I leave you this—" Gil Harmony fished inside his coat pocket and withdrew a tiny nip bottle of whiskey. He continued, "This is my last drink. I bought it twenty-five years ago when I gave up booze, and I've kept it in my desk that whole time. Imagine, they still made the bottles out of glass back then. I promised myself if I ever needed another drink, this would be the last one. I've never needed it."

"Fuck you," Lincoln Harmony muttered under his breath.

He rose to leave, but his lawyer pulled him back down, cupped a hand to his client's ear, and whispered into it.

Linc replied to him out loud, "Books and a goddamn lecture? He's worth *millions.*"

The lawyer shot him a hard look, which Harmony seemed to understand. Linc snorted like a racehorse, nodded in agreement, and settled back into his chair.

They're going to sue, Billy guessed.

"Brock, my son," the image called out in a sudden burst of cheerfulness.

Brock shrank from the screen, and then turned slowly to face it. He looked lobotomized, with the scar on his head and the detached way he floated through the event.

"How are you, my boy!"

He's trying too hard, Billy thought. *Like my old man did when I was Brock's age.*

"Son, I set up a trust for you that will become available when you're thirty-one. It might seem like a long time away, but I think it's good for a man to live without a net for a while, to make it on his own. Like I did. In the meantime, your mother will be living at the beach house, so I want you to have the town house in downtown Providence. Hmm? How's that sound?"

The image waited, as if for an answer. Brock gave none.

"Um, it's all paid for," Gil Harmony continued, as if trying to talk his son into accepting. "And I'm sure your mom can help with taxes and that sort of thing, till you get on your feet. I like the town house because it's close to the court. But it's close to the art school, too. I was thinking, mmm, maybe you could live there and finish up your degree? You're so good at what you do! Your teachers said you're the best they've ever seen. As I always say, find something you love to do, and be great at it. Just like your old man."

Brock lifted his head, exhaled suddenly, and blinked a few times, as if waking from a coma. To Mr. Thybony, he said, "May I step outside a moment?"

"Of course, Brock."

He got up gingerly, and rested a hand on his mother's shoulder a moment. Every pair of eyes in the room followed as he limped out.

"To you, Kit," Judge Harmony continued brightly, undeterred on video, "the best clerk any judge ever had . . ."

Billy found Brock Harmony sitting on the steps of the historic Arcade Mall, leaning a shoulder against a granite pillar and picking his cuticles. He noticed Billy but looked away and said nothing. Billy sat beside him, on a granite step laid long ago by the sons of the men who had fought Cornwallis. Millions of footsteps over nearly two hundred years had eroded a saddle into the rock.

They sat in silence. The air smelled like fried food and tailpipes.

In front of them, private cars, box-style delivery trucks, and students on old bicycles jiggled over the rough combination of cobblestones and potholes on the one-way road. Street people hustled quarters from customers pouring out of Dunkin' Donuts. Businesspeople clicked spiked heels and dress shoes up the granite stairs, heading for afternoon snacks in the Arcade.

"Your father put a lot of pressure on you back there," Billy said, once he had decided Brock had accepted his presence and would not flee from him.

"He's dead," Brock said. He bit off a tiny chunk of cuticle and spat it away. "Which means now I have to become somebody."

Billy considered for a moment what he had said. "You mean, it's time to become something other than Gil Harmony's kid?"

Brock looked at him. He said, "What do you really do for Mr. Smothers? You're no clerk."

"Is it that obvious?"

"If a sixty-year-old lawyer does his own hiring, his clerks will tend to be young, hot, and stacked. You're zero-for-three."

"Maybe his wife hired me for him."

"Maybe you're his investigator."

Zing. *Okay, this kid is sharp.* Of course Brock would be bright; he was descended from the genius who was everybody's favorite law professor.

An old man scraped along the sidewalk, painfully dragging a bad leg. He wore a long, grimy T-shirt stained with yellow circles under the armpits where his sweat had repeatedly soaked and dried. He sipped from a bottle wrapped in a paper bag.

"That guy limps worse than I do," Brock said. "Do you ever just pick somebody out of a crowd and wonder what the hell happened to them? You know, somebody with a deformity, or in a wheelchair or on crutches? Or somebody like this dude, who obviously lives on the street. Some happy new mom, maybe seventy years ago, nursed this guy in the middle of the night. She loved him. So what the hell happened to him?"

They watched the old man cross the street toward them. He blocked a line of five cars for a full minute. When he passed near them, Brock called out, "Hey, buddy—whatchu drinking there?"

The guy squinted at them, suspicious. His lower jaw was offset from the top, as though it had been dislocated long ago and never properly reset. The odor of piss and cigarettes surrounded the man. Billy wanted to look away. *Is there possibly a person in the world who loves this man?* He felt the lightness at the corners of his mouth that preceded that god-awful, uncontrollable, ironic, evil smile. He bit hard on his lip.

"I'm not making fun of you," Brock assured the man. He nodded to the bottle. "I want to buy a sip."

The bum closed one eye and looked down into the bottle, then reached it toward Brock. "It's bad," he warned in a growl.

Brock snatched it, bag and all, swirled it with gusto, and took a long tug. "Ahhh!" Then his face wrinkled. "Oh, my Christ! Peach schnapps? Nasty. How about one shot for my friend?" he asked. He handed the bottle to Billy, saying, "It's my treat. One sip won't kill ya."

No time to argue—Billy needed this interview with Brock. He put the bottle to his lips, let the sickly sweet liquor touch his tongue, and then handed it back to its owner. "Awful," he confirmed.

Brock pulled two fives from his pocket and gave the cash to the startled bum. "There's a liquor store on Westminster Street," he advised. "Get yourself some better booze."

They watched the bum shuffle off. Brock called after him, "Don't you be wasting that money on food!"

"You have an unusual philanthropic streak," Billy said.

Brock smiled and nodded toward the man. "Did you see what he just did? He wiped the bottle with his T-shirt."

Billy laughed. "He's cleaning *our* germs?"

"There's nothing unusual about making people happy," Brock said. "What does it matter *how* you do it, so long as you do?" He folded his hands over his chest and leaned back on his elbows. He stared at the upper floors of the bank tower across the street for a minute. Then suddenly he started a new conversation. "I used to think that the reason I'm on the planet would become obvious for me one day."

"As it did for your father?"

"Mm-hm. My father was here to serve the law. Period. You're not as dumb as I feel, Mr. Povich."

"I don't like people in their twenties calling me Mr. Povich," Billy said. "Why do you feel dumb?"

"Because I can't imagine why I survived that night." His eyes scanned the streetscape, looking for answers in the windows of the downtown offices. "You heard the judge on the video. He sentenced me to be a great man, like he was—but I haven't a clue how to do that. I thought I'd have more time to figure it out. More time to deliberate in his shadow, a cool and cozy place, where not much was expected of me. But now he's gone, the spotlight shines, and the time for figuring is here."

"No thought of law school?" Billy asked, to keep the conversation alive. Interviews are fires that must be stoked with questions.

"Me? Follow in *those* footsteps? Fuck no. Uncle Linc tried that. You see how well that turned out."

"Why don't your uncle and your mother get along?"

"Because she's not in love with him, and never has been."

"Ah."

Brock licked his lips. "I can still taste that awful schnapps," he said. He closed his eyes. "I can still hear the shot."

"You were asleep?"

"You must have read the police report."

"I'd like to hear it from you," Billy said, feeling a pang of guilt for pushing him, and then adding to sooth his conscience, "if you're up to it."

Brock shrugged, eyes still closed. "I'm not going to cry, if that's what you're afraid of."

"That wouldn't scare me."

"It seemed," Brock began, "like the bang was still echoing when I opened my eyes." He opened them now and looked at Billy. "No confusion, no thought that this might be a dream, you know? That shot was real. A *crack*, like from a forty cal, not the chunky boom from my dad's favorite forty-four. I flung myself out of bed and listened for a few seconds. Had my dad misfired a pistol into a wall or something, he would have yelled to let me know everything was all right. As I walked toward my door, I was surprised not to hear his voice. I could hear footsteps downstairs, walking around, not quite frantic... more like *urgent*. Like somebody was looking for something, maybe the cordless phone or the first-aid kit. So as I'm running down the stairs, I'm thinking he hurt himself, and I'm bracing for some horror show in the reading room, while still assuming everything was probably fine. And that's when I ran into . . . you know . . . *him*. Literally bumped into him at the bottom of the stairs. Don't know which of us was more shocked."

"What did he look like?"

"Like his picture in the paper, except no goatee, and not all bruised."

"That was Adam Rackers's old mug shot in the newspaper," Billy said, instantly cursing himself for saying aloud a name Brock had gone out of his way not to mention. "I mean, how did he carry himself?"

Brock searched inside for the memory for a few moments. "Outwardly calm at all times, if you can imagine," he said. "Held the gun with a steady hand. But his voice sounded tightly wound and intense. I thought maybe he was coked up."

"Maybe he was."

"I just stared at him and stuttered, and not too diplomatically. My mouth had disconnected from my brain and I think I asked him what the fuck was going on down here. Something like that."

Billy monitored Brock's face and voice for signs of stress—signs that Billy was pushing too hard. He was a strong kid, and Billy pressed for more. "So he asked you about a wall safe?"

"Which we don't even have at the house in Charlestown," Brock said. His face wrinkled at a memory that did not make sense. "And that's what I told him. Funny thing, he didn't accuse me of lying. . . . I think he believed I just didn't know what I was talking about. And at this point, I realized I hadn't heard or seen my dad. I got real cold and my vision blurred and I may have started to black out. Next thing I remember, he was telling me that a wall safe would be behind a painting or a bookcase or something. He told me to lead him through the house."

Brock shifted on the stairs, leaned forward and rested his chin on his hands, elbows on his knees. He didn't seem in danger of tears, but his eyes were flat.

A portly middle-aged guy lumbered down the sidewalk, shouting into a wireless cell phone earpiece. ". . . *St. Louis advised that Anchorage inside-ops would review the core competencies vis-à-vis the vendor's distribution models. I say it's a value-ad . . .*"

Brock raised an eyebrow behind the man's back and chuckled.

Billy shrugged. "Is he speaking Norwegian?"

Then Brock asked, "Why does Mr. Smothers want you to ask me these questions? Does he think he can protect my mom's assets from Uncle Linc?"

Now, Billy was a nimble liar. How many times had the words *I'll have your money tomorrow* rolled off his lips, sounding as pure as the pope's bedtime prayer? Sometimes such a lie would free him from the steroid-inflated arms of a debt collector, without so much as having his fingers purposely slammed a few times in a car door. Billy had lied so well, his ex-wife hadn't known he was gambling again until the repo men came for the house.

Yet, when facing the fatherless son of a jurist—a father who had made a career of hacking through lies like an adventurer swinging a machete through the jungle—Billy reflexively offered the truth: "Martin Smothers doesn't think Rackers broke in to rob any wall safe. He thinks somebody paid Rackers to shoot your dad."

The words hit Brock like a flick of cold water in the face—a slight jerk of the head from mild shock, and then a heavy-browed scowl, more annoyed than angry. Brock leaned back on his elbows and stared straight ahead.

"A little more than two weeks before the shooting, you scared an intruder from your family's condo—where the judge often stayed when he was working in Providence," Billy said. "Three days later, the police noticed Rackers hanging around your beach house in Charlestown. It looks like he was stalking the judge."

Brock seemed unimpressed. "There's a break-in every night *somewhere* in this city. Some crack addict was probably trying to steal my CD collection."

Billy plowed forward. "Rackers was a full-time shoplifter, and a sadly ordinary burglar," he explained, in an excited voice that pumped life into Martin's hypothesis, even though Billy did not entirely accept the theory. "Never shot anyone before."

"That you know of."

This kid sounds like my old man.

"Point given," Billy said. "But there's no other violence on his record . . . well, except a bar fight or something, um—"

"You don't need my permission to investigate," Brock said, cutting him off.

"But I need your memories."

Brock rolled his eyes. "You're dramatic, Billy," he said. "You should come to art school and sit in my drama class."

"Oh, so you're going back to school?"

"You heard the judge." He sounded resigned to a fate he did not choose, but had no earthly power to change.

"Yeah, the judge," Billy said. "Is it wrong for Martin to want justice for his friend?"

Brock lobbed an imaginary football to a man jogging down the street. "My father thought Martin Smothers was foolish," he said.

He's trying to hurt me, Billy realized. Brock wanted to punish Billy for suggesting somebody might have gotten away with Judge Harmony's murder. The comment glanced off Billy with no damage. Martin was Billy's best friend, but, yeah, the odd little vegan was a bit foolish. Instead of amassing wealth, Martin performed a disrespected virtue—he legitimized justice. By defending villains who inflicted their sick dreams on the community, Martin redeemed all of us who lived under the law. Criminals brutalize us; in return, we brutalize them, by ending their lives in steel cages. The difference between what we do and what the villains do is the criminal defense lawyer.

"He's a little foolish," Billy conceded. "But he's not a fool. And you cannot look me in the eye and say your father didn't respect Martin Smothers as much as any other lawyer."

Brock deflated a bit. "Point given," he mumbled. He looked away, cast a lingering glance at a passing businesswoman in a tight skirt, and then offered, "If I tell you the rest, can you do this without upsetting my mom? She's wrecked on the inside. She wants me to go to law school. Wants me to disown Uncle Linc. Wants me to visit the cemetery every day, even though she hasn't gone since the funeral. And she's nagging me to visit the other guy who survived the crash."

"Stu Tracy?"

"I don't think I can *walk* into that hospital room with just a few scars and a sore foot, and see him lying there, all smashed," he said, a shiver in his voice. "I just can't fucking do it, Billy."

Billy promised, "Everything I do is under the radar. Your mom won't even know. So take me back into the house."

Brock's eyes widened for a moment as he searched for where he had left off. "Really isn't that much more to tell," he said. "I wandered through the house with a gun at my spine, lifting the artwork so he could see there was no wall safe. When I turned down the hall toward the reading room, he yelled, 'I already checked down there. . . . Get away from there.' But it was too late to stop me from seeing. The judge was facedown over his desk. In blood."

Brock's voice was strong, if a little detached. Billy noticed he used the term "the judge" to put emotional distance between himself and what he had witnessed.

"I didn't scream, exactly. I chattered, like in the monkey cage at the zoo. He got rough, shoved me into a few walls until I shut up. Then he suddenly decided we'd leave."

"Just like that?"

Brock nodded. He looked away and told the next part of the story to an imaginary audience on the sidewalk.

"We left out the back door. He told me to guide him through the woods to the road. I was numb from the neck up—I didn't even think of getting a flashlight. He followed me into the woods. It was slow, by just the light of the moon. I was afraid he'd shoot me and leave me in the swamp. Even though I was leading the way, I was afraid to stumble into a shallow grave he had prepared for me. Or that he'd force me to dig my own. The mind comes up with all kinds of scenarios."

"I'm sure," Billy croaked. He cleared his throat and blinked the starchy feeling from his eyes, for what the kid had gone through. He also felt a stir in his belly. His newsman's instincts were buried, but not dead. *This would be a hell of a story.*

"Wanna hear the worst of these scenarios?" Brock asked.

With a nod, Billy accepted the penance.

"Out there in the woods, I got to thinking . . . if a killer forces you to dig your own grave, should you do a good job?"

He went on to describe the carjacking—how Rackers dragged Stu Tracy out of the old Lincoln and forced Brock to drive. He described the harrowing fight against the car's sloppy steering, through snaking country roads, with Stu and Adam Rackers in the backseat. He recalled the moment he realized Rackers would never let them walk away alive, and he described his dangerous gamble, to drive ever faster in a last-gasp effort to force Rackers to hand over the gun.

The crash? A patchwork of visions in his mind, he told Billy, but no memories he could trust.

Billy prodded him with questions. They were probing, intelligent questions, and they belied the thought ringing relentlessly through Billy's skull.

Should you do a good job digging your own grave?

"So he just forced you into the woods?" Billy asked. "Without taking anything? No silverware or jewelry or even the judge's wallet?"

"He had come for a safe. Maybe he didn't want to scavenge for the little stuff."

"Like your mom's diamond earrings?" Billy replied, shooting the kid a raised eyebrow. "Rackers took *nothing* except you, and your father's life." In trying to convince Brock that Rackers was a hired killer, Billy was beginning to convince himself, and he argued with a breathy passion. "That's why we think somebody *paid* him."

Brock thought it over. He shrugged. "He might have just missed the earrings."

"He missed the stones," Billy agreed. "And how a sharp-eyed thief like Adam Rackers could do that is a mystery. That's why it's important you tell me everything that happened."

The color drained from Brock's cheeks. He slid a finger slowly down the line of stitches on his face, slowly enough to count each stitch. Then he said in a low voice, "Something he said didn't make sense at the time."

He paused, waiting for Billy.

"Something you didn't mention to the police?" Billy prompted.

"I didn't think it mattered," Brock confessed. "But when he suddenly decided he was leaving, and that I was coming with him, I was surprised. He hadn't even checked upstairs for a safe. He just looked at his watch, cursed under his breath, and told me, 'The man gets mean when you make him wait.' At the time I thought he was talking about himself, like he was telling me he was *the man*."

Billy squeezed Brock's shoulder. "Who knows what the hell he meant?" he said. As his mouth spoke the gentle lie, Billy offered the young man a silent oath to track down The Man, who had paid a shooter to kill Brock Harmony's father and Rhode Island's best judge.

ten

The train lurched to motion and rolled from an underground bunker near the State House in downtown Providence, heading south on rails parallel to the highway, into the early-morning headlights speeding up Route 95 toward the city. The six-car electric Amtrak coach ground down the tracks with a mesmerizing hum. The steel wheels made a tooting toy horn noise in the curves. The train motored past the windowless backsides of warehouses, under bridges scored by graffiti, past the stacks of used tires piled behind auto body shops that tried to make a good impression from the front. Martin opened his newspaper. The sun rising over his left shoulder made a natural reading lamp. People staggered like drunkards down the aisle toward the café car. Commuters on their way to Manhattan read spreadsheets and magazines, or walled themselves behind their BlackBerries or their iPods. This was an eclectic group in this car, Martin thought, judging by the tones on their cellular telephones, which cried for attention with rock music, circus themes, and the opening bars to the theme from *Hogan's Heroes*.

Martin had been too nervous for breakfast. Now his empty

stomach churned. He found himself at the obituary page. He scanned quickly to be sure there was nobody he knew, and then he settled into the obit of a retired family doctor.

> . . . he was the first sight on this earth for more than six thousand newborns, delivered with calm, with expertise, and with dry wit and contagious poise that gave even first-time fathers the confidence to cut the cord. . . .

Martin smiled. Though the obituaries were unsigned, he knew Povich's writing when he saw it. Everybody was a hero in a Billy Povich obit, because Billy had an eye for what set regular folk apart. That was what also made him a good investigator. An assignment to type obituaries on the overnight shift had been a demotion for Billy, a hint from his editors that his services were no longer required. Instead of sulking, Billy had embraced the job. He didn't type obituaries all night, he *wrote* them. His writing gave the paper a depth of soul it never had before.

Outside the windows, smears of green whipped alongside the train at more than a hundred miles an hour. Greater Providence is so congested, a native to the city can forget how much of the state still feels rural and unspoiled. In South County, the forest opened around the train, and the land pitched gently across miles of perfect green turf farms. Huge diamonds of black earth marked the summer harvest, where the land would be rested and then seeded again. The houses grew larger and farther apart as the train pushed south, over the Pawcatuck River into northeastern Connecticut. For miles, the train hugged the seacoast, traveling a narrow right-of-way between million-dollar estates on the right and the still waters of Long Island Sound on the left. The land met the water at a bulwark of rust-colored boulders and smooth cordgrass that was now more tan than green, as its color faded with the summer. Cabin cruisers neatly filled the slips of private marinas that dotted the inlets.

The train slowed here to highway speed.

Martin leaned his forehead on the window and appreciated the view. A wooden dock, bleached silver by the elements, reached into the water. An overturned aluminum rowboat rested upon the dock, and a stately great blue heron, its beak a stiletto, rested on the boat. A seascape artist could have made use of this view.

If only I were a painter, Martin thought. Instead of a goddamn lawyer who could not ignore a question that pestered him.

He wiped his wet palms on his pants. From his coat pocket he pulled a single sheet photocopied from Gil Harmony's two-hundred-page last will and testament.

Section 167, perpetual maintenance of Midtown condominium.

What the heck was this about?

Gil had commuted to New York by train eight times per month to teach class, so it made sense he would buy a condo for the two nights each week he stayed in the city. He had plenty of money. Why deal with hotels?

But why would the judge establish in his will a generously funded trust to continue to pay condominium fees, and "to maintain the apartment in its current condition in perpetuity"?

The condo may never be sold nor rented, the will commanded. Just maintained. In its current condition. Well, what the hell was its current condition? And why would a dead man need a condo?

Martin reminded himself he was obsessing about four lines tucked into an enormous document that dispersed tens of millions of dollars to charitable causes around the Western world and in Africa.

Christ, why can't I just let it go?

He was reminded of what Mr. Thybony, Gil's executor, had said on the phone.

Let it go, Marty. Let it go.

Martin had called only for an explanation, not to challenge the paragraph on behalf of his clients, June and Brock Harmony.

Thybony had stonewalled him. "It's in there because Gil wanted it that way," he had said.

But why?

"Let it go, Marty. Let it go."

On Gil's video, Martin remembered, the judge had called Ken Thybony the keeper of his secrets.

The condo's address was not in the will, but property deeds are public records, and Gil's deed had been filed in the county recorder's offices. The unit was on the twenty-seventh floor of an anonymous forty-story high-rise. Gil Harmony had owned the condo for two years.

In the marsh to Martin's right, acres of salt meadow hay bloomed deep purple. The two-foot stalks had been combed erratically by the wind like a head of cowlicks. On the edges of the marsh, white birch grew in clumps of four or five. The train passed beaches, sliced through forest that hung overhead to make a tunnel, and sailed over blond fields of wild wheat.

Another train appeared from nowhere. It passed in the other direction with a sudden hiss, in less than two seconds on parallel tracks.

That's the trouble with trains, Martin thought. *Once you're aboard, there's no way to chicken out and turn back.*

If his imagination could have supplied one reasonable explanation for that section of Gil's will, Martin would have saved a hundred dollars in train fare and stayed home. He had promised himself he'd jump the train at one of the scheduled stops if he could come up with some explanation. If Gil had died of a heart attack or in a car accident, this trip would have been easier to skip. But in a murder, no possible clue was too obscure to leave unexamined.

Martin was going to have to knock on the door.

The train left the marshlands and plowed through suburbs, stopping briefly in New Haven, where the concrete buildings near the tracks were crumbling, as if they had been gnawed by some immense steel-jawed monster. The train stopped again in Stamford, overlooking a junkyard with water views, near office towers that grew fatter as they got taller. On the south side of Stamford, civilization overtook the forest; cultivated gardens squeezed out the wild woods. As the train approached New York, plants were confined to reservations inside chain fences.

The sky darkened as the spires of Manhattan came into view. The train crossed the East River on a bridge high above a lonely tug pushing a barge loaded with yellow storage containers. Martin pulled his suit coat tightly around himself, like a straitjacket. The city looked like a bed of nails. He feared what he would find there. Or that he would find nothing at all, no clue to who paid for the hit on his mentor. Or, even worse, that he would somehow learn that he was wrong, and that Gil Harmony had died in a robbery, as a random victim. *Wrong place, wrong fucking time.* Randomness upset Martin. Randomness would mean there was no grand plan for everyone, that fate played no role in our lives, and that nothing happened for a reason. *That there is no god.* Randomness meant there was no right or wrong, and that the term *justice* was shorthand for pushing paper through a courthouse bureaucracy. He shivered in his coat.

On his third step outside Penn Station, a raindrop struck Martin's nose. *No, it can't rain now.* He walked as far as the curb before the clouds unleashed a ferocious downpour. All around him, travelers instantly whipped open black umbrellas like gunslingers with oily quick draws. Who had said anything about rain today? Martin felt like the only person in Manhattan without an umbrella. The first ten cabs he tried to hail ignored him.

Screw this. The apartment was twenty-five blocks away. He turned up his collar, hunched into the slanting rain, and walked. This was the loudest rain he had ever heard, a relentless pounding on cars and streets, on the metal roofs of newspaper stands, and on the stretched fabric of thousands of umbrellas. It was the kind of rain that inspired a man to build an ark.

He was quickly soaked straight through his lucky Boston Red Sox silk boxer shorts, which his militant vegan wife would no longer allow him to keep in the house because, she had decided, they represented the ruthless exploitation of the silkworm. Rainwater gushed along the curbs in little rivers that flowed hard enough to churn tiny white rapids. Martin's socks were soaked and he didn't bother to try to hop the puddles. Passing cars threw sheets of water over pedestrians. The rain soaked Martin's beard and plastered the hair haphazardly against his neck. He passed a junk store selling umbrellas for forty dollars each, and marveled at the proprietor's moxie.

Finally, he found Gil Harmony's condominium building. The doorman didn't want to hear Martin's conspiracy theories about a murdered judge, or any long-winded narrative about a will in probate court in Providence, Rhode Island. Martin finally just paid off the goddamn doorman. Pocketing enough cash to buy a market-rate umbrella, if he had wanted, the doorman discreetly stepped aside. The building's lobby had been done in art deco cream and black, with a pink marble floor partially hidden by a monstrous round braided rug. Good God, how hideous. Alone in the elevator, Martin leaned his head against the brass doors and watched the drips run off his sports coat. His waterlogged clothing conformed to his body like a wetsuit, and Martin realized his potbelly made him look like he was in the third trimester. As he wondered if the bribe he had paid the doorman was tax deductible, the elevator opened to a pair of decorative rubber plants in ceramic pots, and a long white hallway full of doors.

His feet squished down the hallway. Wet, cold, and fearful he was on a fool's errand, Martin thought that nothing on earth could have made him more miserable.

Then he knocked at the late Gil Harmony's condominium.

The door flew open almost instantly. A woman appeared. She was short and broad-shouldered and a little paunchy, with Caribbean skin and a long brown ponytail highlighted with strokes of gold.

"Yeah?" she demanded, and gave him a look-over. "Oh Lord, what the hell happened to you?"

Martin's hands smoothed his sopping coat. "It's raining," he blurted. "I'm looking for . . . is this two seven one six?"

"What do you want?" She had a slight Spanish accent. "I get all the magazines I need."

A voice from deeper in the apartment called out, "Ma? Is that Zach?"

"No, it ain't," she yelled back, and then looked to Martin for some explanation.

"I'm a friend of Judge Gilbert Harmony," Martin stammered.

"Gil's dead."

"I know that, I'm . . . may I ask who you are?"

"I'm his wife."

eleven

Her name was Nelida and her fabric softener smelled like Christmas trees. Martin huddled on a three-legged barstool in her kitchen and watched his linen suit, shirt, socks, and lucky Boston Red Sox boxer shorts tumble in her professional-style clothes dryer. She had lent him a long white terry-cloth robe, with a tasseled gold rope for a waist belt, and the letters *GH* embroidered in scarlet script over the breast pocket.

Gilbert Harmony's robe.

I'm his wife.

She chopped scallions on a maple cutting board. Martin watched her from behind. She wore steep wedge sandals, a loose pair of dark knee-length gauchos, like something a stylish cowgirl might wear to a rodeo, and a clingy patterned top in muted southwestern colors. Her weight shifted from one foot to the other and Martin noted the easy pivot of her hips.

She was not Gil Harmony's *wife*, exactly, she had explained to Martin, after hustling him into the apartment and demanding he strip his wet clothes in her bathroom. For two years, she and Gil had enjoyed something of a common-law arrangement, two nights a week. She was around thirty-eight, he guessed, about twenty years younger than her lover. Martin liked how she moved: smooth and precise, like a dancer.

Her kitchen was mostly white, with Corian countertops, stainless-steel appliances, and a tremendous copper hood over the stove. Six bottles of wine, all reds, dangled in a wire rack suspended from the ceiling, next to a hanging rope of garlic and a cluster of dried parsley. She dropped a handful of scallions into a pan of hissing hot olive oil.

Martin cleared his throat. "You don't have to feed me," he said.

"You said you had not eaten. So you'll have an omelet." She turned down the blue flame under the pan and stirred the scallions with a wooden spoon. "No more arguing with me."

Fine, then. No more arguing. He was starving and his mouth watered at the scent of home cooking.

There was no reconciling this woman, this apartment, even the robe, with the judge Martin had known in Providence. So he stopped trying. The woman was real; therefore, Martin's long-standing image of Gil Harmony was false. Or at least incomplete and in need of a rewrite. Martin imagined Gil's voice in his head. *Even the Constitution had to be amended, Marty.*

Nelida's silence as she cooked for him made Martin feel even more naked inside Gil Harmony's robe. He attacked the quiet. "I'm sorry, um—for your loss." The words came out like a question and Martin regretted saying them.

"A loss unlike I have ever known," she confirmed. Her dainty eyebrows rose and fell, agreeing with what she had spoken. She poured yellow egg batter from a mixing bowl into the pan, and then turned the heat down again. She looked at him. "A loss for you, too. He was your friend."

"And mentor," Martin said, eager to reach common ground with her.

She suddenly snapped the spoon in his direction, pointing to him. "No sausage in this omelet, right? You don't eat meat."

Martin could not help a laugh. "I'm not supposed to eat eggs, either, but I cheat. How could you know that?"

She shrugged and carelessly tested the omelet with the spoon. "Gil told me that if anything ever happened to him, you'd be the one from Providence to find me," she said. "You'd represent his wife, of course. And Gil figured that nobody else would be *particular* enough to find this apartment hidden in his paperwork."

"Gil's partner, Ken Thybony, knows about you," Martin guessed.

She shrugged. "I have met Ken in Gil's company so he knows I exist. Whether he knows that Gil and I were to be married as soon as Gil left his first wife, I couldn't say."

He was struck that she referred to June Harmony as Gil's *first wife*. Would he really have left June? And scandalized his name in Rhode Island? That seemed inconceivable, though Martin had to remind himself he did not know his friend as well as he thought. He summoned the courage to ask, "When was he planning to leave?"

She folded the omelet and then clanked a metal lid over the pan. "Give the egg a few more minutes to set," she said.

"Smells great."

"He would have left as soon as the time was right," she informed Martin, though she did not look at him. Was she embarrassed at stealing a husband? Or did she doubt her own story? "I didn't push him to leave, because his son was still in their house in Rhode Island. That was okay. I knew I had Gil's heart."

Martin was too polite to cross-examine over her alleged hold on Gil Harmony's heart. Maybe she was right; maybe she knew him better than anyone. Or maybe she had bought the same easy lie as every other *comatta* since Moses carried the bad news about adultery down from the mountain.

"Gil was already in semiretirement," she said. "He was working to add a third class to his university schedule here in the city so that we could have another evening together each week. Once he left the bench completely in Rhode Island, he would have moved here and this would have been our home." She gestured to the cabinet above Martin's head. "There are plates in there."

Martin was loath to move around in the robe. He held the edges of the garment in place and spun on the stool. On the inside of the cabinet door he discovered an eight-by-ten photograph that snatched his breath.

The picture of Judge Gilbert Harmony had been taken at a ball game. He sat in the bleachers, beaming under a navy blue Red Sox cap. Nelida sat to his left, in the blue and orange cap of the New York Mets. She grinned in the picture; her chin pressed to his shoulder and she hugged his arm.

Martin had not doubted Nelida's story about the affair, and the robe had been confirmation enough, but he was stunned by the irrefutable proof of Gil Harmony's secret life.

At least she's not a Yankees fan, Martin thought.

She caught him staring at the photo and explained, "It was taken last year."

"A lovely shot," Martin said, admitting the truth. *They look happy*. "Who took it?"

"My son, Jerod."

Martin noticed the empty seat next to Gil in the photo. So this had been a family outing to the ballpark. He pulled a plate from a stack. He stopped himself before he asked aloud why she kept such a lovely photo hidden from view. Of course, he realized, it was tucked away so no visitor would see it accidentally. Never having had his own affair, Martin assumed this was standard infidelity procedure.

She took the plate from him and eased the omelet onto it. She added a fork and a twist of orange and handed the meal to Martin. She scrubbed the pan as he ate. He wondered, *How much did she love the judge?* Enough to slide alone into her empty bed five nights a week, knowing that Gil would be in bed with June? She seemed genuine, but there were a lot of great actors in the world. What if she loved him too much to share anymore? He watched her arms flex as she washed the dishes. She was a forceful, direct person. What if she had demanded that Gil leave his wife, and he had refused?

Suddenly, Martin recalled what Gil had said to June on the video.

I didn't intend for it to happen, all this hurt you're feeling. Some things are, well, just larger than ourselves.

Of course. Seemed so obvious in hindsight. Martin had assumed at the time Gil was apologizing for somehow crossing fate and getting killed. Gil must have figured June might learn about the affair, maybe even that Martin would discover the mistress.

Hmm, so he didn't intend for it to happen? Small comfort in that. *Some things are larger than ourselves . . .* sounded like a confession of love. Maybe he did intend to marry Nelida, or at least he did the day he made the tape.

He finished the food and left the plate on the counter. "Brilliant," he announced.

She smiled with satisfaction at his empty plate.

"Tell me," he asked, probing something that bothered him. "Why did Gil warn that I might find you, should something happen to him? Was he expecting something to happen?"

Her face darkened with dread and her hands began to twist a dish towel into a rope. She started to speak, but paused, and then turned toward footsteps coming from the hall and asked, "Are you going out?"

A young man of about twenty poked his head into the kitchen, gave the mostly naked lawyer on the barstool an up-and-down inspection, and answered, "I'm going to Zach's."

"I thought he was coming here."

"I screwed up. I'm late."

Nelida gestured to Martin. "Jerod, this is Mr. Smothers," she said brightly. "He was close to Gil."

The two men seemed more in tune to the awkwardness of the moment. Martin glanced to the dryer to see his boxer shorts tumble past the porthole. He nodded hello to Jerod. Nelida's son was obviously an athlete who had worked hard honing a V-shaped torso. The hair above his ears was shaved to swathes of stubble, leaving a patch of black curls atop his head. He wore a long green New York Jets football jersey with the number 28, and big round eyeglasses in wire frames, looking similar to the fake glasses Martin often provided for his clients, to make felonious people look studious in front of a jury.

"Are you packed?" Nelida asked her son.

"When I get back."

"Leave yourself time because we have a long drive."

"Mm-hm," he promised as he left.

Martin waited until the apartment door banged shut to ask, "Are you traveling?"

"To Providence," she said. "For Gil's memorial. You'll be there too, I'd assume."

The funeral had been for family only. The bar association had organized a public tribute for the legal and political communities to pay respect to Judge Harmony.

"Gil's clerk is organizing the speaking program at the memorial," Martin said. "She asked me to say a few words."

And June Harmony, too.

Nelida read his mind. "There were reasons to stay hidden when Gil was alive," she said. "Not anymore. I won't dishonor our relationship by being ashamed of it. You can help. You can tell them that I am coming and I'm bringing the son Gil treated like his own."

The dryer buzzed and Martin's clothes collapsed, as if from exhaustion, to the bottom of the drum. Nelida stepped toward the dryer but Martin raised an index finger and froze her in place. "Why did Gil think something might happen to him?"

She retreated a few steps and grabbed the counter, for strength, perhaps. "He had a threat."

"Judges get threats all the time," Martin replied. "Convicted men being led away in chains yell all sort of crazy stuff." *My own goddamn clients.*

"This one was from the mobster, Glanz."

"Rhubarb Glanz?"

"Gil sent his son to prison. I suppose you did not represent him, Mr. Smothers?"

"My clients are not so rich."

"Glanz swore he would have revenge."

"I don't remember hearing of any threat," Martin said, challenging her, to measure how she reacted.

"The threat was in a restaurant on Federal Hill, a few weeks after the sentencing. Gil and his clerk were having lunch and talking about some cases when Glanz and two big goons walked in. They told Gil he should reduce the sentence he had imposed on Glanz's son. When Gil refused, they told him he would regret his decision, and that he would pay. Not in so many words, but Gil got the message."

"There must have been witnesses to this threat."

"Just his clerk."

"Well, that would have been enough evidence to get the police involved. Maybe not enough to file charges, but certainly enough to have some protection assigned to the judge."

She looked away. "Gil didn't report the incident," she said. "He didn't want protection. He told me not to worry, and that he probably would not need it."

"He what—?"

Oh. Of course. Gil Harmony could not have undercover cops

following him to Mets games with his secret second family. Martin looked down to his bare feet and the curling yellow toenails that suddenly embarrassed him. He needed his clothes. He needed to get out of there. He needed to find a phone, to reach Povich and turn him on to Rhubarb Glanz.

twelve

"Bo, don't make funny faces at the blind guy," Billy ordered.

"Grandpa's doing it," the kid replied in self-defense.

"Nobody likes a tattletale," the old man said.

Stu Tracy laughed in a happy gurgle. He said, "I won't be blind when they take these bandages off. And then I'll see what those faces look like."

"Do I have to dial nine to get an outside line?" Billy asked, the room phone in his hand.

No answer.

"You talking to me?" Stu said.

"Yeah, what am I thinking? Sorry."

"I can hear somebody making faces at me," Stu said. "And dial nine, Billy."

Bo giggled. "Oh Stu-oooh," the kid called playfully. "Mr. Einstein is making faces at you."

Stu laughed. He said, "Then I guess Mr. Einstein ain't as smart as everybody says."

Stu Tracy's hospital room seemed less morbid since Billy had persuaded Stu to add the Povich family—the kid, the old man, and Mr. Einstein—to his visiting list. After the old man's blood treatment, they visited with Stu.

Bo sat on a folding chair at the head of the bed, next to the old man, in his wheelchair.

Stu seemed less loopy on this visit. He had said the doctors had eased back on his pain medication, to find the right compromise between agony and alertness.

Billy had arranged the visits as much for his old man's benefit as for Stu Tracy. The old man liked spilling his stories to a captive audience, and Stu wasn't going anywhere on shattered legs.

And Stu wanted to live. He was desperate to live. Maybe, Billy hoped, a little of that desperation would rub off on his father.

The old man had been badgering Billy to take him to the park, alone, without Bo, so they could talk, man to man. William Povich Sr. wanted to talk about stopping his treatments. These visits with Stu had helped Billy put off the conversation.

"What was so *special* about the New York World's Fair of nineteen thirty-nine was that all the exhibits were *mechanical*," the old man lectured to Stu.

"Mmm," said Stu.

"Not like today where computers can do whatever magic you tell them to do. This was before the intelligent circuit breaker. Take the Ford exhibit, for example . . ."

Of course, after a few more hours of this, Billy thought, *Stu may lose his will to live, too.*

Billy took the phone across the room and sat on the windowsill, six stories above the highway. Cars whizzed south down Route 95; those coming north into the city crawled three abreast in a blaze of brake lights. He found a dial tone and tapped the cellular telephone number of a loan shark he had used from time to time to cover tardy payments to impatient bookmakers.

Bo grabbed the dangling plastic IV tube running into Stu's right arm and gently shook it.

"Bo!" Billy scolded. "Stu's eating dinner through that tube right now."

"Don't play with his food," the old man added.

After three rings, a gruff voice said into Billy's ear, "Señor Pizza, may I help you?"

Billy knew to ignore the greeting, which was a front. Sometimes the loan shark answered as a tire store, sometimes as a pet depot. One time, he answered as a gynecologist.

"Garafino?" Billy said. "It's Povich."

A pause. "Well, Billy, this is a pleasure. No hard feelings on your end, I see." He chuckled.

Billy scratched his nose where Garafino's thugs had once broken it. "That was a misunderstanding," Billy said.

The shark chuckled again. "Did you misunderstand that I wanted to get paid? What did I say that made you think I preferred you stiff me on the loan? Hmm? Just so we don't have any more misunderstandings."

Billy pictured the loan shark: narrow, squirrelly face; a big schnoz with black hair curling inside the nostrils; one gold canine tooth; eyes so dark they seemed all pupil; bushy muttonchop sideburns that tapered to a short Vandyke, carefully trimmed into a demonic triangle; skintight black T-shirt tucked into silk trousers held up by a big square silver belt buckle with a dollar sign on it; annoying chuckle at the misfortunes of others.

Billy switched the phone to his other ear and turned away from his family. "I don't need money," he said. "I need information."

Garafino chuckled again in Billy's ear. "So what I hear is true, eh? You're looking to get to Rhubarb Glanz."

Billy jumped to his feet. "You heard this?"

"News travels."

In the day since Martin had returned from New York City with the news of Judge Harmony's secret life—and of the threat on Harmony's life made by Rhubarb Glanz—Billy had made at least twenty calls to former cop sources, bookies, and retired legbreakers, looking for information on Glanz. He was alarmed that his hunt for news had raced ahead of his calls.

"I need to know where I can find Glanz—outside of his nightclub, his limo with the dark windows, or that fortress he calls home in Newport."

"You think you can whack him?" The shark chuckled.

Whack him?

"Who the fuck do you think I am?" Billy demanded in a low voice. He heard the chuckle again and realized Garafino was taunting him. Billy needled back, "Do you think I'm *you*?"

The shark laughed. "In your best dreams."

"I want to talk to Glanz. Five minutes—with no cops, notebooks, tape recorders, or any of his goons."

Garafino paused. The howl of a fire engine passed on the shark's end of the phone. Billy heard him slurp a sip of something. Sounding grave, Garafino said, "So you wanna talk to Glanz, eh? Do you puff dynamite like a big red cigar?"

"I won't tell him I talked to you."

"Who knows what you say when they hang you head-first into the cheetah cage at the zoo, eh? Will you light a stick of dynamite in my lips, too?" He slurped something again, and then announced, "Might not be in my best interest to help you. I have to think about it, Billy."

Click.

Billy called into the dead phone, "Hello? Hello?" He slammed it down. "That slimy son of a bitch!"

He turned to see June Harmony in the doorway, and Brock a step behind her in the hall.

"Oh, Jesus, I'm sorry," Billy stammered.

"Slimy son of a bitch!" Bo echoed with glee.

The old man shushed the boy. Billy wanted to shrivel up and skitter under Stu Tracy's bed.

Bo had shouted the curse in Stu Tracy's ear. Stu grinned and listened to the room. He heard the footsteps stop at the door, a thick-heeled shoe. A woman's shoe, he guessed. He heard Billy apologize again, and then step into the hall. Stu's head turned automatically to look at the door, though his face was still bandaged. The grayness he saw seemed three-dimensional, as if it started at his eyes and extended for a long distance. Maybe for infinity. His mind converted the sound of footsteps into jagged blue bursts on the insides of his eyelids, like electric mites dashing across his pupils. He banged his left fist on the bed in frustration. Distracted by the visit from the Povich family, he had briefly forgotten he still could not see.

"What's that?" he whispered. "Who's there?"

"They're hiding from us!" Bo shrieked. "Einstein and I should go under the bed."

"You won't like what you find under there," said Mr. Povich, Billy's hoarse and long-winded father, who was forever moaning quietly about the humiliations of old age, and spinning stories about the New York World's Fair of 1939. Stu's chemically warped mind had imagined the fair as some kind of Jazz Age Burning Man festival, populated by merry naked people in fedoras.

Mr. Povich leaned close to Stu. "I think that was June Harmony."

"The judge's wife?"

"I recognize her from the paper. Mm-mm, a fox."

"Mmmm, a fox!" Bo repeated.

"Stow that kind of talk, boy," Mr. Povich ordered. "Till you're twenty-one."

"What is she doing here?" Stu begged in a stage whisper.

"She heard that I was here, and she's looking for some all-night manly action," said Mr. Povich, in his dust-dry delivery that broke Stu into painful chuckles.

The door latch clicked. Stu heard the door push lazy air out of the way as it opened. He heard footsteps, a lot of them. Mr. Povich wiggled in the wheelchair. Even Bo seemed to sense the solemnity of the moment; the boy was still.

Billy made the introduction: "Stu? This is June Harmony, the judge's . . . wife. And her son, Brock. Um . . . it's okay, Brock."

"He made you drive the car," Stu said, imagining the frightened face in his memories.

There was a long, uncomfortable pause.

They're looking at me. Measuring my freakishness against their expectations. Whistling quietly past the cemetery. There but for the grace of God . . . They are afraid of me; I smell it. I am the greasy thumbprint of Death, so close it puts a catch in your throat.

A woman's voice, strong, maternal: "Thank you for having us, Stu. I thought it was important . . . that is, Brock and I thought it important that we see how you are, what you need . . . if there is anything we may do for you."

Smells like guilt.

Stu waited, listened, and heard a soft sniffling. *So he cries.* Stu had not cried much since that first night, right after the crash. Mostly they kept him too stoned to cry. His parents never cried in his presence. The nurses were too professional to cry. Stu was pleased to hear that *somebody* could cry over what had happened.

"It's okay, Brock," Billy Povich said, tenderly.

"Yes, dear," the woman agreed. "It's all right."

Stu heard what sounded like a hand rubbing a shoulder; such a comforting sound. Suddenly, with a burst of imaginary yellow inside his eyelids, Stu Tracy realized he was the most powerful person in the room.

He cannot help me, but I can help him. The blind and broken man in the bed discovered an almost Christlike power to cure another man's psyche. *Speak the words and he shall be healed. . . .*

Stu mustered depth in his voice and said into the darkness: "There was nothing more you could have done. Nothing more either of us could have done. I don't blame you."

The sniffle erupted into a heavy sob.

"Oh, honey," the woman said softly.

Heavy footsteps pounded out of the room.

"Be free!" Stu called after him. He felt like a healer.

thirteen

Like an errant shotgun blast, a swarm of green flies blew from the trash bin when Scratch threw open the lid. The stench of garbage had hints of onion peel and coffee grounds.

He scanned the restaurant parking lot for people, saw nobody, tightened his insides against a gag reflex, and then boosted himself over the lip, into the bin. He landed with a crunch on plastic garbage bags, knee-deep in trash, and sent up another cloud of flies that buzzed in chaos and bounced off his skin.

"Goddamn stupid flies," he muttered to himself, flailing hopelessly at the insects.

His inner pessimist mocked him. *Yeah, who would have expected flies in a Dumpster? Normally they're full of rose petals.*

Anybody who thinks the poor are noble should hang with me for a day, Scratch thought.

He breathed through his mouth and poked around with his foot. The better the restaurant, the more disgusting the trash bin. Why was that? Were better establishments more likely to pitch rotten meat and brown lettuce in the trash? Did that mean inferior places put bad meat on the menu? He shuddered. That was far enough with *that* line of logic. This Dumpster, painted a lovely forest green, and belonging to one of the best restaurants in Providence, was perhaps the most putrid Scratch had ever entered. He did not think about germs. He had lived long enough in squalor to tune his immune system into top fighting shape. And the puncture wound through his sore left arm had been slathered with Neosporin ointment and bandaged under his sleeve with athletic tape.

He rested his elbow on the steel side of the Dumpster. *Could this steel stop a bullet?* It would stop an ice pick, for sure. Was he crazy for thinking this? *Doesn't matter*, answered his inner pessimist. *That puncture wound is probably going gangrene.*

The money he had carried the night he was attacked had not lasted long at a no-tell motel near the airport. Scratch was afraid to tend bar to earn more, and terrified to go home to collect his boosted loot to sell for cash.

To survive, he had to steal.

Though he preferred to call what he did *swindling*.

In Scratch's gerrymandered morality, anyone dumb enough to fall for a street scam deserved what he got. He had made a little dough with some three-card monty, but that was a minimum-wage hustle, especially while working without a partner whom the dealer can allow to win a few hands, to set up the marks.

He had not given up trying to figure out who had attacked him. His mind's eye saw an image of a possible suspect: the manager of the Greek restaurant where Scratch and his old roommate had pulled the ukulele scam. Scratch smiled at the memory. That had been the *smoothest* job. Scratch and Adam had bought a beat-up ukulele at a junk store for twenty bucks. Scratch carried the instrument into a classy restaurant, devoured a lavish sixty-dollar lunch, and then claimed to have forgotten his wallet. When the owner demanded his money, Scratch offered to leave the ukulele for collateral while he went home for his credit card.

That's where Adam took over the scam. While Scratch was out of the restaurant, Adam came in, fawned over the ukulele, claimed it was some rare antique, and offered the restaurateur six hundred dollars for it. He promised to get a bank check, and left.

When Scratch returned, the sly restaurateur casually offered to buy the instrument. They negotiated three hundred dollars, plus the lunch. Scratch had insisted on cash.

Now Scratch realized how much he missed having a partner.

Adam Rackers had been the best wingman Scratch could have asked for. *What the hell happened to you, man?* Why Adam had freaked out and killed a judge in cold blood, Scratch could not imagine. He had learned of the crime from a newspaper headline, and read the details through the spaces between his fingers as he hid behind his hands. For days, Scratch lived in fear the police would learn that Adam had been crashing at Scratch's apartment.

But no cop ever knocked.

How Adam ended up at the judge's house was a mystery to Scratch. Adam had been a competent B and E man, nimble in tight spaces, a daring climber, and good with locks—they had just finished together a successful spree of nighttime burglaries of Providence town houses. But Adam had never mentioned a job in Charlestown. They had never worked that far from the city.

Scratch's foot finally clinked on glass at the bottom of the Dumpster. He tore open a trash bag and discovered a dozen empty champagne bottles and a handful of corks.

Where was a wine steward when you needed one?

The Krug was probably the most expensive of the lot. Too pricey for his needs. Ooh, he saw that some prosperous gentleman had tried the Pol Roger Brut, the lucky bastard. Scratch squinted into the bottle as he would into a microscope, saw a tablespoon of champagne on the bottom rim, and would have sucked it down, if not for the surroundings. But such uncommonly good champagne had too uncommon a name, and he tossed the bottle aside. He settled on an empty container of Dom Pérignon, with its familiar shieldlike label. When in doubt, stick to the classics. He took the bottle, pocketed one cork, and heaved himself out of the bin.

No stains on his clothing, he was pleased to see. He walked hurriedly with the bottle, letting the wind he created brush the garbage smell from his body. His arm throbbed, and he sighed. Being homeless, hiding in motels, swindling all day—it was too much work. He couldn't do this forever.

Eventually, he would have to find the courage to go back to his apartment.

Maybe then buy a dog. Or a machine gun. Or enroll in ninja school.

In a minimall convenience store, Scratch invested ninety-nine cents on a liter of diet ginger ale—he detested the diet-soda aftertaste, but this bottle wasn't for drinking, so what did it matter?—and then he ducked around the back of the mall. He slowly filled the empty champagne bottle with ginger ale, then trimmed the swollen cork with his penknife until he could force it back down the bottleneck with a few blows from his palm.

With his prop under his arm, he walked back to the sidewalk and felt the music of the moment.

I'm singing in my brain.
Just singing in my brain . . .

He walked briskly and scanned for a well-dressed person who was not paying close attention.

He passed on an earthy-crunchy woman watching her feet, and

an artsy kid in dark glasses. Then he found the perfect partner to this scam:

Ladies and gentlemen, this afternoon's mark will be played by that doughy gentleman in the pin-striped suit who is hurrying along and barking into a cell phone.

Scratch walked square into the man.

The bottle dropped and blew apart on the sidewalk.

"Oh God, no!" Scratch howled. He stared at the broken glass and liquid fizz. He clutched his own head in horror. "What have you done?"

The man froze in place. His eyes grew with alarm. He said into the phone, "I'll call you back," and then folded the clamshell device and slipped it into his pocket. A growing puddle approached his feet. He stepped back from it.

"*You* walked into *me*," the man said, diagramming the collision in the air with his hands.

Scratch squatted beside the broken glass, and lifted the piece with the label attached. "It's our anniversary," he said, sounding sad and detached. "I don't have a hundred dollars for another bottle."

"Get her something else," the man offered, gruff. "Flowers."

The scene had attracted a handful of people, curious how it might turn out. Profanity? Violence? Fellowship? Anything was possible.

"Our five-year anniversary," said Scratch.

"*You're* the klutz. Where'd you learn to walk?"

"Five years ago on this date," Scratch said, softly, strangling his inner pessimist, willing himself to *believe*, and summoning true tears, "the love of my life gave me one of her kidneys."

The crowd said, "Awwwww."

"Oh, what a fucking fine day *this* has been," the man growled. He reached for his wallet. "I'll split it with you."

fourteen

The dead do not complain. But who says they don't expect good service?

"Thanks, mate," Billy said.

He ended his long-distance interview with a retired Australian sportswriter, hung up the phone, and smiled over his notes. His customer would have appreciated Billy's work, near the end of his long night shift on the obituary desk. Earlier in the evening, a funeral home had faxed an obituary that contained a mystery. Billy Povich had just solved it for his readers, and for his customer—the late Robert Hoover.

Mr. Hoover had died at ninety-four, though his mind had drifted through dementia for a decade.

At the nursing home, he had liked to be called "Three-Fists." Wouldn't answer to anything else, according to the slim set of facts the funeral director had gathered for the obit. Mr. Hoover had no family. No one to give answers. No one to provide a biography.

Obituaries with no sense of story, no reflection of the life they represented, were like tombstones with no name.

Here Lies Whatshisface.

They were disrespectful to the customer.

A global search of newspaper archives, a little informed guess-work by Billy, and a transworld telephone interview had uncovered the mystery. Billy typed:

PROVIDENCE—Robert K. Hoover, 94, of the Blessed Angel Nursing Facility, died yesterday at home. In his youth, Mr. Hoover had been well known in his native Australia as "Bobby Three-Fists," the teenage bare-knuckle boxing champion of Melbourne, who hit so fast that one of his dazed opponents swore he had an extra fist.

He added quotes and some history from his interview, finished the obituary with funeral information, and filed it electronically for the editors to lay out in the morning.

Then Billy leaned back in his chair, thumped his feet upon the desk, and waited for that glow of satisfaction for having done his job well. He waited . . . waited . . . waited . . . eh, maybe he was tired. The Doomsday Clock on the wall said six minutes to midnight, but that was what it always said; it hadn't worked in decades. Billy's desk clock said 2:20 a.m. Ten minutes to quitting time. He rubbed his eyes and stared at the giant wall clock, some six feet across. The newsroom annex where Billy worked had originally been a train depot. The soaring space had been divided into two floors, wired for fluorescent lights, and crudely painted a two-toned dirty yellow and avocado. Nobody else was there this late into the night. The space reminded Billy of a worn-out office of some forgotten part of government, maybe a waste-water treatment plant on the far edge of nowhere. The giant clock face, with black iron hands and Roman numerals, reminded Billy of the Doomsday Clock invented by the *Bulletin of Atomic Scientists* to symbolize mankind's flirtation with nuclear disaster. At one time,

Billy thought the clock had come to symbolize his own crisis over his ex-wife's death. Now, it reminded him of his father, and the choice they would make together. Should the old man continue his treatment? Or stop running from Doomsday?

The fax machine beeped and hissed and clacked out another obituary. Billy frowned at his desk clock. What undertaker would be sending obits this late at night? Billy scooped the sheet off the machine. . . . If it needed a lot of reporting he would have to hold it for tomorrow. . . .

Reading the first line, Billy felt himself flush.

His heart beat heavy in his ear, struggling to pump, as if his blood had suddenly thickened.

PROVIDENCE—William R. "Billy" Povich, 40, of the Armory Neighborhood, is going to die tonight.

Violently.

For sticking his nose into somebody else's bizzness. It ain't personal. It's just the way things are.

Good-bye, Povich.

At that instant, a fist pounded the door three times.

Billy jumped, stumbled, knocked over his chair. He stuffed the paper in his pocket and dove behind a desk.

Who the fuck is that?

The fist banged three more times on the glass door. Not as a plea: the knock was a demand—open up, it commanded. Billy lay on his belly, panting, staring at a wasteland of flotsam under his desk: paper clips and pen caps, cracker crumbs and bottle caps. A mousetrap set by the cleaning staff waited under the desk, cocked but unbaited; some quick-witted mouse had already Indiana Jonesed the cheddar off the trigger. Billy could use some of that nimbleness at the moment, he thought.

BANG.

BANG.

BANG.

No longer a commandment; that was a threat. Open this door or I break it down.

Billy lifted his head and peeked at the door. A lone figure bundled in a long dark coat stood at the second-floor landing. He had come up the outside staircase. Had taken the chance that somebody on the street might see him. The newspaper's annex was tucked against a highway overpass. The outside stairs, added after the building had been converted to offices, were shrouded in shadow at this time of night, but they faced the street.

Goddamn it, whose bizzness *did I stick my nose into?*

How was Billy supposed to talk his way out of this if he didn't know whom he had offended? He browsed a list of bookies and sharks in his mind. *Who do I owe? Who did I screw?*

Nothing came to mind.

Well, nothing recent.

The figure leaned against the glass and became a dark blur. The visitor changed tactics, and knocked lightly five times with just one knuckle. The hair on the back of Billy's neck rose and fell like sea grass in an underwater current.

Legbreakers looking to collect a debt knocked *hard.*

Killers knock softly.

Billy snatched his phone from his desk, flipped the receiver off, pounded 911, and fumbled with the hand piece on the floor.

"Hello? Hello?" he pleaded.

The dead sound he heard from the phone was like a call to a tomb. He drummed a finger on the hang-up button.

No dial tone.

Uh-oh.

The visitor knocked softly again, but not with a knuckle—

something harder, something metal. A gun? Why couldn't he just go back to pounding?

Billy quietly replaced the receiver, then slid the phone under the desk so he would not trip if he had to run.

What to do?

His first plan was to answer the door with a flying desk chair. Bull-rush him, fight it out on the stairs. Hope some passing driver noticed the commotion and called the cops. Stay alive until the police arrived. *Maybe win the sweepstakes for the World's Worst Plan.*

On hands and knees, Billy crawled to Plan B.

He hurried through a maze of office cubicles toward the back staircase. Carpet burn scorched his knees through his pants. At the back corner of the room, he waited against the fire door, mouth-breathing in silence, sweating tangy fear into his shirt, until he heard the metallic knock again, soft and chilling. Mustering courage, he pushed through the door and sprinted down the stairs. Billy had always been clumsy going *up* stairs; he was a tap dancer going down. At the ground floor, he yanked open the fire door and shot out the stair-well. He ran past empty desks and file cabinets and a conference table littered with sickly office plants, toward the outside door in the back of the building. Even if the visitor had seen Billy make for the stairs, by the time the guy ran down from the landing and around the office, Billy would be lost in the neighborhood. Bullets don't take corners.

Billy's palm hit the panic bar and the door burst open, revealing a steep concrete ramp leading to a parking lot of cracked asphalt.

He never saw the rope.

His foot caught the trip wire just above the ankle. He had the sensation of diving into a pool. *It was all a ruse*, he thought. *The obituary, the knock at the door . . . to get me to run out the back, away from the street.* His fingers grabbed impotently for handholds in the air. He tucked his left shoulder to take the impact, and hit the concrete with an *oomph*. His chin clacked against the ground. Spit and sharp pain flooded his mouth. He had bitten his tongue. The numbness in his hand told him he had suffered a deep scrape, before it even had time to bleed.

They were on him with the rope in an instant.

"Rides like a floating bed, doesn't it?" the driver asked.

Billy said nothing until the goon sitting to Billy's right elbowed him lightly in the ribs and said, "He's talking to you."

"Nothing beats Cadillac for the ride," Billy agreed from the backseat. No lie; it did ride great. *They're taking me for a ride.*

"This is the DTS model," the driver said. He was a little guy, very pale, anemic-looking. "Right off the dealer's lot. Came tricked out like this, all standard. Is the air too much for you guys back there?"

Billy sighed. "I'm comfortable."

The driver pushed his derby hat higher on his forehead, shot Billy a glance in the mirror, and smirked behind his rainbow sunglasses. Billy hoped the guy could see the road through those shades, though it probably would be better if they crashed; at least Billy had a chance to survive in the car. Bullets don't come standard with air bags.

They traveled south on Route 95, exactly at the speed limit. Traffic was light. A few headlights flew by the other direction; the Cadillac seemed to have the southbound lanes mostly to itself. On the right, they passed the broadcast headquarters of a local rock station. The station's call letters glowed in pink neon in a fifth-floor window. The overnight DJ would be awake, Billy thought. Was there nobody else who could help him?

"Make sure them headlights back there ain't following," said the goon sitting on Billy's right.

"I know what I'm doing," the driver snapped. "Keep him under control."

Though the driver tended to give a lot of orders, the goon on the right struck Billy as the true brains of the operation. He was a steroid freak of six foot four, with a profile like the departed Old Man of the Mountain in New Hampshire. His long goatee had been dyed pure white. The other goon was almost as big, with striking green doe eyes, and a brooding sense of doom about him. Billy had not yet heard him speak.

He took measure of his situation. After binding his feet with rope, taping his wrists together with duct tape—and choking what little fight had remained in Billy—they had bandaged the scrape on his palm with tape and an old T-shirt. That was probably so he wouldn't bleed in the car, Billy figured. He swallowed the blood from the cut on his tongue. No sense spitting on the upholstery and angering these men.

Was it time to talk his way out of this? Or would talking hurry his fate? Did these men have authority to decide how the evening would end? Or were they just following orders? Could they be bribed or threatened? *Bribed or threatened? With goddamn what?*

Escape seemed impossible at the moment. Billy's hands were bound in the *front*, which was a tiny advantage if he had to defend himself. But that was a small favor. He could not run with his feet tied, nor could he survive the tumble if he somehow forced past one of the goons, unlatched the door, and inchwormed out of the car.

Nothing to do but sit back and enjoy the smooth ride.

Twenty minutes south of Providence, and just a mile off the highway, the car bounced gently down a graded dirt road, into a vast sand pit dotted with dark blotches of vegetation. The tires crunched softly on gravel. They drove through the open gate in a chain fence and then passed a portable office trailer, a dozen pallets stacked with bricks, and two piles of new white lumber. This was a construction site. Hard to tell what was to be built here. A mall or an office building, probably. Billy sighed. Were it up to him, they'd be building a police academy and a hospital.

He wondered what time it was. Sometime past 3 a.m., for sure. He wondered what Bo and the old man were doing. He never knew with those two. The old man was an insomniac, and the kid a light sleeper. Billy endured a brief flash of dread . . . what would happen if the apartment caught fire when Billy was not around? The kid wasn't strong enough to take his grandpa down the stairs, as Billy did nearly every day, wearing his father like a backpack and carrying him in silence so not to add to the old man's shame. William Povich Sr. weighed barely a hundred pounds, but that was still too much for Bo.

Would the kid know enough to leave the old man and save himself?

Billy shuddered. He feared the kid would not leave, and that the boy would die from smoke trying to save an old man who didn't want to be saved.

The Cadillac's headlights landed on a yellow Caterpillar backhoe with a wide front bucket and a narrow back pail lined with steel teeth. The driver jammed the transmission into park and shut off the car, but left the headlights on. He reached into the glove box for a long metal flashlight, then got out of the car and slammed the door.

The goon on Billy's left smiled and spoke his first words of the evening, "This is your stop, Mr. Povich." He opened the door and stepped out.

Billy swallowed a taste of his own blood. The bleeding had nearly stopped, but his tongue pulsed with dull pain. Outside, the driver panned the light around a moonscape of sand, revealing emptiness that stretched far longer than the flashlight beam.

The other goon nudged Billy toward the open door. "Out, Povich."

"Are you guys going to tell me what the hell this is about?"

"Plenty of time for productive conversation." He pointed and commanded sharply, "Out."

Billy swung his bound feet onto the seat. *Fuck them and the uphol-stery*, he thought. From a sitting position, he walked on his ass bones until his feet could touch the ground. The other goon grabbed a hand-ful of Billy's shirt and pulled him from the car. He dragged Billy a few steps from the Cadillac and then left him.

So what do I do? Just stand here? He felt like the main event at a fir-ing squad.

Without a word, the driver walked straight to Billy and slammed the flashlight into the crook of Billy's neck.

Billy crumpled, as much from shock as pain. He clenched his jaw so that he would not cry out with weakness that would disgust them and invite another blow. The sand felt cool against his face. The mus-cles in his neck tightened around the bruise and felt like they would pull themselves from the bone. A hand grabbed Billy's shirt and rolled him onto his back. Then the hand pinched Billy's Adam's apple, and the flashlight shone into his face. Billy shut his eyes and turned his head from the light, but the hand squeezed his throat until Billy turned back.

"You must have quite a phone bill," said the bearded goon, from somewhere off to the side.

Shit, are these guys from the phone company? No wonder they're so rough.

"You made a lot of calls about Mr. Glanz," the second goon said.

The bespectacled driver shouted in Billy's face, "What do you want with Mr. Glanz?"

Billy pushed a mouthful of spit and blood over his lip and felt it slither down his cheek. *Son of a bitch, these are Glanz's goons.* Billy was accustomed to violent bill collectors, but these men were different in every way except tactics. They could not be appeased by promises to pay. And they did not care that dead men did not honor their gam-bling debts.

Billy cursed his former self, the Billy Povich of the past two days, who had plumbed many crooked sources for information about Rhubarb Glanz. Billy should have known to be more careful, especially after Garafino had told him of the rumors on the street, about a former investigative reporter trolling for scraps about Glanz. Oh, God, how could he have been so reckless? *Of course* the news would have gotten back to Glanz, who was tapped deeper into underworld sources than anyone else in Providence.

So how to play it?

The truth was dangerous—once he told it, there would be nothing to fall back on. Billy thought about the chain of people who knew of Glanz's threat to Judge Harmony: Martin Smothers; Nelida, the judge's mistress; and Harmony's clerk, Kit Bass. If Billy sold them all out, what was to stop these goons from whacking all three in order, like killing a virus before it contaminated the population?

He could think of no lie they might believe, so Billy said nothing.

Two fingers roughly pried open Billy's eyelid. The flashlight blinded him. "Got a problem understanding the English language?" the bearded goon asked.

"What's wrong with your English?" the driver screamed in Billy's face.

They waited for Billy to answer. Billy's heart slammed in terror against his rib cage. He offered, "The paper wanted to do a profile of Rhubarb Glanz and they asked me to make a few calls." Sweat had filled his ear canal, and his own voice sounded like he was speaking underwater. "But I didn't get anything so they dropped the project."

For a second everything was quiet, except Billy's panting.

"Who's writing this project?" said the talkative goon.

"Why they writing 'bout my father?" the driver screamed.

His father . . . ?

Uh-oh.

Billy had assumed this encounter was just business, a little violence between people used to dishing it out and a client accustomed to getting it. But this was about *family*, and a realm of emotion in which people often made rash and stupid decisions.

"Watch your mouth, Robbie," warned the bearded goon.

Of course, Billy thought, the driver was Robert Glanz, resident of Newport, the younger brother of David Glanz Jr., resident of the Rhode Island Adult Correctional Institutions, courtesy of Judge Harmony.

The big goon squatted beside Billy, grabbed a handful of Billy's shirt, and pulled him close. "Who's writing this story?"

"Nobody. The editors dropped it. They gave up."

"What gave them the idea in the first place?"

"Don't know." Billy had answered without hesitation and was pleased with himself. If they could be taught to see Billy as just a bottom-rung plebe, who just made a few calls on the order of The Man, maybe he could slip out of this.

Robbie swung the light from goon to goon to check their expressions.

"We'll see," the bearded one said. He pushed Billy back to the ground and then nodded toward Doe Eyes. "Fire up the Cat," he commanded.

Without a word, the gloomy goon swung himself gracefully into the backhoe and wiggled onto the seat. The engine huffed to life, and then snarled at being woken in the middle of the night. Bug-eyed lamps mounted atop the cab threw harsh white light onto the ground. Bits of reflective minerals sparkled in the sand. The goon seemed like an expert at piloting such a machine. The Cat backed away from the party with a series of warning beeps, then turned a sharp semicircle and dropped the wide front bucket to the ground. The goon spun the seat around and worked a separate set of controls. The hydraulic limb at the back of the machine uncurled like a scorpion's tail, and the pail scooped a mouthful of earth. With jerky motions, the pail swung to the side and dumped the sand. It swung back to scoop again. The sand from the hole was darker than that on the surface; it looked damp.

They are digging my grave.

Billy faced the revelation without emotion. He recalled his conversation with Brock Harmony, who had feared his kidnapper would force him to dig his own grave. Would Billy prefer that Glanz's goons did a good job? Did he want to be buried in a proper grave, *deep* under the soil, in a sandpit that soon would be a parking lot?

No . . .

To just disappear without leaving a body is to risk becoming a sad joke. A Jimmy Hoffa for the modern day. He preferred to be buried *shallow*. Snacked upon by coyotes, perhaps, but at least a fair chance to be discovered in time to head off an urban legend.

At least he would not have to endure that *conversation* with his father. The old man would have no choice but to continue his treatment. He would have to stay alive for the sake of the boy. They would need some kind of home health care service. How would the two of them manage? They would be indigent without Billy. Maybe Medicaid would pay.

Billy looked around in wonder. So *this* was what a murder scene looked like during the act. He had been to plenty of murder scenes—as a reporter, the day after the crimes. He had for a long time been struck by how an ordinary place, even a beautiful one, can leave a chill once it becomes the scene of a violent death. Like the orchard where a young drifter hanged himself in anonymity. Or the all-night restaurant where a gangster died in a shower of bullets. Or the rolling fields of Gettysburg, where Billy swore he could feel the breeze left behind by cannonballs. Haunted places, he had called them, though Billy never believed in doomed spirits that walked the earth. He enjoyed a deep breath, despite the diesel fumes. Maybe this would be a good time to believe in ghosts.

The backhoe tucked its pail against the cab and suddenly fell silent. Billy felt pain in his wrists and realized he had unconsciously rubbed them raw against the tape, trying to break free.

"Good enough?" asked Doe Eyes.

"Fine," said the Beard.

"You want me to square off the corners?"

"And be here all night?"

From the Cadillac's trunk, the driver gathered three short-handled shovels, like for moving coal in the old days. He javelined a shovel to each of the goons, then swung his own shovel by the handle, like a majorette, and cracked Billy across the thigh.

So sudden the blow, Billy howled and grasped for his leg. Robbie chuckled as he beat him. Billy pulled himself into a fetal tuck, understanding without irony that he was close to leaving the world in the position he was carried into it. The flat side of the spade punished Billy's shoulders and ribs and the backs of his legs. The blows struck with a *slap* on soft flesh, and with a ringing *plink* when they hit close to bone.

When Robbie had decided the beating was good enough, or maybe when he just got tired, he stopped, panting, and stabbed his shovel into the ground. He spat in the sand and commanded, "To the hole, okay, boys?"

The two goons pulled Billy to his feet, dragged his battered body to the edge of the trench. The hole was about six feet long and five feet deep. They had done a fine job digging, but Billy was not glad about it. He felt nothing. Such a deep hole. They leaned Billy over it.

I am Hoffa.

"For the last time," the bearded goon said, with a beleaguered tone of disappointment, as if Billy were a child who had let him down. "Why were you calling around for dirt about our employer, Mr. Glanz?"

I will not sell out Martin.

Billy swallowed blood. "Told you guys already," he croaked. "The whole truth."

They spun him into the hole.

He landed on his tailbone and slid to the bottom of the trench. Billy wiped sand from his face. Five feet below the surface the sand felt like an icebox. Above him, a thousand stars were out. He thought for a moment how there were more stars in the universe than grains of sand in this entire pit. The flashlight beam shot all over. The beating had left him numb, but Billy had the sense that no bones had been broken. Well, maybe a rib. He inhaled deeply and analyzed the pain. To be so analytical at such a time . . .

Shouldn't this bother me? Why am I not upset?

He heard a shovel bite into the earth. A clump of sand plummeted onto him and landed with a *whump*. He spit sand from his lips. Another clump struck his chest and splashed into his eyes. The three men worked in a rhythm, quickly shoveling sand into the hole. They were good at it. Like maybe they had filled a lot of graves.

They are fucking burying me alive.

Billy struggled feebly, but was knocked back by the rain of sand that fell faster and piled ever heavier on his body and his legs. His hands frantically cleared the sand from his face and he gasped for breath. *How will the old man break it to Bo?*

At the thought of the boy, Billy screamed into the night, his cry hoarse and desperate.

"Something you'd like to say, Mr. Povich?" Billy recognized the bearded goon's voice. "We're happy to take a break."

"This is tiring," agreed Doe Eyes. "How about we rest while you talk?"

"Oh Jesus!" Billy cried out from beneath a mound of damp earth.

They had broken him.

Sobbing into the sand, struggling for air, Billy told them in fractured sentences of the judge's mistress in New York, and of Martin's meeting with her. He told them of the theory that Rackers was paid to kill the judge, and he confessed that he knew Rhubarb Glanz had made a threat.

He sold out Martin, the mistress, and the clerk.

The sand fell no more. Billy never heard the three goons walk away. Just the pop of three doors and the crunch of the tires fading to nothingness in the night.

fifteen

Billy lay still as the silence swept up after the sound of the car. Glanz's goons had just left him in the pit, under what felt like several hundred pounds of sand. Did they leave him to escape? Or leave him to die? They probably didn't give a damn. They had not been ordered to kill Billy, or he would be dead. They had been ordered to get information in whatever manner proved effective. Turned out, a kidnapping, a beating, and a premature burial proved highly effective. Mission accomplished, so they went home.

They didn't care enough about Billy to free him or even to finish him off.

He was pinned on his back, twisted slightly toward his left side, under a cone of damp sand several feet high, the point of which looked to be about at his thighs. The sand sloped steeply toward his head and had begun to fill the bottom of the trench, where Billy had frantically cleared space to breathe. The other side of the pile sloped less sharply toward his feet. Billy realized they had intentionally spared his head the worst of the sand to allow him to talk. Had he been fresh, untenderized by a shovel, and not bound hand and foot, he might have wormed his way out of the pile. But for the moment, he was trapped. His hands were near his mouth, and he used an index finger to brush sand from his eyes and to swab inside his nostrils.

Screaming for help would probably just waste energy, which his injured body would need to survive a cold night. The work crew building this project would arrive in a few hours. Then he could scream, assuming they didn't have a day off or a union strike.

The part of his brain that enjoyed torturing the rest of him created an image of Bo and the old man struggling in gray smoke. In this fantasy, Billy could smell charcoal and hear smoke alarms screech. He could see Bo tug at the old man's arm, but the boy could not move him and the smoke got thicker and their movements . . . slowed . . . down. . . .

Jesus Christ! Enough!

He shook the image away. This scenario was one in a million. Maybe one in ten million. Why couldn't he stop thinking about it? He sighed. He obsessed, he figured, because the stakes were infinitely high. *My boy's life.* He would talk to Bo. Later today after he was rescued from the trench. Make the kid promise to save himself. Billy thrashed angrily against the prison of sand, and relished the pain that assured him he was alive and awake. He knew talking to Bo was no good—the boy would promise anything, but he'd never leave his grandpa.

Not while the old man was alive.

"You're a fucking burden!" he heard himself scream aloud. "You cheating son of a bitch!"

He screamed in his mind: *Die if you want.*

Billy stopped his struggle and lay very still. He cursed the dark notion in his head. *Die if you want.* He denied it. *Not my thought. Not my thought.* The tears he could not deny, burning lightly like diluted acid in his eyes. He realized he was losing consciousness, blending dream and reality. He saw his son and his father in the apartment again.

There was no smoke. They were eating breakfast in the middle of the night and watching an infomercial on television about that mechanical bed that rose up and down at the touch of a button. *Operators are standing by....* Side by side they sat. His father and his son. Two old pals with the same blue eyes. The true source of Billy's anger suddenly revealed itself. He was not afraid of losing his son in a fire, not really. He was enraged by the knowledge that the boy would never abandon the old man *who had abandoned Billy.*

He bit hard and crunched sand between his molars, and thought about the three decades after the old man had left the family. And then he seethed at the irony, which seemed at the moment the product of a god with a sick sense of humor—after the old man's bad health had finally broken him and brought him to Billy's door to claim the unearned love that was his by blood, he wanted to stop his treatments, and leave Billy again.

Billy imagined footsteps, dashing lightly in the sand.

He pictured Bo running toward him, but the footsteps were too quick and rhythmic to be those of a little boy, and the fantasy dissolved.

He withdrew from his dreamworld and felt the snap of reality in the stabbing pain in his rib.

He listened.

The footsteps grew louder, too loud not to be real. Nearly on top of him, they stopped. He held his breath and stared out from the hole.

The dark outline of a human figure eclipsed the stars.

Billy did not flinch. He breathed silent, shallow breaths. Should he call out, or stay invisible, buried under shadows? Trapped and beaten, barely conscious, he had never been so vulnerable. Fear throttled him and he said nothing.

The figure wavered over the hole for what seemed a long time. Its feet sent tiny avalanches of pebbles down the side of the trench.

Then a woman's voice softly and urgently called, "Povich?"

Billy gasped. A familiar voice he could not place. But the voice was real; he was sure of it. Tears flooded his eyes again; he had never heard such beauty in his own name.

"I'm—I'm here. I'm in the sand."

"Are they gone? All of them?"

Billy did not know for sure, but he could not take the chance she might become afraid and leave him. "Yes," he ventured. "We're alone." He wondered who she was, and she read his mind—

"It's Kit Bass," she said. "I was Judge Harmony's clerk. I saw you the day they opened his will, though we were not formally introduced."

After a half beat of silence, Billy offered, "Well, how do you do?"

She chuckled softly. Billy recalled her face: narrow and a little mousy; two dozen freckles, heavier on one side than the other; small upturned nose; eyes that looked sleepy when she smiled, as if she had just woken to something—or someone—who made her very happy.

"Those three men work for Rhubarb Glanz," she said. "The little one is Robbie—he's Glanz's son. Ain't he a son of a bitch? The day will come when I kick his ass. According to my research, the other two used to be cellmates, if that tells you anything. I've been following them since my own run-in at Glanz's nightclub. Tonight, I saw them drive behind your office."

"They sent me a fax. Maybe from a laptop, I don't know. Got me to run out the back door, into a trap."

"I ducked down in my car when they drove away. They passed under a streetlight and I recognized you riding with them." She paused. "Forgive me, Mr. Povich—"

"It's Billy, please."

"—but I didn't know if you were mixed up with them. So I followed you. Robbie Glanz always drives at exactly the speed limit so it's easy to keep a safe distance without losing them." She paused. "You're not really Martin Smothers's law clerk, are you?"

"His clerk makes a lot more money than I do."

"You're his investigator." She didn't bother to wait for confirmation. Dropping to her knees at the edge of the hole, she said, "How bad are you hurt?"

"I'm trapped in here, buried." He thought about the question and realized he had not answered it. "I'm fading out."

"It's so dark. . . . I have a flare in my trunk."

Billy shuddered; she was asking permission to leave his side.

"My car is hidden up the road about a mile, as close as I dared to leave it."

A mile? "That's gonna take nearly an hour to hike up and back," Billy said. "I don't know if I can stay awake."

She stood and dusted off, chuckling as if she had just heard something cute and naive, like from the mouth of a child. "See you in twelve minutes, Billy," she promised. "Five and a half minutes to the car, five and a half back. Sixty seconds to open the trunk."

With that, she dashed off.

The flare's fluttering red glow turned a small circle of the moonscape into Mars. Like an enormous firecracker, the flare hissed dangerously and reminded Billy of what Garafino, the shark, had told him about messing with Rhubarb Glanz. *Do you puff dynamite like a big red cigar?*

Kit had found a long-handled shovel at the construction site. She wore loose-fitting shorts and a tight half tank. Her skin glistened in the red light. Her thighs were braids of muscle. Her thin arms, hanging from squared-off swimmer's shoulders, were deceptively strong, and she filled the shovel with big helpings of sand. She worked to free him as rhythmically as the goons had to bury him.

Twelve minutes, she had said. Billy doubted she had been gone even that long. This woman was *built for speed*, he marveled. He watched her dig for a few minutes. He thought about Gil Harmony. How did the judge inspire so much loyalty from one law clerk?

Billy said, "The day they opened the will, I left before the judge came to you on the video. I'm curious. What did he leave you?"

She smiled sadly and kept digging, though a little more slowly. "His Bible, that's all. No money, which he knew I wouldn't have taken. Just his mother's old family Bible, which stayed in his desk when he served in the state senate, to remind him that Somebody was looking down on him. When he was appointed to the bench, he used that Bible to swear his oath of office."

"I didn't know he was a religious man."

"Not outwardly pious. Congregationalist. Liked the social aspect of church. But I know that he prayed."

"Why do you think he left you the Bible?"

She stopped for a moment, leaned on the shovel. "Because he wanted me to know that he'd be looking down on me." She smiled sadly at Billy, and then went back to work. "We should call the cops when I get you out of here. What they did violates chapter eleven of the criminal code, sections five and twenty-six dash one, felonious assault and kidnapping. With their criminal records, they could each get up to forty years."

"They won't."

"Well, even if they pleaded down to get concurrent sentences, they're looking at hard time."

"We're not calling the cops."

"What—? That's ridiculous. They nearly killed you."

"My word against theirs. They have better lawyers than the state. They'll never do any time."

"The grand jury can make their lives miserable. Maybe an indictment would put a scare into them?"

Billy sighed. Kit knew the General Laws of Rhode Island by heart. But she never studied under a professor like Rhubarb Glanz. He told her, "One hour after Robbie Glanz gets a subpoena on a pissy little charge like this, I will accidentally fall down a flight of stairs to my death. Maybe more than once."

"They can't—I'm a witness."

"They'll kill you, too."

She heaved a shovel of dirt with a grunt and said, "So what are we supposed to do? Cower in fear of these assholes? Let them do whatever they want to us? What about *the law*?"

"If you're going to take down the king, you better aim for the heart. We have to nail Rhubarb Glanz."

"Rhubarb Glanz wasn't here tonight," she said. "We can't prove he told those men to leave you buried, where you would have died of exposure."

"The sand is now quite warm, thank you, like a five-hundred-pound blanket."

"Billy!"

Sharply, he informed her, "We're going to take down Rhubarb Glanz for hiring a street punk to shoot Judge Harmony in cold blood."

He had stunned her. Kit's hand covered her throat. "I was there," she whispered, "when Glanz made the threat."

"I know. Tell me what happened."

She explained softly, "Glanz came in with those two big goons and demanded Gil reduce the sentence he had imposed on David Glanz Jr., the son." She closed her eyes. Sweat droplets raked her cheek. "I'll never forget it. Gil and I were at lunch, talking about some decision he was writing. I remember clearly that after Glanz made his demand, Gil took his napkin from his lap and dabbed the corners of his mouth, staring through Glanz the whole time, before he slowly stood and told that old mobster where he could get off—not in those terms, of course—"

"Of course."

"—because Gil, *the judge*, I mean, was a gentleman. Glanz didn't even blink. He had to know a man of Gil Harmony's moral stature would never bend to a threat like that."

She looked at Billy and seemed to be waiting for him to agree. "Naturally," Billy said, absentmindedly. Her face distracted him; he noted how her dark eyes and her hard jawline softened when she spoke of the judge.

She shoveled in silence for a minute, sending tiny shock waves through the sand and into Billy's body.

Then suddenly, as if the thought just struck her, she blurted, "You just said you knew? You knew about the threat? How could you? I wanted to report it to the cops afterward, but Gil persuaded me not to. He said it wasn't a serious threat, and that Glanz was just protecting his standing with his crooked employees. 'All for show,' Gil said to me, before we both swore an oath of secrecy. Nobody knows about the threat, not even . . . his wife."

Oh, Jesus Christ, Billy thought in horror. *She loved the judge.* Kit's face screamed it. She could barely force herself to acknowledge out loud that Gil Harmony had a wife. Billy felt the creep of the death smile on his face and turned his head to the sand.

"How could you know this, Billy?"

Billy concentrated on the pain in his ribs and obliterated the smile.

She waited for the answer, one hand on her hip like an impatient traveler at a bus stop. Her posture sent a subliminal message that the shovel would do no work until Billy admitted how he knew of the threat. She drilled him with her eyes.

Give it to her straight. She was tough and had wanted Billy to know it. He would not embarrass her with mercy.

"I heard it from Mr. Smothers," Billy said, "who heard it in New York from the judge's mistress, who had heard it from the judge."

Kit stepped backward. Her lips silently formed the word *mistress*.

She looked away a moment, perhaps reconciling old memories and nagging questions with this new information. Then suddenly she returned to digging, faster and more violently than before.

Billy watched the flex of her muscles. She had not protested or probed for more information about this mistress.

Kit had not been the judge's lover, Billy decided. The revelation about Gil Harmony had obviously surprised her, and no mistress would be surprised by a second mistress. Though the cynic inside Billy warned him to be careful. Maybe she was playing him with that subtle twitch of rage at the corner of her mouth. As Martin liked to say, there were a lot of great actors in the world.

The flare sputtered. Kit cleared the sand from Billy without another word and then cast the shovel aside. She helped him crawl free.

Pain provoked ironic laughter from Billy that trailed off into a groan and a cough. He flexed his arms and legs in a quick self-diagnostic. Nothing broken, he confirmed. The bone bruises on both elbows and his shins would be with him for a few weeks. A dark red paste of congealed blood and sand smeared his raw wrists. He had not taken any blows to the head, probably because unconscious men keep their secrets, and the goons had needed Billy to talk.

I've taken worse beatings, Billy thought with a trickle of pride.

He leaned against the side of the trench, grimaced at the deep pokes of pain in his rib cage. The duct tape around his wrists had lost its tackiness in the sand, and Billy slipped his hands from the cuff. Kit untied the binding from around his ankles.

"So how do we do it?" she asked, a hard starch in her voice. "How do we fucking take down Rhubarb Glanz?" She looked him up and down. "Can you walk?"

Billy waved off the last question. "In a minute." He spat grit from his mouth. "We tried confronting Glanz to find a connection to the judge's death, but Glanz is too well protected."

"Following Robbie never led me to the father," she agreed.

"Until we find a weak spot in his defense, we should work on the shooter, Adam Rackers. We trace him backward to Glanz. There must have been some meeting, or a connection through a bagman. There was a payoff *somewhere*—nobody kills a judge for money without insisting first on a deposit."

"What can we learn about Rackers that the police couldn't?"

Billy wiped a finger inside his armpit, then cleared the sand from under his lips. "The police get their information from good citizens," Billy said. "We're not under those kinds of limitations."

She shot him a sideways look as the flare sputtered out and abandoned them in a moonlit crater of sand. Without the hiss of the flare, the silence was more unsettling than the darkness.

"Do you know those kind of people?" she asked.

"I have sources," Billy confessed. Another thought came suddenly to him and he wondered if his conscious mind had suppressed it until she had freed him from the sand. He told her straight:

"I sold you out to them."

sixteen

Martin nearly hurled himself at his assistant's feet.

"Thank *God* you're here," he blurted. "Do you have my speech? You're smiling. That means you do? Is it any good? Will it read like I wrote it myself? I don't want people to think my employee had to write my speech for me. Don't look at me like that! Do you have my shoes?" His assistant held up a plastic grocery bag. "Oh, Christ, thankfully! Does it always echo in here like this? Son of a *bitch*, I hate that echo. Do I seem nervous? Is it humid in here? Christ, it's like a rain forest in this State House." He blotted his forehead with his necktie.

Carol patted Martin's arm. "Easy, boss," she comforted in a velvety voice that clashed with the stir of devil in her huge round eyes.

"What?" Martin said. "What's the grin?"

"I was mingling in the audience before I came up here. I saw the judge's *comatta*."

He shushed her. "Not too loud!" Though he was sure nobody could hear them in the ricochet of voices, amped through a PA system, which echoed off marble floors and walls and careened through the alcoves and stairways of the Rhode Island State House. This was where a young Gil Harmony, barely out of law school, served two terms in the state senate.

Carol inspected her boss. "Your shirttail is coming out." She opened his jacket, one side and then the other, clicked her tongue, and pointed to a black spot on his shirt. "That silly fountain pen exploded in your pocket again, so keep this coat buttoned up."

"Oh, fuck." He jammed his shirttail into his pants.

"And don't worry about the speech. It'll sell."

"Is it profound?"

"Makes the Gettysburg Address read like a dirty limerick."

Was she joking? Would she joke with him a few minutes before Martin had to read a speech about his murdered mentor? Martin stuck his little pink hands on his hips. "Now quit that," he ordered. "You know I have no ear for hyperbole."

Carol pulled a pair of size 8½ leather cap toe oxfords from a shopping bag. "Why can't you keep these at the office?" she asked.

"My wife can smell dead cow straight through a filing cabinet."

Martin kicked off his hideous 100 percent nonanimal, faux leather plastic loafers. He paused a moment and glanced around unconsciously to make sure his militantly vegan wife was not around. The upper reaches of the state capitol were empty. *What makes a taboo so exciting?* he wondered. He enjoyed a tickle in his potbelly and felt the stretch of his grin as he slipped his feet into genuine cowhide shoes he would never dare bring near his own house.

Martin and Carol peered together over a third-floor balcony rail, into the State House rotunda. Far below, the memorial service for Justice Gilbert Harmony was under way. More than a hundred well-dressed people competed for standing room on four great staircases that led into the hall. The rotunda is a soaring space befitting a cathedral, built of pillars and balconies standing upon each other, from the brass seal of the state embedded in the white marble floor to the high point of the capitol dome, 149 feet above. For a century, the rotunda has been the site of protests and celebrations, public announcements and government denouncements. More recently, it had become a backdrop for wedding photos.

As an indoor courtyard open to each floor of the building, the rotunda is bright, and seems built of equal parts air and rock. Veins of black swirl though the white marble pillars, the staircases, and the balcony rails polished as smooth as a beach stone. Four arches near the top of the space are gilded in gold, and decorated with murals of ladies in flowing gowns and laurel leaf crowns, holdings books and swords to represent literature and justice. The dome that caps the rotunda is 50 feet across, painted a blend of blue and white, like the sky.

Blue velvet ropes protect the ten-foot state seal in the rotunda floor, which is surrounded by ornamental brass streetlamps, each supporting ten frosted-glass globes of light. At a podium next to the seal, a retired senator mumbled at eighty decibels through a PA system that splashed his voice monstrously against the marble.

"... *my goooood friend-d-d and colleeegggg ...*"

Martin wiggled his toes inside the glorious leather and asked Carol, "Did you see June Harmony?"

"Front row, protecting her territory," Carol replied.

A dozen metal folding chairs had been set up in three rows before the podium. June Harmony was conspicuous in a long black dress. She sat at attention, yet gazed off as if she had not noticed the crowds, the podium, and the speaker. Her spectacular diamond earrings twinkled in the light.

"So you told her about Nelida?" Carol asked, gently prying for information.

"I felt like a little boy confessing to my mother that I had broken a family heirloom," Martin admitted. "She didn't flinch."

"Of course not. She knew. At some level, the wife always knows."

Martin glanced at Carol and was relieved that she did not look back at him. Carol was a generous soul—she would not force Martin to acknowledge that June Harmony may have had the world's oldest motive to kill her husband: jealousy.

"June didn't try to bar Nelida from this event," Martin said.

"To take action against the mistress would affirm that June considered Nelida a threat, and June Harmony is too proud for that," Carol said. "Have they met eyes?"

"I fear for this building when they do."

"Do you see where Nelida is standing?"

Martin could not miss her. "Behind the great seal," he said.

The judge's mistress wore a navy blue pantsuit and a yellow shirt so bright a hunter might wear it to avoid getting shot in the woods. "She's certainly not in hiding."

"She staked out territory as close to the podium as possible," Carol said. "It's her first public claim on the judge's life. She waits just off to the side like a gathering army before an invasion. Is that her bodyguard with her?"

"That's her son, Jerod," Martin said, feeling a squirt of embarrassment at the memory of meeting Jerod in New York while Martin was in a robe, briefly out of his briefs. Jerod looked impressive in an athletically tapered gray suit coat. "Nelida says Gil treated her son like his own blood."

"I noticed Jerod when I was mingling earlier," Carol said. "His eyes darted everywhere. He feels out of his element."

"How was Brock?" Martin asked. He picked the kid out of the crowd, at his mother's side and mimicking her posture.

"Zombified."

Martin's eyes drifted to a slender woman in a swishy black skirt: Kit Bass, the judge's clerk, carrying a legal pad and hurrying among the attendees like a worker bee in a crowded hive. She approached Gil Harmony's old friends one by one, landing with a whisper into her hand cupped to their ears, probably telling each of them when they would speak. With a scratch on the legal pad, she would fly off again.

"Povich says that woman, Kit Bass, loved the judge too," Martin said, more to himself than to Carol.

"Which one? There? The clerk?"

"Too young for him."

Carol laughed. "From his perspective there was no 'too young.' And from hers, nothing smooths wrinkles like money and power."

Martin sighed. "I'm stuck with these wrinkles, and the oatmeal masks my wife wants me to wear."

"Do you good, maybe." She smiled and did the sexy little hair flip she liked to do when she teased him about his age.

He scoffed, "Oatmeal masks. Cucumbers on the eyes. She has a skin cream with carrots in it. Why do women put food on their faces? And why can't anybody make a shampoo that doesn't smell like dessert? With a beard like this, do you think I want it stinkin' like witch hazel and huckleberries?"

Martin spotted Lincoln Harmony. The judge's brother looked down on the memorial from the second-floor balcony. He leaned against a pillar, arms crossed, occasionally nodding to people to accept the condolences of politicians and lawyers who had caught his eye.

"Is the brother drunk?" Martin asked.

"He's anxious," Carol said. "See the leg bouncing? Read that as impatient. Hmmm. And with his flat mouth-line and crossed arms, I'd say he's waiting for something."

"Maybe he's just nervous about speaking to this crowd. No shame in that. I should head down there."

They walked together down a side hall painted butterscotch and cluttered with the serious portraits of men who had served as Rhode Island governor. Each governor in history had a portrait somewhere in the State House, regardless of whether his administration ended in success, failure, or incarceration.

Carol slipped Martin two typewritten pages. "Your speech," she said. "Don't read it too fast. Breathe now and then. Pause at the spots I've indicated, and make sure you look up and make eye contact with somebody."

Martin read the first line:

Long ago, as a young attorney, my friend Gil Harmony taught me that lawyers save as many lives as doctors, by serving the truth.

He sighed, folded the speech, and tucked it into his pocket. "A beautiful opening," he said. "But I'm going to feel like a liar, knowing what I know about Gil."

"He was a complicated man," Carol said. "Pick the truth about him you loved, and serve that one." Her hand, resting lightly on his shoulder, felt like an iron guyline that steadied him inside a hurricane.

They passed an oil portrait of former governor Ambrose Burnside, known for wearing a beard over his cheeks with a clean-shaven chin. The Civil War general didn't want to command the Army of the Potomac—he warned President Lincoln he was no good for the job. But Burnside got stuck with the command anyway, nearly lost the war at Fredericksburg, and had to be talked out of a suicide charge at Confederate troops. Though a disaster on horseback as a general, he gave the world a new hairstyle, known as *burnsides*. Somehow, the dyslexia of history mangled the name into *sideburns*.

Martin was suddenly struck with new respect for Burnside. At least the general knew his limitations. *Do I know mine?* Martin's drive to find Gil Harmony's killer had succeeded only in killing the judge's reputation. Rumors of an out-of-town mistress bubbled through the legal community, and they carried the ugly, unspoken suggestion that Gil's behavior might have been responsible for his murder. Martin felt he had strangled the judge in the grave. Plus he had nearly got Povich buried alive.

At the floor of the rotunda, Martin left Carol in the crowd and took the seat reserved for him behind June Harmony. He tried not to look at Nelida but could not resist. She stared back and lifted her chin an inch in a greeting nobody else would notice. Her son, Jerod, leaned in front of his mother, which Martin interpreted as a gesture of protection, as if he were ready to take a bullet for her.

The speaking program of earsplitting echoes continued. Martin read over his speech. With his leaky fountain pen, he edited a word here and there. Carol was brilliant and Martin dreaded her graduation from law school. She'd ace the bar, of course, and he'd immediately offer to make her his partner. But then they'd have to hire a new assistant, and they'd never find someone as good as she.

A man brushed roughly past Martin's elbow, dragging the scent of cigars. Martin looked up to see Lincoln Harmony leaning over June. She glared up at him. He smiled sweetly and handed her a white envelope, which she reluctantly accepted as she would a dead rat. He clapped her twice lightly on the shoulder, and then grinned at Martin and shot him with a finger gun. Then Linc staggered off into the crowd.

He's got to be fucking hammered!

June gripped the envelope in the middle, as if to tear it in half, but then changed her mind, slid a pinkie under the flap, and took out a document. Martin leaned forward and read over her shoulder.

A subpoena.

Linc Harmony was contesting his brother's will.

seventeen

The close-up photos of a dead man's body were like a morbid Frankenstein puzzle. A bicep, part of a shoulder, left pectoral above the nipple, right shoulder blade. The autopsy photos had been printed in black and white, and Billy knew the dark spots on the colorless skin were bloodstains. The pictures of Adam Rackers on a slab in the morgue purported to show identifying marks such as moles and scars, but only the inscrutable tattoo seemed to have belonged to an individual. The Old English letters spelled *dismas23* in a curved frown on Rackers's shoulder. What the hell did that mean? Some kind of gang name?

Billy laid out six pictures before him, roughly re-creating Rackers's dead body on the kitchen table. He sat on his father's foam doughnut to protect a bruise on his tailbone. His wrists were loosely wrapped in gauze. Six ibuprofens had drawn a thin cushion over the pain throughout his body. He felt like an abused tackling dummy at the end of Patriots training camp. Worse than the physical pain, he felt a pressing anxiety. He had done no better than the police in tracing Rackers's movements the weeks before he shot the judge. The cops had been thorough. They had checked Rackers's last known address, a Pawtucket duplex on an island of residential streets jammed among industrial buildings, in a neighborhood no outsider could find without a map. Rackers had skipped out on his lease three months before he died in the wreck. Nobody in the old neighborhood had ever seen him again. Rackers's residential fingerprints stopped there. No change of address through a cell provider, no credit applications in the Internet databases, no contact with government or the utilities, other than the cop who spotted Rackers casing the judge's neighborhood shortly before the killing.

Where the hell had he been hiding?

Billy's street contacts had reported rumors that Rackers and a partner had been feeding discount loot to local fences, but nothing specific. And nobody could provide an address for Billy to track down.

A low murmur floated down the hall.

Billy stared toward the source and listened. That was his father's voice, though Billy couldn't make out what he was saying. The old man was talking to himself again. And not just a stray thought subconsciously expressed by the lips—his father was having monologues in his bedroom. This was not the first time. He tried to remember when the old man started giving speeches to himself. Maybe a few weeks ago? Two months?

Need to ask him about that . . .

The laptop computer on the table suddenly shouted: "Missed it by THAT much!"

Billy had no clue how Bo programmed the computer to quote *Get Smart* whenever e-mail arrived. He glanced at the clock: 2:45 a.m. Who the hell was e-mailing at this hour? He turned the volume down so not to wake Bo.

The old man's wheelchair glided into the kitchen. Mr. Einstein lay across his lap. "That's my e-mail," he said.

"You better give that doll back to Bo," Billy said. "If he wakes up without Einstein, he'll be scared. What were you doing with that thing?"

"Talking with him," the old man said dismissively. "Open that e-mail! It's a reminder to bid on my world's fair item."

"Don't you have enough useless trinkets?"

"Not nearly. Lemme at that machine. Just takes a second." He held up a palsied hand and waved for Billy to get out of the way.

"Can you do this without Bo?" Billy asked. "This is a computer, not a butter churn. Never mind. I'll do it for you. Why do you always wait till the last possible second to bid?"

"So nobody can come in after me and steal my items. Quicker!"

Billy followed a link to an online auction site. He scoffed, "Is this what you're buying? What the hell is this thing? A piece of paper? You're bidding on old paper?"

"It's an invitation," the old man said, sounding anxious. "There's three minutes left! We gotta bid!"

"An invitation to what?"

"To the opening ceremonies of the world's fair. An original invitation! FDR was there, you know. He spoke to a huge crowd about the world of tomorrow—that was the theme for the fair." His fingers slashed the air for emphasis. "April thirtieth, nineteen thirty-nine. That was also the anniversary of the inauguration of George Washington. One hundred fifty years to the day, General Washington took the first presidential oath of office in front of a huuuuuge crowd."

"Did you have good seats for the inauguration, old man?"

"What—? Seats to who?"

"How was George's speech?"

"Eh?" The old man's mouth dropped open and he squinted at his son from behind thick eyeglasses.

Billy sighed. Sarcasm was completely wasted on his father. "How much are you bidding?"

"Thirty dollars. No, thirty-five!"

"For a piece of paper?"

"We're gonna lose it!"

"Fine then, thirty-five dollars."

"Log me in," the old man commanded. "The log-in name is g-r-o-v-e-r-w-h-a-l-e-n. Uh-huh. And then two. Uh-huh. No, the number two, don't spell it out. Jesus on a skateboard! Where'd you learn to type? Okay, okay. The password is Ziggs."

"What the hell kind of log-in is that?" Billy asked as he typed a bid of thirty-five dollars and clicked to confirm. "Okay, you're the high bidder."

The old man relaxed. He wiped his palms on his long flannel nightshirt and explained, "I named myself for Grover Whalen. He was the New York City police commissioner who said, 'There's plenty of law at the end of a nightstick.' Heh-heh. They don't talk like that today. Then he was president of the world's fair of thirty-nine. I'm saluting him for what he did for the fair. Don't you understand how these auction places work? Nobody uses their real name. It's like a nickname. Christ, I shouldn't have to explain this . . . ain't you younger than me?"

"Not feeling that way right now," Billy said. He refreshed the Web page. "Hey, you won. Congratulations on your new piece of paper."

The old man smiled. His wrinkles looked like contour lines for a very bumpy life. Then suddenly he wheezed and grimaced in pain and Billy instinctively reached for him. The old man waved him back, banged a fist on his own chest, coughed three times, sputtered weakly as if he were about to die in the chair. Then he pulled himself clear of the cough and took a loud, deep breath. He moaned, grumbled about the indignities of old age, spat into his hand, inspected the clear foam, and then wiped the mess on the tail of his nightshirt.

"Copy down the seller's address," the old man commanded, sounding hoarse. "So I can send him a money order."

Billy wrote down the address. "Why do you buy all this crap?" he asked.

"I'm leaving it to Bo," the old man said.

"You're leaving the kid this invitation? And the ashtrays, and the dinner plates you won't let anybody use, and the salt and pepper shakers—"

"Those shakers are in the *original* box," the old man interrupted. "And they're only going up in value. The giant world's fair mechanical pencil writes perfectly fine, and the jackknife has a mother-of-pearl handle."

"What's the kid supposed to do with this junk?"

The old man paused. "Bo's going to remember me," he said. He frowned and looked away, then scraped a fingernail over some crusty stain on the arm of his wheelchair. "The more stuff I have to give him, the more he'll have to remind him. I don't believe in hell, and if there's a heaven I can't be sure I'm going. But I'll have my immortality through that kid. He knows me through the world's fair, see? It's my only hobby, the only passion I got left, and the only thing I know more about than his father, okay?"

Billy confirmed gently, "You're the encyclopedia of this fair, Pa."

"You're goddamned right I am. Did you know that the centerpiece of the fair, the Trylon and the Perisphere exhibits, inspired the magic castle in Disneyland? See, someday when Bo takes *your* grandkids to Disney, no matter how old he's gonna be, he'll think of the fair, and he'll think of me. Might even tell his kids a story or two they can pass along to *their* kids." He looked at Billy. "This invitation is the last piece of the collection. We end with the beginning. . . . You wanna have that discussion about my treatment now?"

A python flexed around Billy's throat. He gestured vaguely to the spread of pictures and notes on the table. "Pa, I gotta work. . . . This case I'm on is, ah, a real bitch."

The old man slowly spun 180 degrees in the chair. As he rolled out, he warned without looking back, "Don't put me off till it's too late. Never think of the future—it comes soon enough."

Billy gave him a double take.

The old man read his mind. He shook the doll and said, "Yeah, I'm quotin' Einstein."

"Missed it by THAT much!"

Billy woke with a start and lifted his head from the table.

I'm half blind!

He blinked his eyes. No, he wasn't blind—he had fallen asleep on his notes, and a photograph had stuck to his face. He peeled it off, then winced at the pain in his back, which sizzled down his hamstrings.

The photograph reminded him of his minor breakthrough in identifying Adam Rackers's tattoo: *dismas23*.

Not that the discovery had helped at all.

He tapped the computer's space bar and dispelled the screen saver. Rubbing the sleep from his eyes, he read the clock in the bottom corner of the display.

Oh, shit, 6:33 a.m. He had slept the night at the kitchen table. No wonder his back hurt.

The Web page he had studied a few hours before was still on the screen. The page listed Catholic saints throughout history. It was there Billy had found Saint Dismas. He was the "good thief," who had asked for a blessing while being crucified next to Christ. Dismas was the patron saint of criminals. Billy had never known criminals had their own saint. The numeral 23 he had not been able to decipher for sure. Maybe it had to do with the mention of the good thief in chapter 23 of the Gospel According to Luke, or maybe that was a coincidence.

He clicked the e-mail message that had woken him. It was for his father:

Dear groverwhalen2,

Congratulations on winning the bid for the World's Fair Open-ing Ceremonies invitation. I promise to ship the item within 24 hours of receiving payment.

Best—

cancanman036

What the hell was a cancanman036? Who would do business un-der a nickname like that? His father planned to send money to this unseen person on the West Coast. Who knew where cancanman036 even got this thirty-five-dollar invitation? He could have stolen it from a geriatric invalid at the nursing home next door.

Billy pushed himself from the chair, and gasped as his body tight-ened like a clamp. He heard his father's voice in his mind, *Welcome to my world. Feel good?* Clutching the back of his chair, he rolled his shoulders and gently forced his back to straighten. "Oh! Oh!" he cried quietly, in surprise. The pain was like having the nerves yanked from his legs, the way an electrician pulls wires through a pipe. He grew lightheaded and feared he might pass out, until the muscles loosened and the pain slowly diluted through his body. He found aspirin in the cabinet and chewed five tablets with no water. He kept the aspirin paste under his tongue for a minute before he swallowed, because he had heard it got into the bloodstream faster that way.

"Ain't you the picture of health," said the old man. "Who did this to you? I thought you were paid up with the bookmakers."

Billy turned to face him, felt a twinge in his lower lumbar, and froze. "Didn't hear you come in." He rolled his upper body around his hips. "Hey, Pa, did I hear you talking to yourself again this morn-ing?"

The old man bristled. "So what if you did? This apartment is in America, ain't it? I got my free speech rights, even in this second-story gulag with no elevator."

Billy turned his hands up in surrender. "I bow to the First Amendment. Talk all you want."

"I'm skipping treatment today," the old man declared.

Oh, fuck, not now.

"We never had our discussion," Billy said, not daring to look at him.

"That's your fault. I don't have forever to wait."

Billy turned to his father. The old man wore a short housecoat over threadbare cotton pajamas. His knees were parted. His legs were so goddamn thin, just sticks and angles, like a grasshopper's legs. "Pop—"

"Any news on my world's fair item?"

Billy licked his lips and accepted the old man's detour around the discussion of his slow suicide. He said, "Just got an e-mail from someone named cancanman-zero-three-six—"

Billy stopped, struck by a thought.

The anonymity of the Internet . . .

"Well, what did he say?" the old man demanded. "He better not be backing out of this auction. I won—fair and rectangular."

"Pop, can we look people up by their nicknames? At this auction site?"

"Yeah, nicknames and home cities. But you can't see their real names unless they want you to. Am I not getting my world's fair invitation?"

Billy shuffled to the chair and plopped down. His hands trembled as he tapped the address for the auction site. "Show me how."

Together, the two Povich men—one of whom was still mystified that a microwave can make a frozen sausage so hot it explodes, yet somehow knows not to set paper plates on fire—navigated the site's various search features until they found a place to type a nickname to locate any member.

"Who you looking for?" the old man asked.

Billy typed *dismas23* and commanded the machine to search.

One exact match.

Hometown: Providence, R.I.

"Huh. You found somebody local," the old man said. He clumsily slapped a photograph on the table, and turned it to read the inscription on Adam Rackers's shoulder. "Dismas-twenty-three? Who is this feller supposed to be?"

Billy was too far along to begin an explanation. "How can I see what he's been selling?" he snapped.

"Click his history." He pointed to the screen.

What a history!

Billy browsed page after page of recorded transactions. Over the past twelve months, dismas23 had been a clearinghouse for women's fashion, high-end electronics, new DVD movies, designer sunglasses, wristwatches, rare silver coins, and sterling tableware.

The old man let go a low whistle. "This guy's made a fortune online."

"Would all of these people have sent him checks or money orders?"

"He only accepted electronic transfers," the old man said, reading the screen. He shifted in the wheelchair, and Billy caught the faintest whiff of aftershave and dirty hair. "I'm afraid of those transfers. What's wrong with money on *paper*? What if I hit a bad key and send my bank account to some teenager in Poland? Uh-uh, boy."

Billy could not be sure dismas23 was Adam Rackers, but the clues were persuasive. There were no new auctions listed under that nickname after Rackers's death, and several of his most recent buyers had posted complaints that they never got their merchandise. Dead men don't visit the post office.

"We're so close," Billy said. "How can these people help us find him?"

"See if he bought anything," the old man suggested.

Billy clicked the buttons to exclude all sales from the list of transactions. A much shorter list of purchases remained. With the old man's shaky guidance, Billy found the one item dismas23 had bought within the last three months of Rackers's life—the period for which he had no known address.

The object was a tiny eyepiece, for which dismas23 had paid sixteen dollars.

"What the hell is that?" the old man asked.

"A loupe," Billy said. "It's like a magnifying glass or a little microscope. Jewelers use them to examine gems, to help decide what the stones are worth. Hmm. Now, why would Rackers buy a loupe?"

"Why would *who* buy a magnifying doohickey?"

"Just a guy I'm trying to find, Pa."

"This guy in the pictures you got spread out here?"

"Sort of."

"Ain't he dead?"

"He was alive for the time I'm trying to find him."

"What—?"

"Why would he buy a loupe . . . unless he was going to examine some gems. . . ."

"If you wanna find this guy, why not ask the photographer who took these pictures? Doesn't look like he'll be moving too fast."

"Let's concentrate on the loupe, okay?" Billy asked.

The old man harrumphed and tightened the drawstring of his housecoat. His waist was as thin as a child's. Billy looked away. In his youth, William Povich Sr. could have benchpressed Greenland, or so it had seemed to Billy.

"Sixteen bucks for that doohickey," the old man said with a chuckle. "I told you there were deals on this site."

"Pop, please," Billy said after a deep breath. "I need to find where this guy was living."

"Well, then ask the seller where the heck he mailed the doohickey. Had to send it somewhere."

Billy slapped his own forehead and thundered, *"Now* you goddamn tell me!"

In a far corner of the apartment, Bo's tiny voice echoed: "Now
you goddamn tell me!"

The old man punished Billy with a dirty look, then called down
the hall: "You hush with that talk, Bo."

"Yup!"

"Change outta your jammies and get me the newspaper on the
porch, okay?" the old man ordered.

"Yup!"

Billy sighed and typed a message to the seller, icedealer177. "I'll
just ask him for the address, right?"

"Won't work," the old man said with a sour face. "Say that you're
interested in what he's got for sale, on the recommendation of dismas-
twenty-three."

"Why so complicated?"

"If some stranger asks anonymously for the address of one of your
customers, what would you do?"

Billy huffed impatiently. But he took the old man's suggestion,
deleted what he had typed, and wrote a new message.

He sent it.

They waited.

"I guess that's all we do right now," Billy said after three minutes.
"If I don't hear from him, I'll send another message every twenty-
four hours. Eventually. . . ."

"Missed it by THAT much!"

Billy and the old man looked at each other in surprise. Billy opened
the message:

> To groverwhalen2 . . . i offer many items for sale, on the inter-
> net and through special arrangement. where is dismas23? is he
> mad i sold his address to junk mail marketing list? an oversight on

my part. tell him i remain VERY interested in the arrangement we discussed. i am prepared to offer best price, if quality as good as he says.

icedealer177

The old man scratched his scalp and shed dandruff flakes into the air. "That don't make sense," he said.

"He's a diamond dealer, Pop," Billy said. "By the look of it, not a scrupulous one. Rackers bought a loupe from him, so Rackers must have gotten his hands on a stone. You can't just list stolen diamonds on the Internet, can you? This guy must have offered a black-market deal to fence whatever rocks Rackers had stolen."

"Have there been any diamond robberies the last few months?" the old man asked. "I ain't heard of any."

Billy searched his mental record of front-page headlines. "Naw, nothing like that. That would be a big story." He sighed and read the message again. "Maybe Rackers hadn't gotten a diamond yet. Maybe he was planning to steal one, and was preparing ahead to fence it."

"That's bad luck."

Billy glanced at the dead man's pictures on the table. "Apparently."

The old man would not let go the point. "Do you schedule a victory parade before you play the game?" he asked incredulously.

"I get it, Pop."

"Because Fate—she gets pissed when you do that."

"Mm-hm."

"I should know. I've had it with Fate and she's had it with me. That lady . . . is a bitch!"

"That lady is a bitch!" sang Bo brightly as he stomped into the kitchen with the newspaper.

Billy glared at his father, but the old man refused to look at him.

The kid still wore his Atomic Thunderbolt pajamas: red booties and gloves, little blue shorts, and an off-white shirt with a red splotch on the chest, like someone had splattered him with a paint balloon. Billy could not understand why Bo had taken to an obscure comic book character from the 1940s. The Atomic Thunderbolt never even had his own cartoon. This was the old man's influence, of course. Billy's father thought everything was better in his day, even the superheroes.

Bo staggered into the kitchen like a four-foot hurricane and threw his arms around Billy.

From the corner of his eye, Billy watched the old man recoil.

So much can happen in a split second. His father's lips spread into a snarl, and the heat of jealousy burned in his eyes. In an instant, the emotion was gone, forced back beneath his face.

The reaction startled Billy. He held the kid by the shoulders and gently moved him to arm's length, then laughed as if it were a game.

"Weren't you supposed to change?" Billy asked.

The kid hugged himself, and his costume. "I want to show Stu," he said.

Billy looked at the old man. "Treatment day, Pop," he said. "We should get to the hospital, so the kid here can show Stu Tracy his superhero pj's."

The old man glared bitterly at some spot on the ceiling. "Stu's blind, for Christ's sake."

"I want to show him," said Bo.

The old man papered a smile over his rage and took the newspaper from Bo. "Fine, then. We'll see Stu after I get my blood scrubbed, okay? Why don't you pick a movie for us from Billy's collection."

The kid snapped to attention, broke off a crisp Atomic Thunderbolt salute, then ran recklessly down the hall.

"That was shitty of you," the old man growled. "A betrayal."

"Let's type a response," Billy said cheerfully, locking his eyes on the screen.

"You only delay what I have decided is inevitable."

Billy spoke aloud as he typed: "Dear icedealer-one-seven-seven, thanks for the e-mail. My friend, Dismas-two-three, is currently, um . . . out of commission." He paused, thinking.

"Dismas authorized you to take over the deal," the old man urged, unable, even in betrayal, to resist being part of the action.

"Yup," Billy said as he typed the suggestion. Then he added, "But my friend left town rather suddenly and you need to send me his mailing address so I may pick up the appropriate item for the transaction."

"That's a fucking whopper," the old man whispered.

"I hope this guy is greedy enough to buy it."

He sent the e-mail.

They sat together in silence. The old man emitted hot anger like radiation. *Christ, like sitting next to a hunk of uranium.* Billy sensed that his father could not stand to be near him, but was too curious about the e-mail deception to leave. The old man dumped the newspaper from its plastic bag and snapped the paper into shape. For two minutes he read in silence, then showed the front page to Billy and demanded, "This the case you're on?"

A front-page photo showed the State House memorial for Judge Harmony. Two smaller photos showed June Harmony delivering a speech, and Martin Smothers at the podium, with his jacket open and a nasty black spot on his shirt.

"That's my case," Billy confirmed. "Not that I've gotten anything out of the investigation, except a beating and two pounds of sand in my ear."

The computer said, "Missed it by THAT much!"

Billy hurled the paper over his shoulder and banged the key to open the e-mail:

> To groverwhalen2 . . . if dismas23 is your friend, what is the item?

"Shit, we're bagged," Billy said.

"How are we supposed to know what the item is?"

"Exactly, Pop, this is a test. And we need to send the answer fast, or this guy's gonna get too spooked to deal with us."

"Well, it's a gem. Tell him it's a gem."

"Not specific enough." Billy pushed himself from the chair and moaned at the pain. "So goddamn close!" He paced the room, ignoring the complaints of battered muscles. He wound up to kick the newspaper, but stopped and slowly lowered his foot.

He stared at the pictures of Martin and June Harmony. Something about the two of them together held his attention. . . . What was it?

Holy shit.

He needed a phone. Billy barked, "Where's the goddamn cordless?"

"There!" The old man pointed.

Billy snatched the phone from the countertop and began to dial Martin Smothers. "No," he scolded himself. "Not something Martin would know offhand." He hung up, and then dialed a new number: the cellular phone of Martin's assistant, Carol.

His father stared up at him helplessly. "What? What's going on?"

On the second ring, a voice like a phone sex operator oozed into Billy's ear: "Hello, Billy boy."

"Thank God, Carol. I need help fast!"

"Mmmmm. I hear that from lots of men. Why should I help you?"

"Because I know you're a goddess."

She laughed. "You have passed the test. What do you need?"

"The police report on the judge's murder—somewhere in there it mentions June Harmony's earrings, the expensive pair left out in a jewelry dish the night Rackers killed her husband. I need to know the specifics about those stones. Details, details—whatever you know."

"Her diamond earrings? Of course," Carol purred. "I saw her

sashaying in them yesterday at the memorial. Oh, gorgeous stones! Colorless, ideal cuts, just blazing. A pair of perfectly matched solitary diamonds in platinum bezel settings. Mmm-mm. Four carats total weight. Worth about two hundred thousand." She lowered her voice and cooed, "A man gives me stones like that, I might be tempted to overlook a *comatta* in New York City."

"I am madly in love with you," Billy joked.

She laughed. "Keep that between us. I don't want my business out in the street."

"Gotta go!" He hung up and pitched the phone into his father's lap. The old man caught it in the housecoat.

"You got the answer?" the old man pleaded. "Billy?"

Billy typed furiously:

Dear icedealer177 . . . diamond earrings, perfect match, four carats total, platinum bezel settings . . . we still on?

Send.

Billy dropped his head on the table with a thud. "I hope that was fast enough."

"Aw sure," the old man said. "This is e-mail. How does he know you weren't taking a dump?" He scraped a finger on his white neck stubble. "Who's this person you're madly in love with?"

"Smooth segue," Billy said.

The old man's eyes widened. He shrugged in innocence. "What?"

Despite the pain in his chest and the anxiety crushing him from every direction, Billy laughed out loud.

The answer came two hours later, about the time Billy had convinced himself that his hunch about June Harmony's diamond earrings had been wrong.

Billy waved his hands over the keyboard like a magician for good luck, then opened the e-mail:

> To groverwhalen2
>
> my terms are unchanged for the stones. you and dismas23 carve your own split. leave me out of it. i don't want to know. this is the address i mailed the loupe. . . .

The address was in Providence.

Unfuckinbelievable, Billy thought. All that searching for Adam Rackers, and his address was a five-dollar cab ride from Billy's apartment.

eighteen

A midnight mist slipped silently up the bay and followed the river into Providence. It spread invisibly, except in the glow of street-lights, where it looked like static. The cold mist landed on Billy's skin as softly as frozen spider's silk. The streets seemed especially quiet, as if the city were discouraged by the sudden chill that confirmed the death of summer and foretold another New England winter.

Billy stuck his hands in his pockets and listened to the city. Some unseen foot kicked a can that clanked and echoed. A passing car splashed through a deep puddle. Voices shouting over each other at a neighborhood bar momentarily grew louder whenever somebody opened the door. A church bell rang twice, the second *dong* coming before the first had died out. Billy's shoes tapped unevenly on the sidewalk. He limped against the pain of a bruised hip.

Kit Bass walked in stride beside him. She made no sound at all. Kit wore old Nike racing flats—an outdated model the company had not made for years—loose cotton slacks, black fleece sweater, and a knit watchman's cap. She had tucked every strand of her hair under the cap; if Billy had not known better, he might have guessed she was bald.

A car roared up suddenly from behind. A passenger laughed hideously at them out of the window, which startled Billy and flushed him with fear. "Hoo! Hoo! Hoo!" the man added as the car sped on, to molest some other pedestrians.

"Fucking drunks," Billy muttered. "A drive-by laughing."

"Why are we going in the middle of the night?" Kit asked. She wrapped her arms around herself.

"If it's locked, we're breaking in," Billy replied. "Not what you should do in broad daylight. And heck, I took a vacation day to do this."

"Ever been convicted of B and E?"

"Never convicted of anything. Why?"

"Second offense is a four- to ten-year sentence. That's in the General Laws, title eleven, chapter eight-dash-two."

"What's first offense?"

"Two-year minimum."

Billy whistled and pretended to hike a fedora high on his head. "Working for the court, do you get an employee discount?"

She looked at her shoes. "I'm on a leave of absence until I learn who paid to kill the judge. I won't quit until I know what happened."

Billy noted that she no longer referred to Judge Harmony as "Gil." He was *The Judge*. Her choice of language imposed distance between Kit and her former boss, though the intensity of her words still sounded like love. She grabbed Billy's elbow and asked him, "Why did you bring me here tonight?"

There were so many reasons. He shared a few of them. "Because I owe you for saving me," he said. "Because two people can search a house twice as fast as one. Because you worked for the judge, and you're chasing the same truth that I am, and I thought you deserved to be here." Left unsaid was that the encounter with Glanz's goons had rattled Billy, and he did not want to go alone.

"What do we hope to find?"

"I have a little gambling hunch, the kind I've learned to pay attention to," Billy admitted. "Rackers's payment for shooting the judge didn't come in cash. He was being paid with June Harmony's diamonds, which he apparently believed would be in a wall safe in the judge's house. He planned to shoot the judge, and collect his payment on the way out. Rackers had already arranged to sell the stones to a shady rock dealer over the Internet."

Billy paused to let her process his theory, then added, "What I can't get my mind around is why the hell didn't he take the stones? They weren't in a wall safe—the house didn't even have one. They were lying in plain sight. He'd have to be as blind as Stu Tracy to miss them."

"Who?"

"Not important. As a wild guess, I'd say the real killer, the one we're looking for—"

"Like maybe Rhubarb Glanz?"

"Or maybe his kid, Robbie, or one of his goons, offered a deal for Rackers to kill the judge, in exchange for the combination to a wall safe."

"But there was no safe."

"Rackers didn't know that. So he killed Judge Harmony first, then looked for a safe. Brock came running downstairs and scared the shit out of Rackers. So he put the kid to work checking for a safe, but in his panic didn't see the stones in plain sight."

"So he was calm enough to break in and kill the judge in cold blood, but too panicked to put a pair of diamonds in his pocket?" In a robotic voice, Kit said, "Does-not-com-pute."

Billy grinned at Kit's first show of whimsy since he had met her. Maybe she wasn't completely hard-minded and in love with only the judge and the law. She had, he realized, punched clean through his theory. "That's why we have to search his home," Billy said, "whether or not we violate title eleven, chapter eight-dash-my-ass, of the General Laws."

The apartment where the diamond dealer had sent the loupe was on the third floor of a triple-decker. In the vestibule, the doorbell for that apartment was listed under the name Gary Gleason.

"An alias?" Kit asked.

"A roommate, maybe," Billy said. "It's hard to carry off an alias. Fake driver's license, fake credit cards—those things are hard to get, expensive to maintain over time, and a good way to get noticed by the IRS or the FBI or some other set of government initials."

He checked the inner door of the vestibule.

Locked.

"So what do we do?" Kit asked. "We can't just ring the bell."

Billy crouched to examine the lock on the inner door. Very old. Poorly maintained. A wide crack between the door and the jamb. He stood and leaned a shoulder on the door. "Spare me the legal citation, okay?"

"What?"

Billy rocked back, then violently drove his shoulder into the door just above the lock. It burst open. Billy staggered into an inner hallway that smelled of piss and dust. He gathered himself, stood at attention, held the door for Kit, and swept his hand through the air like an overdramatic doorman.

"Billy!" she said in a stage whisper, cut with giggly laughter. "I've just witnessed my first real crime!" She hurried inside. Billy let the door wheeze shut. The corridor continued to the ground-level apartments. To the left, battered wooden stairs and a decorative banister led to the second floor.

Kit waved a hand in front of her nose. "Stinks in here," she said. "What is that awful smell?"

"Poverty," Billy replied.

She went on about the smell. Billy barely listened. His attention was on a string of small spots near the base of a banister post. The hallway light was no better than forty watts, so Billy could not be sure, but the dark streaks on the wood looked like dried blood. He scraped some away with a fingernail and sniffed it.

Crusty, sharp-smelling blood.

He hid the discovery from Kit, wiped his fingers on his pants, then leaned close and briefed her:

"We're going to the third floor. If we run into anybody, we ignore them. We do not make eye contact. We do not strike up a conversation. We will look like we belong because we will *believe* that we do. If anyone questions us, we tell them to fuck off and we keep moving with absolute confidence."

Without waiting for an answer, he started up the stairs. Thousands of footsteps over ten decades had pressed the creaks out of the old staircase. Billy was pleased to climb it without making a racket. Kit followed close behind.

At the second-floor landing, a black cat with a regal white shield on its chest watched them from a corner. The cat held its ground as they passed. It hissed once, not aggressively, just a friendly warning to tell Billy and Kit to keep moving, and to mind their own business.

More streaks of dried blood spotted the banister on the staircase to the third floor. The stairwell seemed colder than the outdoors. Billy blew into his hands. Someone had pilfered the lightbulb in the ceiling lamp at the top of the stairs. The landing was dark. Billy pulled a small hiker's headlamp from his coat, turned it on, and panned the beam around. Under the white light, the bloodstains that speckled the floor were deep burgundy.

Kit took three loud, choppy breaths and pointed to a smear on the doorjamb. Billy put the light to it. More blood. He slipped on the flashlight's elastic headband and wore the light like a coal miner.

He looked at Kit. She squinted and turned away from the brightness. Her cheeks and nose were red from the cold, or maybe from fear. Her nostrils shone wet. Tension had raised ripples in the skin over her brow. Billy slowly scanned her with the light. Her hands were steady. Her stomach rose and fell with each deep breath. He held the light on her shoelace, coming undone, until she reached down and tightened it. Should they have to run, he wanted Kit to have every advantage.

She nodded that she was ready. Billy winked, then turned to the door. It was dark wood, with a brass knob and deadbolt fixture. An index card taped to the jamb had a name in block letters: GLEASON, G.

Gary Gleason, same as the mailbox downstairs.

Billy pressed an ear to the wood. Two sounds competed to be heard: the rush of water through old pipes and the heavy drone of a refrigerator, right on the other side of the door.

He drew a handkerchief from his pocket, wrapped the doorknob to keep it free of his fingerprints—no sense giving any detectives the wrong idea—and turned the knob. It resisted a moment, then smoothly rotated a half turn and clicked when the bolt snapped into the door. *Holy shit, unlocked.* Who would leave his door open in this neighborhood?

Now what. Should they knock?

Oh, well, what the hell.

Billy pushed open the door.

What he saw brought a flash of horror that broiled his skin and raised a sweat.

A thick stripe of blood, like from a housepainter's brush, slashed across the side of a white refrigerator to the left of the door. The refrigerator was wide open; it cast a dim yellow glow that cut the room into triangles of shadow and light. Bottles of beer lay scattered across a floor stained deep red.

Footprints and scuff marks in the blood marked the scene of a savage fight.

Chairs and a table had been tipped over. What looked for a moment like a human arm lay across a counter, a bright glob of congealed blood where the wrist would be.

Billy's eyes widened at a human form across the room. He aimed his flashlight at it. A male mannequin, missing an arm, stood over the scene like a wounded survivor, shell-shocked to silence.

Billy stepped toward the door. Kit grabbed a handful of his shirt and pulled him back. He turned to her and whispered, "This is what we came for."

"We have to call the authorities," she pleaded.

"As soon as we're done, we'll drop the dime, anonymously."

He turned away before she could argue, and stepped into the room, taking long strides onto islands of white linoleum between the bloodstains. Several identical women's business suits were piled in a heap at the feet of the mannequin. The security tags were still attached, so he guessed these suits had been boosted from some local department store. That seemed more like Rackers's style than shooting a judge.

He glanced back to Kit, who was still in the hallway, looking pensively at the carnage across the kitchen. Billy waved her inside. She came haltingly, then quietly closed the door behind her. With the door shut, Billy felt free to speak.

"I'm going to explore," he said. "Look around in here but don't touch anything."

"Look around for what?" she asked, but Billy did not answer, for he had noticed a blood trail leading down a wide hallway. The drops were spaced a few feet apart, and he imagined they had been left by a wounded man running at top speed. But running where? Into the bathroom?

No, he decided.

Running for the door.

The deduction calmed Billy's roiling stomach. With so much blood, he would not have been surprised to find a body splayed on the floor. But if the bleeder had been wounded in the bathroom . . . he must have escaped the apartment, down the stairs to the street.

He walked silently past a battered sofa and a storage chest, which sat across from a small bathroom. Shards of broken mirror on the bathroom floor reflected his headlamp, and scattered light around the room like a poor man's disco ball.

This is where the fight began.

The light switch was just inside the bathroom door. He couldn't think of a reason to stumble around with a flashlight in an apartment with perfectly good utilities, and he clicked on the light.

No dead body. Whew. He stepped inside.

The top half of a broken mirror hung above the sink, reflecting the blue shower curtain across the tiny room. He noted a toothbrush in a glass on the vanity. He watched a soap bubble pop on a glistening wet bar of Ivory. On the floor, blood had spattered the chips of broken mirror. The ten-inch shaft of an ice pick stuck out from the wall at shoulder height, like a giant nail. The tool's wooden handle lay splintered on the floor.

Billy swallowed hard and closely examined the ice pick, until his imagination began to guess how it might feel to have that metal slide through his guts, and he had to turn away.

The toilet lid was up, the water inside clear, and the old porcelain bowl stained with rust. A few magazines were scattered.

He walked back to the hall and turned toward the bedroom.

Wait . . .

He froze, thinking . . .

Holyfuckingshit.

Gooseflesh erupted over his body. He looked desperately at Kit, who was in the kitchen, grimly leaning over the counter for a closer inspection of the mannequin arm. Billy tried to warn her but the words never left his thoughts.

The soap on the vanity . . . why is it wet?

Somebody else was there.

Billy looked again toward the bedroom, dark and unexplored. The line of sight from the kitchen door went straight down the hall. If Kit and Billy had surprised somebody using the bathroom, Billy would have seen him duck into the bedroom.

But he was convinced he had heard water running when he listened at the apartment door. Distracted by the gore in the kitchen, he had forgotten about the noise. So they *had* surprised someone . . . someone who was washing his hands . . . who had heard the door . . . and killed the light. . . .

So where did he run?

Or . . . did he run at all? Billy's head slowly turned, more slowly than the red second hand of a clock, until he stared straight at the shower stall.

The curtain hung motionless.

He shivered against another wave of goose bumps.

nineteen

Of all the fucking no good luck!

Scratch shrank in his shower stall into an uncomfortable squatting position, with his tailbone against the tiled wall and his ass on his heels, coiled like a spring—the position should provide the best leverage to explode from the shower and make a run for his life. Except that he had squatted there so long, afraid to move, barely breathing, hardly blinking, he could not be sure his legs had not gone numb.

He listened to the footsteps coming closer. *Oh, Jesus Christ, is he coming back?* Scratch screamed orders to the intruder in his mind: *You've already searched the bathroom. Remember? Two minutes ago. Are you thick or something? Nobody is here so go the hell away!*

Scratch had been *positive* he had not been followed to his apartment. Not after riding a cab from the airport to the train station downtown, and then hopping a second cab from the train station to the city park, through which Scratch had shadow-hiked along strolling trails that circled the duck ponds. Not to mention the ten-minute ride on a rickety three-speed bicycle he had liberated from a backyard on the Cranston city line. No way he could have been followed; his trail was scrubbed.

Had they been waiting for him? This was his first time home since the attack. He only wanted some spare cash, fresh clothing, his favorite marked deck of poker cards, and a shoe box stuffed with resalable PDA cell phones, which Adam had pilfered from Radio World before he died in the wreck. Eh, maybe a few beers, too. Just some necessities to make life on the lam more bearable.

And then to be caught at home with his pants down. Not down, actually—but unzipped. Either way, big trouble. He hadn't heard them at the door until it was too late to run. He practically had to drag himself by the collar into the shower stall, from which the masked attacker had plotted Scratch's murder.

But there he squatted, hiding from an intruder in the place an intruder had hidden from him.

Scratch was beginning to detest irony.

To be murdered in his bathroom after escaping a murder in the same damn bathroom would be too much.

A woman called softly from the kitchen, "Billy? Have you found anything? Billy?"

No, Scratch answered silently. *There's nothing to find. Now split.*

The woman's voice had a nasally thickness. Something about her pronunciations suggested she was well educated. Who was she? Did hit men bring their wives along? Were they on a date? *Hang on, babe. We'll get to* Phantom of the Opera, *soon as I waste this guy.*

Scratch's left leg began to quiver. From fear? From the stress of squatting? He couldn't be sure. He clutched his knee with both hands, as if to choke it to death if it didn't calm down.

A sliver of broken mirror crunched underfoot on the other side of the curtain.

Whoever this guy was—*Billy*, the woman had called him—he was standing directly in front of the shower stall.

Scratch waited, waited. . . . His eyeballs stung, and he realized they had dried out from not blinking. He blinked the pain away and wondered, how long was this guy going to stand there?

"Billy?" the woman called again, more urgently. She was coming down the hall. "I've checked in the kitchen—" She stopped suddenly. "What? What's wrong with you?"

With a ferocious grunt, the man suddenly punched the shower curtain. It bulged where Scratch's head would have been, had he been standing.

The woman shouted, "Billy!"

Scratch sprang into the curtain like a bull into the matador's cape. The man said, "*Oomph*," hurtled backward, and skidded on broken glass. Scratch tore past the curtain, raced to the door. He stiff-armed the woman square on the forehead and crushed her out of his way.

"Hold it!" the man screamed.

Uh-uh.

"We gotta talk to you!"

Busy, sorry. No time to be executed. Call my agent.

He dashed to the bedroom, the way he had entered. The window to the fire escape was open and he scrambled through it. A hand grabbed his foot. Scratch slammed his feet together and caught fingers between the heels of his shoes.

The man yelped and Scratch pulled free.

He dragged himself on his elbows, then rose to crawl on hands and knees, then triumphantly gained his feet, like a swamp fish evolving from water to land in the space of two seconds. Down the iron ladder he toe-tapped. The man thundered down behind him, laboring heavily. His clip-clop limp was no match for a cat burglar.

And once I hit earth . . . whoosh!

Scratch dropped to the porch roof, then to the ground, and glanced up. The intruder was still between the first and second floors; he might as well have been a mile away.

Good-bye, Mr. Slow Motion. Tallyho!

Scratch turned to run and saw the woman sprint out the front door. What comedy! She was trying to run him down. Scratch aimed his feet toward Asia and made like Man o'War down the home stretch. Running was easy for Scratch. In every scam he ever pulled, running was Plan B. He had employed this secret backup plan more frequently than he liked to admit. But he had never needed Plan C, because nobody had ever caught him.

I'm singing in my brain . . .
Just singin' in my brain . . .

The woman jumped his back from behind and Scratch went down.

Bang. Forehead to pavement.

Brief hiatus from reality.

He thought he blacked out for a split second, but he must have been away longer than that. By the time he remembered there was no Plan C, the man was there, and the guy's knee had found Scratch's throat.

"We're going to talk," he informed Scratch. He was panting, and Scratch took pleasure in knowing he had made the guy work for it.

"I got nothing to say to you."

The woman pleaded, "You *have* to help us."

"Guess again, Miss Speedy McFly," Scratch taunted. He still could not comprehend how the hell she had caught him.

The man sighed. He ground his knee in a painful little circle, and looked off into the starless night for a moment. Then in a calm voice suitable for a lecture on monetary policy or greenhouse gas emissions, the intruder told Scratch:

"Over my life I have made many bad wagers based on some wild hunches. The National League and the money line in several World

Series, for instance." He passed fingers through his hair, and seemed to relive a painful memory. "On occasion I have lacked sufficient funds to finance these mistakes of judgment. Whenever that happened, I would be visited by some of the most sadistic and creative debt collectors in New England. These men have massive, mutant fists, propelled by chemically enhanced muscles—steroids, human growth hormone, EPO—whatever. They have been schooled inside the state's finest correctional facilities in the arts of damaging somebody else's body. They are men of pain. The Picassos of torture. Men who think you'll shit silver if they squeeze your skull hard enough. Over the years they have taken turns brutalizing me in ever more clever and original ways. Take it from me, these are experiences you never forget."

The guy interrupted himself with an ironic chuckle. He offered a sad smile to the woman.

Then darkness gathered on his face.

He turned hard to Scratch and informed him: "I have learned a lot from these men. And now you and I are going to talk."

twenty

Billy learned quickly that Gary Gleason was afraid to be called his real name, and that the Q&A would go more smoothly if Kit and Billy just called him Scratch.

"I had nothing to do with the judge," Scratch claimed for the third time. He dabbed a damp washcloth on the scrape on his forehead.

He had decided to talk.

Funny thing about threats—they often worked, even a bluff with no true violence backing it up. Though Billy might have brought himself to slam Scratch around a bit to make the threat more realistic, he'd never have *damaged* him.

But Scratch didn't know that.

The three of them had walked together to the bloodstained apartment, for privacy. Billy had forced Scratch onto the sofa in the hallway. Billy stood in the bathroom doorway; Kit guarded the route to the kitchen. Scratch seemed vaguely intimidated by Kit; he shot puzzled glances her way.

Kit unnerved Billy, too. He could not have tortured Scratch into talking, but he suspected Kit might have.

"Is that your blood all over the kitchen?" Billy asked.

Scratch pulled up his sleeve to reveal a forearm wrapped in cloth tape. "Sore but getting better," he said. "A clean wound."

"Who attacked you?"

"I thought that *you* did." Scratch looked past Billy into the bathroom. "And that you had come back tonight to finish the job. How did you find me?"

"We found the apartment," Kit said. "Why was Adam Rackers getting his mail here?"

"He had moved in. Adam had some problem with his old landlady."

"What problem?" Billy wanted to know.

"He didn't want to pay her the rent." He grimaced as he gently squeezed his wounded arm.

"So how did you guys make your livings?" Billy asked. Scratch's eyes suddenly shot toward the bedroom, as if he were contemplating a second run for freedom. Billy cut off the thought: "Look, Gary—Scratch, I mean, whatever—we're not cops."

"Just tell us," Kit demanded.

"We know you two weren't trading international stocks down on the exchange, or selling real estate on Ocean Drive, so where did the money come from?" Billy asked.

Scratch looked from Billy to Kit, and then back to Billy. He cleared his throat. "None of this would be admissible in a court of law," he said, "because you're holding me as your prisoner. It's not a confession by free will. Case law is very clear on this point."

"Oh, fuck you and start talking," Kit said sharply. "This ain't a deposition."

Scratch refused to look at her. He frowned and wiped sand off a wet spot on his knee, where he had rolled over in the street after Kit had tackled him. Then he explained, "Adam was my wingman when we pulled our street hustles. I dealt the cards, so to speak, and Adam set up the marks. He was so good at it, pretending to be excited when I let him win. Even people who assumed it was a scam were taken in by Adam. He was a great, great fucking actor."

"Rackers played the stranger in the crowd," Billy said, "who won money from you at three-card monty?"

Scratch nodded. "Something like that. Most scams need two elements—somebody to set the terms and a second person to drive up the price. It's about creating demand. Making people believe they're getting a good deal." He smiled, reliving old victories.

"Rackers had a lot of burglaries on his record too," Billy said.

"He was great in tight spaces, and could slip through a window faster than most people can run through a door," Scratch said. His little testimonial sounded like a eulogy. "I've seen him slide up old drainpipes that a squirrel wouldn't have trusted. He was an urban cliff climber, like maybe he was raised by mountain goats."

"Then why was his police record so long?" Kit said. "How'd he get caught so often?"

"Sometimes he was as smart as a goat too."

Scratch pulled his legs up and rested his heels on the sofa. For an instant, some fatherly instinct in Billy wanted to order those dirty shoes off the furniture, but Billy reminded himself that this was not his house, and Scratch Gleason was not Bo Povich.

Scratch continued, "Adam was a stupid fuck sometimes, no common sense. He always assumed things would work out for the best. He couldn't see the hazards of a particular job, and didn't plan for contingencies. You can't just *assume* that everybody keeps their best silverware in a suitcase in the curio cabinet, right? You can't just *assume* that a middle-class house won't have a silent alarm—things like that." He clicked his tongue. "But managing risk is something I understand, so the partnership worked . . . mostly."

"You've been in jail too, haven't you?" Kit asked.

"Aw shit," he said, "nothing but a few months of shock time from some hard-ass judge who thought he'd scare me straight. What he did was scare the recklessness out of me. Did me a favor. Made me a better crook than I ever was." He flashed a yellow-toothed smile at Kit. "That's why I insisted we unload as much merchandise as possible over the Internet. It's slow and labor-intensive for us, but anonymous and safe so long as you space out the items." He made a chewing motion, as if he had gum, and suddenly seemed to be enjoying himself. People do love to boast about what they're good at.

Billy snapped his fingers twice to get Scratch's attention, as he would to a dog. Scratch glared at him for breaking the mood. Billy demanded, "Tell us about Rackers's connection to Judge Harmony."

Scratch turned his palms up at Billy, as if to push away any accusation. "I told you I had nothing to do with that. Adam never mentioned going back to Harmony's place."

Going back . . . ?

Billy and Kit exchanged urgent looks.

Her eyes narrowed in rage. Her fists clenched, as if she were holding two imaginary ice picks.

Scratch watched their faces in horror, realizing he must have slipped up, but not yet seeing how. His eyes wandered, looking backward over the past few seconds, until his eyelids slowly closed, his lips tightened, and understanding spread over his face. He lowered his head into his hands. "I never actually went *into* the judge's condo," he said, speaking in the general direction of Billy's shoes. "And I never even saw the beach house, or even knew about it. That was all Adam."

They waited in silence for a few moments. There was no need to pepper Scratch with any more questions. Hiding behind his hands, he gave them what they had come for:

"A couple weeks before Adam shot the judge, he had an idea to break into some pricey condos downtown, you know? Some corporate apartments and executive city homes, that kind of thing."

"Judge Harmony's condo," Kit said.

"Adam ran the addresses through a real estate database," Scratch explained. "The judge was on TV all the time—had written all them books. He had big dough. So yeah, his place was a good mark. I didn't even know he had another house in Charlestown. And I didn't know he had a wife or a kid, none of that. We cased the building a few nights. Not just Harmony's apartment, the whole complex, but we noticed the judge's schedule. He traveled a lot. Spent half his nights in some other bed, hmmm? Rich men like a change of scenery sometimes. They get bored easy."

Billy thought of Nelida and Jerod, the judge's secret second family.

Change of scenery, all right.

He thought of his father, too, looking to see the scenery beyond this world. The old man was bored with who he was, and what he had to do to survive. Just like the old man's marriage—when he got bored, he skipped. Billy's mind played with the odd sight of his father at a hotel bar in a faraway city, milking a whiskey, flashing his blue eyes and testing pickup lines on the Grim Reaper.

Miss Reaper, haven't we met before?

If we had, you'd know it.

You have lovely bone structure.

Call me Grim.

"You listening, man?" Scratch asked. " 'Cause I don't wanna tell it all over."

Billy extinguished the daydream. "You watched the judge's place. Fine. Saw a bunch of executives taking their *comattas* home for the evening. What happened the night of the break-in?"

"Adam did the entry. A thing of beauty. Used the condo's landscaping to his advantage. Shimmied a thirty-foot white birch. At the top, he leaned his weight toward the building, bent the tree, and rode it like a parachute to a second-story balcony. Once he let go, the tree snapped back—no ladder for us to hide. See? You'd be surprised how many paranoid people put three deadbolts on the front door but don't lock the slider to the balcony." He clapped a hand on his knee and marveled, "My God, Adam was fuckin' talented. We were such a great team, man. We could steal anything. Adam once told me, 'Together, we could loot the moon.'

"On this night at the condos, I stayed below with a garbage bag. Adam went in and out of the apartments. The balconies are only about four feet apart, so he just stepped across the railings. About half the places were open. He'd duck in while I kept watch. He didn't dare use a light, so he'd just grab what he could find in one or two minutes and send it down to me in a pillowcase on twenty feet of twine. Most of the stuff was crap, but this was like beachcombing. You dig up a dozen bottlecaps for every silver dollar." He chuckled and sneaked a peak at Billy, who glared the grin right off Scratch's face.

"At Harmony's apartment, he was inside a long time. Felt like five full minutes, but might have been less. He came out in a hurry. Jumped back down."

"He jumped?" Kit asked, incredulous. "From the second story? Don't be bullshitting us, Gary."

Scratch cringed at the use of his real name. "It's not such a hard jump," he insisted. "The floor of the balcony is twenty feet off the ground. Adam was almost six feet tall, and closer to eight feet when he hung by his arms. That means when he was hanging from the bottom of the balcony, his shoes were twelve feet from the ground. Big whoopee. He landed on damp dirt and cedar chips. Adam made jumps better than that all the time. We both did. Anybody could. Just don't forget to roll on impact." He looked up to see if anybody challenged his math. Nobody did.

"I pulled him up when he landed," Scratch continued, adding a shrug to indicate this was where the story got fuzzy. "He told me almost got caught, that somebody got the drop on him, and we had to bug outta there. Like I said, I'm the cautious one, so I started to run. Adam grabbed my shirt and told me to chill. 'Let's just walk and not attract attention,' he said. He told me not to look back. Just keep walking. When we got back home, he wasn't interested in going through the shit we stole. Told me to split it myself, because he trusted me."

"And was that unusual?" Billy asked.

Scratch rolled his eyes. "We're crooks, man."

"Forget I asked," Billy said, feeling a little silly.

"Adam and I didn't work together much after that," Scratch said.

Billy smiled at his semantics. *Didn't work together.* Since when was stealing and running street cons considered *work*? Hammering rivets or teaching sixth grade is work. Even typing obituaries in the middle of the night—as glamorous as peeling vegetables, and nearly as well paying—at least offered a firm claim on honest work.

"We both always did solo jobs—nothing we ever talked about, you see? So I didn't think much about it, until Adam got himself killed in that car wreck." He leaned his head back and looked up to a ceiling stained with blotches of mildew, like a fading Jackson Pollock masterpiece in green, black, and brown.

"I never could have imagined Adam doing something violent like that," Scratch said. "That wasn't his personality. Maybe the judge threatened him, and Adam wrestled the gun away, um . . . and then shot him accidentally, or in self-defense."

Kit mocked him with a snort and a laugh.

"That's the only explanation I can think of," Scratch offered.

"It's bullshit," Kit barked. "Think again."

Scratch seemed to tire of Kit's acerbity. "I knew Adam," he informed her with a jab of a pinkie in her direction. "My wingman wouldn't have killed anybody. He was harmless. . . . At least the way I knew him he was." Scratch spread his hands. "He slept right here on this sofa, for Christ's sake. Would I have let a killer sleep in my pad? Adam was spiritual. He thought of himself as the good thief."

"Saint Dismas," Billy said.

"Hey . . . how did you know that?"

Billy ignored him. He took a step backward into the bathroom and looked over the sofa. What a strong spine Rackers must have had to sleep on that sagging thing. He imagined Rackers stretched out there, asleep with no sheet, under a threadbare cotton thermal blanket. Billy couldn't help thinking that a legal giant such as Judge Gilbert Harmony should have been slain by somebody more impressive.

Of course, Harmony *had* been killed by somebody bigger—whoever had hired the triggerman. Though Billy had doubted Martin's theory in the beginning, he had come to believe it as strongly as his winning hunches. His eyes settled on the wooden storage trunk set like an end table at the side of the sofa.

"Is that his?" Billy asked.

"Nothing valuable left in there," Scratch said. They stared at him, and he shrank defensively. "What was I supposed to do? He owed me his half of the rent. So I hocked his Harry Winston wristwatch. Do you think he's squirming in the coffin, wondering what time it is?"

Billy brushed a pile of T-shirts off the box and flipped open the lid. Shoes and papers, old receipts, compact discs, hardcover books, and a hundred other odds and ends filled the box halfway, like an oversized junk drawer. Billy plucked a stubby plastic cylinder from the mess and held it to his eye.

"Is that it?" Kit asked.

"Is what?" said Scratch.

"A loupe," Billy explained. He tossed it to Kit, who snatched it and studied the lines in her own palm. "It's for examining precious stones—diamonds, for instance."

"We didn't have any stones," Scratch said, cautiously. He seemed to detect a trap in Billy's tone. "Adam and me liked home electronics and high-end clothing . . . common household stuff. One-of-a-kind items, like family heirlooms, are too hard to sell. See? Internet auction sites have ten thousand identical digital music players for sale, and who knows which ones fell off the back of a truck? You guys sailing on my drift? I'm first mate on the good ship *Anonymous*."

"Are heirlooms really hard to sell?" Billy asked. "Or just too dangerous?" He stared a hole in Scratch's forehead.

"Put it this way, there's a buyer for everything if you dare to take the risk. I was the cautious one, remember?"

Billy pulled items from the chest, announcing what they were as he tossed them aside:

"Polarized sunglasses, missing one lens," he said. "Scented candle, blackened wick, smells like a Christmas wreath."

"I told him to pitch that thing," Scratch said. "If I wanted to breathe the forest at night, I'd sleep in the park."

"One brass doorknob."

Scratch explained, "He was going to learn to pick locks."

"One *Frommer's Chicago*. One mini walkie-talkie, no batteries. One petrified Snickers bar with a bite out of it. One DVD copy of *Horny Hawaiian Homemakers*, part two, the *Block Party Diaries*, in high definition."

Scratch raised his hand. "Over here," he called. Billy flipped the movie to him.

"One hardbound Bible, abridged version. Looks like agate type on tissue paper. Still has the price tag on it."

"Jesus Christ," Kit muttered. "He thought enough to shoplift it; he should have tried reading the thing once in a while. I wonder what's the cosmic penalty for stealing a Bible?"

"Hmmm," Billy said. "One unmarked eight-by-eleven envelope, sealed with a spot of wax on the flap."

Scratch leaned in for a closer inspection. "That little shithead," he growled. "He was afraid I would snoop in his personal papers? I'm insulted."

"You sold his wristwatch," Kit reminded him.

Scratch snapped his fingers sharply. "That was my inheritance."

Billy slid his thumb under the wax and popped open the envelope. Inside he found another envelope—business-sized, and addressed in typewritten letters to Adam Rackers, at this apartment address. The top had been slit with a letter opener.

"Postmark is Providence," Billy noted. "There's no return address."

Inside, Billy found a single newspaper clipping, undated. The clipping showed a photo from a charity ball. The handsome couple centered in the frame looked into each other's eyes as they danced together on a parquet floor, next to a twisting interpretive ice sculpture as tall as the people.

Billy read the caption silently to himself and felt his blood pressure spike. He said to Scratch, "The good ship *Anonymous* just got torpedoed in the bow."

He held up the clipping and read the caption aloud:

"Judge Gilbert Harmony and his wife, June, ruled last evening's festivities a big success from gavel to gavel, as they danced the waltz at the International Ballroom. June looked marvelous as usual in a platinum Vera Wang mermaid gown. And everyone was checking out her new bling: a pair of ferociously sparkling, perfect diamond studs, whispered to reside in the friendly neighborhood of four carats. We plead guilty to envy."

Scratch's face paled. He rubbed his scalp nervously and asked, "Who writes that crap?"

"Where did Rackers get this?" Billy demanded.

"I dunno. Somebody mailed it to him. What's the date?"

Billy checked the postmark. He looked blankly to Kit. "This was mailed two weeks before Rackers shot the judge."

"That confirms it!" she shouted. "Billy—you were right!"

"I never seen this before," Scratch interjected. "Um, in case anybody was beginning to suspect me of anything." He clutched his head and muttered, "I should set sail on the good ship *Get the Fuck Out of Town*."

"These diamonds were supposed to be Rackers's payment for killing the judge," Billy said. "Whoever mailed this clipping wanted to prove June really had these amazing stones, which Rackers thought were worth doing murder. After he shot Harmony, your wingman searched the house for a wall safe. My guess is, the person who sent this clipping offered Rackers the combination to the safe, in exchange for killing the judge."

"But there was no wall safe," Kit said. "Your friend, the con man, got conned."

Scratch's head ping-ponged between Billy and Kit. He fingered the wound in his arm.

"Whoever mailed this letter is as guilty as Adam Rackers," Billy continued. "You listening, Gary? That's why Adam bought the loupe—to inspect the earrings before he sold them to a shady ice dealer on the Internet. He probably didn't want to get cheated."

"After he stole the diamonds," Kit said.

"What we still need to figure out," Billy said as he withdrew into his own thoughts, "is why Rackers upheld his half of the bargain, but didn't take the stones."

twenty-one

Cool autumn wind swept three-pronged sycamore leaves across the parade ground, in waves of tan and deep brown. He tested the park bench with his hand to be sure its wooden slats were dry, then settled onto it. Though he was taking a calculated risk, he felt safe: anonymous behind wraparound sunglasses, a baseball cap pulled low on his head, and his jacket collar turned up.

The sun rising above the giant armory building felt warm on his face. The morning light gave the yellow-brick castle a buttery look, against a background of blue and stirring white clouds. The Little League baseball field at the foot of the castle—with a muddy infield peppered with footprints, and three brown patches on the grass that marked where the outfielders always stood—was abandoned.

Across the street, fifty pigeons sunned themselves on the sloping slate roof of an old Victorian house. *Why that house and no other?* he wondered. A few birds pecked aimlessly at the slate. He imagined tossing a rock up there to scare them all into the sky at the same time. A homeless man in mismatched winter clothing paused on the great granite steps of a nearby apartment house and furiously scratched a lottery ticket. A jogger in striped tights wheezed down the paved path at the edge of the parade field, on the far side of two rows of immature American sycamores, which stood at attention like twin columns of guards. The wind carried bursts of pop music and Spanish lyrics from a boombox surrounded by ten teenage girls on the other side of the park. He craned his neck to watch the girls for a moment. He decided they were too far away to bother worrying about.

Here, at the intersection of two narrow asphalt walkways that wound through the park, he had found the Povich boy.

Such a sweet child. He played with an Albert Einstein doll. Who had ever heard of such a thing?

He didn't *want* to harm the boy. Who *wanted* to do things such as that? Just crazy people. He was pragmatic, not crazy. But he needed information. This information was for his personal survival, and if the child withheld such critical data, then the child was a threat. It would be no different than if the boy had attacked him.

Who could blame me for acting in self-defense?

"So which house is yours?" he asked the boy, sounding breezy and friendly.

The child pointed across the parade ground, past the empty tot park, past a clump of gnarled pine and the stone memorial to the scholar who had donated this land to the public, to a boxy red and black Victorian with a long, distinguished black awning that covered the front stairs and stretched across the sidewalk, to the street.

"But that's a funeral home."

"We live upstairs," the boy said. His attention was on the microcassette recorder in his hands. "Mr. Metts runs the funerals. He's my friend. He lets me use his telescope."

"Isn't *that* swell!"

The boy offered the tape recorder and two batteries. "Do you know how to put these batteries in?"

The child placed the recorder into an outstretched hand.

After a glance to the funeral home, some two hundred yards across the field and partly screened by trees, he questioned the child: "Does your dad know you're out here in the park by yourself?"

"Billy ain't home. Grandpa's watching me. Are these the right batteries?"

"Double-A, yes they are. And they fit in here like this—you match up the plus signs. See? Plus means positive. One faces up, one faces down. It's important they go in the right way." He snapped the battery cover back onto the little machine and returned it to the boy. "So where's your grandpa?"

"In his room," the boy said. "He can't go down the stairs by himself. I'm not supposed to go past the jungle gym, but I'm on a mission."

Trying to sound awestruck, he leaned toward the child and whispered, "Really? Well, can you tell me your mission? I promise I won't tell anybody." He traced an X over his heart.

The boy tugged the bottom of his windbreaker and peeked at his house. He whispered, "I think Grandpa has been making tapes for me. I can hear him talking through the wall. He says my name all the time."

A golden leaf suddenly blew between them, and the little boy grinned and stomped it. The child continued, "I think the tapes are supposed to be a secret. He made six of them already."

"Let me guess—you took one of your grandfather's tapes, and came way, way out here into the park so he can't hear you listening to it."

The boy grimaced as his plan was laid bare. "Is that bad?"

"Nah. We can listen together, if you'd like. Would you like me to work the tape player?" He gave the boy a sly, sideways look. "That way, if your father or your grandpa asks if you played one of the tapes, you can say no and it won't be a lie." He smiled at the boy and pumped his eyebrows.

The boy's brow bunched above the bridge of his nose as he considered this amendment to his plan. The computations took several seconds. Then his face relaxed. The boy nodded and handed over the device. The kid suddenly hopped on the bench and sat on his own little hands.

How shocking!

He's sharing the bench with me.

How marvelous to find a human being completely without guile. In this cynical world? Had it been so long that he, too, was without cunning? What a shame that this boy was destined to outgrow his instinct to trust.

What a crime that I am hastening this child's cruel transition to grown-up.

"The tape is cued and it looks all set, so I'm just going to play it. Okay?"

The boy nodded.

Click.

The tape hummed for a few seconds, and then a whispery old man's voice cut in:

"Hiyah Bo! This is Grandpa again. If you're listening to this particular tape, then you're turning sixteen years old! Happy birthday, my boy! I hope you remember your grandpa. Remember me? Hmmm? By now I been dead quite a while.

"You're probably looking forward to getting your license soon. Don't stand for your pop telling you to wait till you're eighteen. That's no way to meet girls. You gotta have wheels, boy! I don't know what kind of cars they're gonna be making in the future, but here's another tip: don't fall for the trap of automatic transmission! Learn to drive a standard shift. The fillies will think you're the big man on campus.

"Heh-heh.

"And this brings us to the lesson for today. The stick shift is frustrating to learn to operate, but keep in mind that depressing the clutch simply disconnects the wheels from the engine, so you're just coasting, okay? Then you can safely change gears. The trick is finding the sweet spot on the clutch and

hesitating there a fraction of a second when you let it up. Every clutch is different. You'll get it. Just be patient.

"And then, well, maybe you can drive by the old boneyard and say hi to your grandpa? Okay? Good-bye for now. I got another tape for when you're old enough to vote. So we'll talk again soon.

"Ahhhhh, I sure miss you, boy. I'm looking down at you right now. . . . Heh-heh. Or maybe looking up! Either way, you know that your grandpa loved you."

The words seemed to confuse and upset the child. "Click it off, please," the boy begged.

"Okay."

The boy looked away, wrapped both arms around the Einstein doll, and kicked his little sneakers in the air. His grandfather was preparing to die. How sad for this little boy, yet how beautiful for the old man to leave him messages from beyond the grave.

What profound sadness I feel for this child, for what he has heard and cannot possibly understand.

The jogger in the striped tights shuffled along, completing another lap around the park. He was pleased that the jogger made his revolutions, and that those teenage girls still danced and smoked cigarettes across the park. They would stop him if he tried to take this child against the boy's will. They made it too dangerous to steal this child away.

Good!

Though he trembled over what the boy might know, he wanted the child to live . . . to someday learn to drive a standard shift.

"How's your father doing?"

"He's okay," the boy replied. The kid slapped the lamppost beside the bench and rattled its glass globe. "Look at all those birds on that roof!"

Gently, gently.

"Has your father been real busy? Is that why he's not home today?"

"He's doing a case with Mr. Smothers. That's his friend. He's a lawyer. He don't eat meat."

"Hmmm, that must be interesting work. Does your father say how the case is going?"

"Can I have my recorder back?"

"How's the case, Bo? The case! Does he have any leads?"

Keep your voice low, give him the smile, a thousand watts.

"He told Grandpa he found somebody he was looking for."

"Huh. That's soooooo interesting. Who might that be? The person that he found?"

"Some guy."

"His name, Bo." Smile, smile, sweat gushing down the inside of his shirt. Deep breath. Bulging vein in temple pulsing like a quasar. "What . . . is . . . his . . . name?"

The kid rolled his eyes around, and then his whole head. He tucked his bottom lip behind his front teeth, smiled, and said, "Mm-mmm . . ."

"You can remember, can't you? I'll bet you can! A smart boy like you can remember!"

"Scratch!"

He gasped.

Jesus Christ, he fucking found him.

That goddamn Povich had made the connection. But how? *Deep breath.* Didn't matter how. Scratch had proved too slippery the first time he tried to take him out, in the apartment Scratch had shared with Adam Rackers. He had to find the little thief again, to cut off the trail before it led back to him. This was self-defense. Self-defense was permissible. Soldiers and cops who are forced to defend themselves are not murderers. They're victims.

"Can I have my recorder back?"

"Sure, let me wipe it clean on my shirt . . . okay? Don't want you taking a dirty recorder back home. There you are! That sure was an interesting tape. I wouldn't think too much about it. It would be best if you put it back where you found it, and didn't mention to anyone that you took it. Hmm?"

The boy looked down in sorrow at the recorder in his hand. Then he looked up, into black sunglasses. "You won't tell either? Promise?"

"I promise! Hope to die, stick a needle in my eye." He drew an imaginary zipper over his mouth. "Let's both swear to *never* tell anyone that we met each other in the park today. All right? Then nobody will ever know that you took your grandfather's tape. Deal?"

The kid hesitated a second before accepting the outstretched hand. He shook with enthusiasm.

"Deal," said the boy. "I promise, hope to die."

twenty-two

Martin ordered a club soda, then changed his mind and asked for beer, then changed his mind again and demanded a malt whiskey, as it was, neither chilled nor mixed. Just put it in a goddamn tumbler. He downed a sip, gasped at the burn, and informed his waitress he would be outside on the patio.

"It's awful cold," she said.

"I'm awful weird," he snapped. Her eyes got huge. Martin immediately felt guilty, apologized, tipped her double, grabbed a burning oil lamp from an unoccupied table, and stepped outside to the patio overlooking the river.

The typewritten note that had been delivered by courier to his office requested that he arrive by seven thirty. Martin was a few minutes early. He set the drink and the lamp on a round pub table, then collapsed into a plastic chair. He was the only customer who dared drink in the cold, and had the outdoor patio to himself.

Night had fallen. The city blazed in colored lights. The glow scrubbed the night sky of all but the brightest few stars.

The brick patio ended at a grass slope that slid steeply to the riverwalk. WaterFire, the downtown river festival for which Providence had become renowned spread out below him in Waterplace Park. Bonfires raged in floating braziers, suspended above the water on pontoons. The fires cast red embers like confetti into the night. A trail of floating bonfires led from the basin, down the river, and out of sight. Hidden audio speakers played the hypnotic voices of an all-male chorus, chanting what sounded like the prayers of Gregorian monks. Hundreds of people strolled the riverwalk below Martin, moving as slowly as the placid Providence River, which the city years ago had rerouted into man-made granite trenches and calmed to a slumberous pace. Couples walked arm in arm. Groups of teenagers strolled in clumps. There were no loud voices, and nobody hurried. The fires seemed to infect people with a sense of quiet reflection.

Martin inhaled a deep breath of woodsmoke. The flames, the music that seemed to come from nowhere, and the smell of burning cedar and soft pine usually combined to drive away whatever stress he carried in his body.

Not tonight.

Martin shivered, and not just from the chill. He felt suspicious and guilty, like he was meeting a mistress. That was precisely what he was doing, though she was not his mistress.

"Hi, Marty."

He stood to show his manners, and gestured her into the chair across from him. "Good evening, Nelida. Can I, uh . . . get you something?"

"Maybe later."

She wore wool pants, a knit turtleneck, fleece mittens, and a puffy down jacket that probably would have gotten her safely to the peak of Denali. "At least you're dressed for the cold evening," Martin said as he sat.

"Your note said you wanted to talk outdoors, so I bought this coat at the mall today."

"My note?" Martin said, alarmed. "I thought this was *your* meeting. You sent a note by courier, to my office."

They both realized at the same moment they had been set up. Martin bolted up and scanned the crowd.

A deep voice commanded, "Oh, sit down, Mr. Smothers! You're going to pull a muscle."

Martin whirled.

Lincoln Harmony walked gingerly from the restaurant with two martinis and a tumbler of whiskey on a tray. He closed the door with his foot and lamented, "Too cold for the waitstaff, apparently. Oh well. My physician says I could use the exercise."

He set one drink in front of Nelida, explaining, "It's gin, vermouth, and blackberry brandy. It's called a Desperate Martini. Fitting for you, wouldn't you say? Hee-hah!"

To Martin, he said: "Another whiskey for you, Mr. Smothers. And since this round is on *my* tab, I thank you for drinking the cheap stuff." He set the glass in front of Martin with a heavy clink, and a tooth-filled sneer.

"And for me, ah, something called a Fine and Dandy—the bartender recommended it," Linc Harmony cooed. "Don'cha *love* places like this?" He put down his drink and cast the tray on an empty table. Then he dragged over another chair, sat clumsily, and waved Martin into his seat. He sipped his drink. "Mmmmm! Triple sec. Orange bitters." He made the sign of the cross in the air over the drink, like a priest at the altar, and pronounced it "Lovely."

Nelida gaped at him.

"We haven't been introduced," Harmony said to her, with a frown and a roll of his eyes toward Martin, "and Mr. Smothers is *completely* without manners. I'm Gil's brother."

"Lincoln," she said. She held out her hand to shake, though she kept it closer to her body than to his.

Harmony pinched her fingers for a moment, and then mocked her with an exaggerated grin that involved his whole face. "Gil must have told you *all* about me," he said. "Pillow talk can be endlessly enlightening. Hm?"

Nelida looked at Martin. He reassured her with a little nod. *This guy's hosed but he ain't dangerous.* She turned discreetly to the crowd, lifted her chin, and subtly feathered her fingers in a tiny wave.

Martin followed her eyes.

Nelida's son, Jerod, stood like a sentry on the riverwalk, hands on his hips, staring up at them. Either Nelida was afraid to walk the streets alone, or her son had an overprotective streak. Or, Martin conceded, maybe Jerod was right to be paranoid for his mother, considering that her lover had been shot through the eye.

Martin grabbed the initiative. "So, Lincoln—your *honor*, I mean— to what do Nelida and I owe the pleasure of these invitations?"

"Oh, just can the phony politeness, Marty," he said, and then slurped his drink.

"What the fuck do you want?" Martin asked.

Harmony laughed out loud. It seemed Martin had sincerely delighted him. "That's the way, my boy! We don't all have to speak as my brother did—all stuffy and Elizabethan, like he had a hardened titanium rod pounded up his arse."

To Nelida, Harmony encouraged, "Drink up! Blackberry brandy is good for you. The inventors of that goddamn food pyramid recommend five servings of fruit a day." He roared at his own wittiness.

Martin's brain wobbled inside his skull on a cushion of whiskey. He pushed his empty glass away, eyed the full one, and thought: *What the hell?* He sipped the booze Linc Harmony had bought for him. Nelida did not touch her drink. The way she frowned at it, it could have been chilled Drano with a splash of iodine.

Linc Harmony downed the rest of his drink like a frat boy doing a liquor shot. He wiped his mouth on his sleeve. Then he leaned over the table and said, "I called you two lovebirds together—"

"We're not lovebirds," Martin interrupted sharply.

"You both loved my brother in your own ways, so don't get all literalistic on me. This ain't about you! This ain't your party, Marty." He snorted and laughed. "Marty party!"

He gassed Martin with his breath. Martin thought for a moment of lifting the oil lamp, to ignite Linc Harmony's fumes right in his goddamn face. Boom!

"You're June's lawyer, so you probably already know that I'm challenging my brother's will in probate court," Harmony said. "That video Gil made was an embarrassment. I get his *law books*? Who gives a shit?" He jammed a meaty finger on the table. "I sacrificed growing up with that guy, and he owes me."

They should not be having this conversation outside of a courtroom, Martin thought. *I should grab Nelida and walk away.* But instead, he taunted Harmony: "Were you not loved enough as a boy? Did your brother get all the hugs from your daddy?"

Harmony aimed his finger at Martin. The nail was healthy pink and buffed into a perfect arc. "You have no right, and no idea what it's like to see your father's love, which you have earned, go to somebody else!" He rose a few inches out of his chair, and for a moment seemed that he would challenge Martin to a fistfight, but instead he overtly picked a wedgie out of his ass and then dropped back to the seat. "All I want is what I deserve rightly, by blood!"

Spit spray landed on Martin's face. He closed his eyes until the desire to throttle Linc Harmony faded away.

"Why bother Nelida with this?" Martin asked.

Harmony turned to her. His eyes widened with surprise, as if he had forgotten that she sat with them at the table. He grinned at her untouched martini, whisked the glass away by the stem, and sampled the mix. "Oooo, you don't know what you missed." He took a long pull of the drink. "You see, Nelida, you're going to be my star witness in court. My lawyer will question you at length, and in *meticulous* detail, about what you did with my brother. All the particulars. Where? How? And how often? See? I want to know if he preferred satin sheets to cotton. Strawberry body lotion or coconut? The little white woody pill, or the little purple one?"

"What good would all that do?" Martin said. "You're contesting your brother's will, not divorcing him on grounds of adultery."

"Well, we have to ask these questions," Harmony said in a breezy voice. "How else will we discern my brother's state of mind and competence? Hmm?" His left eyebrow rose in an upside-down V. "Of course, if June would rather avoid all that nastiness under oath, much of which no doubt will be splashed in the press, then maybe we can reach a mutually agreeable arrangement, eh? I'm not looking for much, just the one-third share of Gil's estate that I had expected."

"You're an asshole," Martin said.

"You're nothing like your brother," said Nelida. She stared at him in wonder.

"Oh, I beg to differ," Harmony said to her. "Gil and I are exactly the same." He leered, inspecting her body from the ankles to the chin. "When we see something we want—we take it, and to hell with the consequences on anyone else. Doesn't that smell familiar?"

"You're still an asshole," Martin reminded him.

"One-third of the estate, and June can have his damned law books back." Harmony downed the rest of the martini. "The postmortem revelations of Gil's affair must have been terribly hard on June. Why not suggest to her a way to end the pain? Look at the cost-benefit, man! This deal is a bargain."

"She already knew about the affair," Nelida blurted.

Both men stared at her. She looked away and cupped a hand over her mouth. Too late. The words were in the atmosphere.

She sighed and then helped herself to a sip of Martin's whiskey. "June figured it out," she said. "She's not a foolish woman. She confronted Gil about a month before he was killed. He told her he loved me and Jerod, and that he would be leaving her. June's as tough as rocks. She handled it. The hard part was Brock. Gil wanted to stay in the house until he and Brock could work things out. The weekend Gil died, he had planned a father-son getaway at the beach house in Charlestown, so that Brock and he could fish together like they used to, and talk like men."

She stared into the glass. Silence fell over the table.

Lincoln Harmony broke the quiet with a soft belch. He tapped a fist on his chest. "Well, a fascinating story I cannot wait to record under oath." He stood. To Martin he said, "You take my offer back to your client."

Martin watched Harmony ramble unsteadily away.

"That bastard . . . ," Martin began, but Nelida was not listening.

She dabbed a tear with the tip of her finger and met eyes with Jerod, who stood unmovable and stone-faced on the riverwalk. People strolling the cobblestone path parted around him, the way a river yields to a boulder.

twenty-three

The battered Ford Contour sedan that Scratch bought off the back
lot of an auto-body shop in Cranston had cost four hundred in
cash, twenty for a half tank of gas, a hundred for a fudged inspection
sticker, and one boosted Nintendo Game Boy for the borrowed license
plates. A man on the lam inside his own state cannot be registering
cars: the DMV would want proof of address, and Scratch intended to
remain a moving target until he discovered who had tried to kill him.
That was Plan A. He would switch motels every few weeks, so he
would establish no utility accounts and no permanent phone number.
His mail would be forwarded among shifting addresses, so unless his
attacker worked for the U.S. Postal Service, Scratch should be un-
traceable through government records.

The car was Plan B.

The Ford was such a shitbox: no radio, dinged all over, and the
engine coughed like a chain smoker. The front passenger's window
had fallen inside the door, and had been replaced by a transparent
plastic sheet and some silver duct tape, which had proven, sadly, more
waterproof than the actual window on the driver's side. The plastic

flapped in the wind and reminded Scratch of the bag the attacker had worn on his head.

But at least the car ran.

Damn thing was reliable; started every time. If Scratch needed to put miles between him and a bag-headed man with an ice pick, he was confident the car would get him at least to New Jersey, despite the expired tags.

The gas mileage on his four-door sled was passable, but trips were expensive because Scratch took crazy circuitous routes everywhere he went. He was terrified of being followed.

Already today he had logged fourteen miles on a six-mile trip to the post office, to ship some boosted loot to his satisfied Internet customers.

He idled at a red light on a four-lane suburban highway near the airport. A lumbering 737 rolled away from him. The jet got smaller and smaller, then suddenly pulled a wheelie and lifted off. *Going to someplace safer than here.*

The streetlight turned green but Scratch did not move. The car behind him beeped after about two seconds. *What took him so long to honk? This being Rhode Island.*

Still, Scratch stayed put. More honking. Cars streamed by him in the right-hand lane. Drivers trapped behind Scratch jerked their cars around him and roared their engines to punish him for costing them precious seconds on their way to Hooters.

His light went yellow, then red.

Scratch pounded the gas, spun the wheel, and made a squealing U-turn in the intersection. He floored the pedal and screamed down the street, watching his mirrors for a tail.

Nope. Nobody back there.

He meandered down back roads along Narragansett Bay, generally heading south, enjoying brief vistas of the bay between waterfront homes and stands of shedding hardwoods. He turned north onto a commercial strip, tucked his car behind an appliance shop, got out, and raced around the building on foot.

Nothing unusual. Nobody seemed in a hurry to get him, or to get away from him.

Back on the road, he pulled his red-light U-turn again before zig-zagging back to his motel near the airport, confident that no attacker could have followed him *in a fricking helicopter.*

He parked in front of his unit—why not? Nobody knew he had bought a car.

The late-afternoon sun melted into the roof of an apartment house across the street. Another jet banked overhead, turning a graceful circle. For reasons Scratch had long forgotten, jets in the air reminded him of Benjamin Franklin.

Franklin was perhaps the smartest Founding Father. What if Ben Franklin were suddenly transported in time to the present? How would Scratch explain thirty tons of flying metal with no apparent moving parts?

Well, Ben, it has to do with the shape of the wing, and the way the air molecules move around it.

By george, Master Scratch! What in heaven's name is a molecule?

All those years watching jets and Scratch still wasn't prepared to meet Ben Franklin.

He scooped up his mail inside the storm door and let himself into his dreary brown flat. The one-room apartment smelled oppressively like cigarettes. Scratch had even tried burning Adam's pine-scented candle, which had done nothing to clear the air.

He could have scraped nicotine off the walls with a spatula, pressed the brown goo into squares, and sold it as smoker's gum.

He tossed the keys on the dresser and sorted his mail. Grocery store flyers and solicitations addressed to "Resident" went to the trash.

Hmm, somebody had used the post office's overnight service to send Scratch a thick five-by-seven-inch envelope with some bulky object inside.

The envelope had originally been addressed to his former apartment, to which he would never return, especially after being waylaid there by Billy Povich and that creepy fast chick with the short temper. The post office had slapped a yellow sticker on the package with his current address, which would be changing in another few days.

He tore open the envelope and dumped into his hand an object carefully bound in plastic tape and bubble wrap. He removed the padding, but still didn't know what it was.

"Huh."

Some little electronic device, made of hard plastic, about the size of a cellular phone, but not as heavy. What the hell was this thing? A small compartment in the back held two alkaline AAA batteries. A plastic clip on the object was meant to attach to something, though it was too narrow to snap onto a belt.

The front of the device—if he assumed the batteries were in the back—showed a small silhouette of a dog stamped above four letters:

F.I.D.O.

"Cute," Scratch said aloud.

He repacked the item in bubble wrap and checked the envelope for a return address—none.

"Huh."

Somebody must have sent Scratch the wrong item from an Internet auction. He opened his laptop to check his recent auction bids, then changed his mind. No, what probably had happened, he decided, was that some seller Scratch had patronized in the past had crisscrossed his records, and had sent Scratch an item meant for another customer. And the poor buyer had paid for express shipping, too.

"What a bummah!" he said.

Scratch put the doohickey aside—maybe he could resell it later.

He realized he had forgotten to search the apartment.

Gripping a twenty-inch hunk of steel muffler pipe as a club, Scratch poked in the closest, peered under the bed, and—*oh God, yes!*—peeked behind the damn shower curtain. For good measure, he looked inside the dresser. Not that anyone could fit in his underwear drawer, but, in theory, a person could cut out the drawers with a power saw, and then conceal himself inside the empty shell.

Nope, just underwear in there.

He was alone.

He left the club on the nightstand, then locked the dead bolt, engaged the chain lock, and shoved the dresser against the door.

He fell backward onto the bed and exhaled a deep breath polluted with fear. That calmed him.

Finally, for this evening, peace.

The pressing sense of doom hit Scratch around 4 a.m. The feeling was not like somebody had dumped a load of bricks on his chest, more like someone had piled the bricks on him one at a time, until he could not sleep, and hardly could breathe. He stared at the clock until 4:16, then got out of bed and pulled on his jeans. He hated these ambiguous bouts of paranoia but had learned to listen to them. He knew that if he did not get up and be sure he was safe, he would not sleep again this morning.

With the muffler pipe in hand, he repeated his in-house intruder check: closet, under the bed, shower stall, dresser. Other than a cockroach under the bed, which he whacked dead with the pipe and left there as an example for the others, he was alone.

He slid the frilly window curtain aside and looked out to the parking lot. Nothing unusual. His car was where he had parked it. He saw nobody in the predawn gray. Muffled truck traffic had already begun to hum around the airport.

Everything seemed normal. Everything seemed exactly like the day before, and the day before that.

Well, not *everything*.

He dumped the little doohickey out of the envelope in which it had arrived. This was the only thing different from the day before.

He read the letters on the device. "Fido, eh? What the hell are you, fido?"

Scratch flipped open his laptop and powered it on. He plugged the modem cable into the wall and dialed into the Internet. He had no accounts with a service provider, but he had bought a dozen log-in names and passwords from a guy in a bar, and they had proven useful. As long as the rightful owner of the account was not currently logged in, Scratch usually could get online for free.

Using a dial-up Internet connection was breathtakingly slow compared to the broadband line at the public library. Scratch tried to be patient, but using the outdated technology was like crossing the country in a covered wagon. The anticipation increased the pressure on his chest. He massaged his breastbone. Finally, the machine gave him a solid connection and a search site.

Scratch typed the keywords: "F.I.D.O." and "dog" and "batteries." Click.

After another minute of waiting, he had his answer: F.I.D.O. Inc. was the name of a high-tech company in Massachusetts. Its logo was the silhouette of a German shepherd. The acronym stood for Find Intrepid Dogs Online. The company Web page gave a sales pitch:

Your answer to lost pets!
The F.I.D.O. Global Positioning System device attaches easily
to your dog's collar.
Shock tested and water resistant.

The F.I.D.O. unit sends out a silent signal detected by GPS
satellites anywhere in America.
The system allows you to easily pinpoint the location
of your lost pet through our Web site.
Accurate to 30 feet!

No more calls to the pound. No more "lost dog" posters.
Get F.I.D.O. for your pet and sleep soundly tonight!

Scratch read the advertising again. He grabbed the device. *What the hell . . . ?*

A GPS locator beacon?

And it already had the batteries. . . .

A chill combed over his skin.

"Oh, no."

It's . . . goddamn . . . turned . . . on.

"Fuck!" he cried.

He threw down the device like a hot hunk of charcoal, grabbed the pipe, and bashed F.I.D.O. to S.H.I.T.

He hit it five more times than necessary, and then dropped the weapon and crushed his fists into his eyes. They were onto him! How could Scratch have let this happen? He slapped his open hand on his forehead.

Slap. Slap. Slap.

"Stupid! Stupid! Stupid!" he berated himself.

Okay, stop hitting your own head and fucking THINK!

No time to waste. This motor lodge would be his tomb.

Gotta go!

He stripped a pillowcase and dashed around the room, ransacking the place, stuffing his valuables in the bag in a panic, as if he were robbing himself. As he gathered his essentials, he thought ahead.

Time for Plan B.

Drive!

One-half tank of gas in the car. Not a problem. Can always gas up on the interstate. With the seasons growing colder and winter on the way, he would head south.

No! That's what they'd be expecting.

Haaaa-ha-ha! Scratch would drive north.

Not so far as Canada—no sense trying to cross an international border in a junkyard car with bogus plates.

How 'bout Maine! What's that rhyme? *The rain in Maine is wetter than Spain.* Or something like that. Whatever! He would go to Maine, way up there, near the Arctic Circle for Christ's sake, past Bar Harbor, to the frozen tundra where the tourists rarely trod.

That's untamed land, where a man could find a fresh start, shoplifting from department stores and selling shit on the Internet.

Scratch heaved the dresser out of the way, threw open the locks, and ran out with a Santa sack of his own stuff over his back.

The Ford's door opened with a meow and Scratch heaved the pillowcase to the passenger's side. *Remember to drive the speed limit*, he reminded himself. *Don't get pulled over for bad plates.* The keys jingled. His hands would not stop shaking. He pumped the gas and stabbed the key at the ignition.

The rope was a blur.

It came from behind, slipped quickly before his eyes, then clamped tight above his Adam's apple.

He didn't have time to scream. The rope tightened around his throat and choked his scream back down.

Scratch pulled and writhed against the rope that strangled. He kicked his feet and flailed his arms, bashed his elbow against the window, tried to twist away, but the rope just cinched tighter around his neck. He picked desperately at the rope with his fingernails and ravaged his own skin. The man choking him from the backseat breathed heavily in his ear. The gurgle Scratch heard was from his own throat.

In the mirror he saw the eyes of his attacker, those dead gray eyes from the shower.

How goddamn stupid. Always check the backseat.

Scratch smelled rubber, asphalt, and oil. His cheek rested on a tire. *A spare tire?* He was in blackness, folded up in the trunk of a car.

My car, by the sound of it.

The engine wound dangerously high. They were going fast.

His chest made a wet whistling as he inhaled. His damaged windpipe seared with pain. His hand explored the damage, found his throat, burned raw, and the rope coiled around it. He fingered the cord around his neck. Nothing but nylon clothesline rope. Probably cost twenty cents a yard. Something you'd hang your wet knickers on.

He knew there would be no negotiating when the car stopped. He could not speak, nor fight, nor hope for escape. He could not even lift his head from the tire. Why had he even woken up? These extra moments of consciousness were unnecessary, he thought, even cruel. Only by accident did Scratch still live, and not for long. The attacker had one reason to be driving the car.

To dump the body.

Scratch faded out again.

If he dreamt, he did not remember. A car door slammed and the vibrations woke him. The engine was off. He heard the crash of waves. Gulls squawked. They were at the beach.

Footsteps circled the car. They sounded hollow. Like a man walking on a dock.

Scratch heard a grunt and a low "Eeeeee!" Someone strained himself against a heavy load.

He felt slight movement and heard the wheels grind forward. The footsteps followed behind the car. They got faster and faster, until they became the sound of running. Why was he *pushing* the sedan? Had they run out of gas?

And then the footsteps stopped.

Scratch was thrown against the trunk lid when the car hit the water. The Ford bobbed once, and then the bay poured inside. Frigid. Salty.

I'm singing in my brain.
Just singin' in my brain.

He was not worried for his soul. Heck, he was a swell guy. He had robbed the middle class to give to himself, but never hurt anybody. If the decision were left to Scratch, he would have enough compassion to forgive himself, and open up those platinum gates.

Is God any less compassionate than I?

He said a funny little prayer for justice, not through the cops or the courts; he never trusted either.

He prayed for Povich.

twenty-four

Billy slept with his hands folded on his chest like a dead person. Bo twirled the flashlight beam over his father's eyes until he was sure that Billy was asleep. Then he turned out his light, and he and Albert Einstein went on their mission. With Mr. Einstein held tightly to his chest, Bo did not feel alone. He did not have to wear a mask, as he once did, in order to have the courage to complete his mission.

He listened to Grandpa mumbling inside his room. Grandpa was making another tape for Bo for when Grandpa was dead. The mumbling scared Bo. It sounded like witches.

He padded silently along the hall and stepped down to Mr. Metts's funeral home, one stair at a time. The new red carpet felt good on his bare feet.

Six white couches lined the walls in the waiting room. That was where Mr. Metts kept his telescope, which Bo liked to play with, but not right now. Mr. Metts had set up three rows of folding chairs in the center of the room. That meant a dead person was there. Bo hurried past the brown coffin. "Be right back," he promised. The flowers stank and his nose itched. The carpet in this room was not as soft as the stairs but it still felt good.

The coffin in the next room was black and silver. It lay flat on a low table. The bundles of roses beside the coffin were black too. Bo was afraid of them. They bloomed big and healthy and they smelled good, but they looked dead. He hurried through the room.

In a hallway, he stopped at a white door marked with a gold sign that said PRIVATE. He dug a key out from under the carpet, as Mr. Metts had showed him, and unlocked the door to visit his friend Sal.

Inside the closet, Sal's coffin stood on one end. Bo got a little scared and crushed Mr. Einstein in his armpit. He peered up to the glass window set in the coffin, and to the gray face with black witch's hair in the window.

"Hello, Sal," he said. "It's me."

Bo knew Sal's story by heart. Sal was part of the traveling circus in 1929. Maybe he had been a clown, but Bo did not know. When the circus came to Providence, Sal died. Mr. Metts's grandfather was supposed to bury Sal, but he did not get paid. So he made Sal a special coffin with a window and put him on display, until Sal's family would give him the $125 they owed for the burial. The family never paid.

Bo saved all his money, every nickel he got from Billy and his grandpa, to bury Sal.

"We're up to fifty-three dollars," Bo said. "I thought you'd be happy." He looked at the corpse, saw the stitches through the lips, and looked away. "I'm not wearing my mask, because I have Mr. Einstein. Grandpa gave me a paper tube to roll my dimes." He laid a hand on the shiny brown wood. "When you get buried you'll see my mom. She won't be alone anymore." He felt he might cry and he shut the door. He moved Mr. Einstein to his other arm. Then he cracked the door and whispered inside. "I have to go, Sal. I want to say good night to the others."

Bo locked the door and returned the key.

He went to the room with the black coffin. He stood beside the casket for a minute. Then he reached out with Mr. Einstein and lightly brushed the doll's long white hair on the black wood. Nothing bad happened. He let Einstein rest on a chair, and then went to the coffin again. He held his flashlight in one hand. The coffin had two doors, a big one and a small one. He pressed his palms under the small door and pushed.

The dead person inside was a man. He was very old.

He looked like he was sleeping but Bo knew he was dead.

Fear shook Bo's arms. He could barely speak. He whispered, "Hello, sir. Tomorrow you'll be buried and then you won't be alone. Good night."

He quickly lowered the lid. Then he snatched up Mr. Einstein and hugged him until he stopped trembling.

Two more to go.

The person in the next coffin was a woman. She was very old, like all the dead people he visited. She held pink rosary beads in her hands and looked like maybe she had been saying them when she died. Bo spoke to her as he had the man, and then let down the lid.

The third coffin was deep inside the funeral home, down a long hallway that was very dark. Bo lit his flashlight. The shadows on the walls looked like monsters. He held up Mr. Einstein to lead the way, and followed the doll.

The last coffin was white. He gasped when he saw it. It was very small.

It was the size of a boy.

Bo stepped slowly toward it. His feet did not want to go but he made them do it. They had to do what Bo wanted. The carpet in this room was scratchy. He wished he had his mask. This coffin had two doors like the others but the doors were the same size. He didn't know which one to lift. Bo stroked the white wood with Mr. Einstein's hair. Then he tucked the doll down his shirt so Mr. Einstein was hugging him.

He pushed up one of the lids.

Inside were a little boy's legs and feet. The legs wore black pants and white sneakers, small enough to fit Bo.

This dead person was not old. Bo's arms quaked and the lid dropped. The noise startled him.

He yelped and collapsed to the floor, in tears.

He backed away, whimpering, clutching his doll, terrified of the dead boy in the tiny white casket. Bo and Mr. Einstein ran away from him.

twenty-five

Bo dozed over his oatmeal, head on his fist, elbow on the table. His other hand still gripped the spoon stuck in the bowl.

"Look at that kid," Billy whispered.

"I told you oatmeal was boring," said the old man.

"And what's with the outfit today?"

Bo wore his school clothes: new blue jeans, a collared polo shirt, and fleece sweater with the Flying Elvis logo of the New England Patriots. But instead of his little white tennis sneakers, the kid had paired tube socks with the shiny leather dress shoes from his church outfit.

"Bo?" Billy called.

The kid woke with a startled look. His hand jerked and the spoon flung oatmeal like a catapult against the kitchen cabinet. The gob stuck there for several seconds, and the three Povich men watched in rapt fascination as the oatmeal slowly unglued itself from the cabinet door and hit the counter with a splat.

Ziggs had seen enough; the cat jumped from the table and fled.

"You should never wake a sleep-eater," the old man scolded.

"Why are you so tired this morning, Bo?" Billy asked.

"I'm not tired."

"Did you not sleep well last night?"

The kid shrugged and heaved a giant spoonful of oatmeal into his mouth. "Can't talk wit' my mou' full," he said.

The old man chuckled at Billy. "He's using your own rules against you."

"Where's Mr. Einstein?" Billy asked.

The boy looked away and chewed. "He's busy. Has a new job. Top secret."

Billy's son was still such a mystery to him. After Angie was killed, the boy seemed to handle the death of his mother better than Billy had survived the loss of an ex-wife. How someone so small could be so tough . . . Billy turned away and blinked the tears from his eyes. Mr. Einstein was "busy" in Bo-speak, which meant that the doll was gone. It had been replaced by some other coping system, the way the doll had replaced the Halloween masks the boy used to wear around the house to give him courage to face the pain little children were not meant to see. The timing could not have been worse. The child was terrified of being alone. And he had abandoned his crutch right as his grandfather had decided to let himself die.

"Maybe you should stay home from school today," Billy suggested.

"Whaaaaat?" the old man whined. "He needs to learn."

"He can't learn if he's asleep in class."

"But he's already missed too much school already, coming to the hospital for my treatments, visiting Stu Tracy. Do you want him to fail?"

"I want him to be healthy."

The old man's tone softened. He reached out his gray corpse hand and smoothed the boy's hair. "I can't watch him proper today," he said. "I got dirty blood and I feel like hell."

"I'll stick around and watch him."

"What about your investigation?"

Billy sighed. "I'm at a dead end," he confessed. "I've traced the shooter back to his last apartment, and proven, at least in my own mind, that somebody paid him to kill the judge. But I can't make the leap to the next link in the chain."

Bo sipped milk. He watched Billy over the rim of the glass. Then he wiped his milk mustache on his sleeve, and announced: "I want to go to school today."

"The kid doesn't want to be a ditchdigger, thank God," grumbled the old man.

"You sure, Bo?" Billy asked.

The kid shrugged, sipped more milk, and then explained, "Mr. Metts will have three funerals downstairs today."

Huh . . . ? What was he saying? That he didn't want to listen to three eulogies through the floor? That he was tired of living above a transfer station for human remains?

"Do you want us to move, Bo?"

The kid shrank from Billy. He grabbed the table. "I never want to leave. *Ever.*"

He drove Billy speechless.

The phone rang.

"I got it," Billy offered, and threw himself from the table.

"You wanna wake up for school?" the old man asked. "Try some coffee. Makes you all tingly inside. Math is easy on coffee."

Billy sighed and carried the cordless down the hall. That was all the kid needed—drugs to make him more hyper. The phone chimed again in his hand.

"Yeah, hello?"

"Billy, man," a low voice purred. "I'm glad I caught you home. Heh-heh. A man in my position don't leave his voice on tape."

Garafino!

Billy instinctively clutched his wallet, then covered his thrice-broken nose.

Wait a sec . . . I'm all paid up with this guy. "You got me mixed up with some other client. I'm current with you."

The shark laughed. "Billy, man, you're my favorite. When you need cash, you call me first."

"I'll try the bank next time."

"Fuck the banks, man! When you don't pay them, they give you a lot worse than a punch in the mouth. How long does one punch hurt? A few days? The bankers kill your credit for the rest of your life." He laughed again. Then his voice fell; he grew serious and sounded like he was talking out the corner of his mouth: "You, er, still looking to get to Rhubarb Glanz?"

Billy switched the phone to his other ear. He watched Bo sip from the old man's coffee mug and make a sour face.

"You there, Billy?"

"Yeah. How do I find him?"

"That big Catholic cemetery, man, in Cranston? It's like the only place he goes alone. Later this afternoon, four o'clock, when the cemetery kicks out all the cars and locks the gate. Officially, the place is closed at four, but they don't mind if one old man walks around the gates. You'll know him. He'll be the dude dropping roses on his old lady's grave. Sweet, ain't he?"

"What are my liabilities?"

"Better than usual. No guns in the cemetery, and no goons. Glanz likes to keep these visits in the family. Just his fucked-up kid, Robbie, who'll drive him to the gates, and then wait in the car on the street. But be careful. Robbie's protective of his old man . . ."

"I've noticed that."

". . . so you'll have to neutralize the son if you wanna whack the papa."

Billy flushed with anger. "I don't want to kill him, you goddamn maniac, I want to *talk* to him."

Garafino giggled, showing a sense of humor Billy never saw when he owed Garafino money. "Call it what you want," the shark said. "Just leave my name out of it."

"You're taking a chance telling me these things," Billy said, suspicious all of a sudden. "Why help me?"

"Oh, dude, 'cause you're a good shit and I like you, man."

"That's crap. Why are you helping me?"

The shark paused. Billy heard the flick, flick of a cigarette lighter. And then a deep breath, and a long, slow exhale. Funny, the power of the mind—Billy swore he could smell smoke.

"I'm helping you, Billy, because I'm into some things, okay? Things that are *so fucked up* you would not even believe it. Dangerous things. Heh-heh. Loan sharking ain't half of it. I'm gonna need my friends. I built up a lot of favors over the years, but the people who owe me are all snakes, see? They'd shoot their own mothers for cab fare and doughnuts. I think it's in my best interest to know at least one honest man who owes me a favor."

twenty-six

The cemetery began at the gates and stretched for nearly a mile, along ponds and marshlands, small stands of evergreens and white birch. Roads of sun-bleached asphalt the blue-gray color of gunmetal carved through the grass. The development of the cemetery over the decades could be mapped by the sugar maples that lined the roads; the bigger the trees, the older the graves.

The stones closest to the entrance marked family plots laid down in the 1800s. To identify the resting places of entire clans, the eclectic stones were eight, ten, or twelve feet tall, carved with relief figures from the New Testament, adorned with stone crosses, biblical passages, and the wisdom of many lifetimes chiseled forever into the granite:

Joyous is he who bathes himself in The Word . . .

See always as a child sees . . .

Books by day, by night, wine . . .

These huge grave markers reminded Billy of the battle monuments spread over the fields at Gettysburg.

He walked with his hands in his pants pockets. The afternoon was colder than he had expected. Tiny American flags at the graves of veterans flapped in a breeze that chilled. Strips of low clouds spread over the graveyard in a lumpy gray weave. Slivers of blue bled through the clouds here and there. Two cars raced past Billy toward the exit, before the gates were shut to traffic at 4 p.m.

In just a few minutes' walk, the city faded away, as if it no longer existed beyond the gates. Billy wondered, what was it about cemeteries that seemed to radiate silence, which blotted out the noise around them? He saw no other living person once the gates had closed. People had paid their respects already and had left, though there was still more than an hour of good daylight before dusk. Billy couldn't decide if being alone in the cemetery was a good thing or a bad thing.

The remoteness was *good* if he had to force Rhubarb Glanz to talk; but *bad* if things went wrong, and somebody got the drop on Billy.

No, it's good, he decided.

He intended to learn the truth about Judge Harmony's murder, no matter the cost. He walked on.

The rows of stones appeared endless, stretching in straight lines beyond a gentle rise in the land. Tombstones in this part of the cemetery dated to the 1940s; they were smaller than the old family markers, but larger than contemporary headstones. Most were bone white or gray, with a few pink ones scattered among them. Billy came upon a seven-foot white obelisk, on which was mounted an oval locket about the size of his hand. The name on the stone was Manzi. Billy couldn't help himself. He lifted the locket to see the rugged face of Mr. Manzi in a crisp black-and-white photograph. The picture had been taken when Manzi was a strong young man. He had a wide face, thick neck, ink-black hair, and a droopy walrus mustache. Billy guessed he might have been a blacksmith or a stevedore. Unlike the dour people in many old photographs, Mr. Manzi grinned with joy. He struck Billy as a man who had been fun to know.

"May your bones rest gently," Billy whispered.

He followed the path to a twenty-foot cross set in a pile of stones at the intersection of two cemetery roads. There he turned left, following directions he had copied earlier that day from the cemetery map in the church hall. Sugar maples two feet thick were spaced every thirty steps along the road. They still held most of their leaves this October, and the wind swished through them. Billy noticed movement from the corner of his eye. A big black crow hopped from the top of one tombstone to the next with one flap of its wings. The bird seemed to be following him. Billy stopped to watch it, and the crow complained five times: Caw. Caw. Caw. Caw. Caw.

He smiled at the bird. *Okay, let's keep moving.*

He crossed a stone bridge that carried the road over a thick freshwater marsh, with open-water ponds beyond it. Sparrows flitted among the tall reeds and brown grasses. He noted that the wetlands were shaped like an hourglass and that the bridge crossed the narrowest point. That was respectful of nature; Billy liked that. A hardwood forest crowded against the road, and then suddenly fell away to reveal a vast plain of green. This was the newest section of the cemetery. Though the stones were all around the same size, the range of colors was more spectacular than in the cemetery's older neighborhoods. The stones were black and smooth like opal, light pink, deep red, shimmering blue, and a rainbow of grays. These people were barely dead, and Billy recognized many names from obituaries he had written for the paper. A tombstone was sort of an obituary, he thought, though highly edited. The inscriptions were two-line news stories to provide the bare essentials: name, date of birth, date of death.

Everything else was detail.

This section of the cemetery would be where Billy would bury the old man. And where someday Bo would bury Billy.

Unless this plan fails today.

Then Billy might be first into the dirt.

A cellular tower stuck up like a needle in the distance, and he remembered he must call Kit. He fished Martin Smothers's spare cell phone from his pocket and dialed.

Kit's phone rang with jungle drums. She pulled the car to the curb about two hundred yards from the cemetery gates and answered.

"Hey, Billy!" Kit said. "Are you in place?"

"Walking there now. You?"

"Perfect timing. I'm going to wait for them here. . . . Are you nervous?"

"I was just thinking," Billy said dryly, "that if things go wrong they can bury me where I lay. Save money on renting a hearse. Shit, it's quiet out here."

"Better than those old family plots near the highway."

"Yeah, what a kick in your dead ass—to be laid to rest in a pasture, and then have your great-grandkid sell the land for an interstate."

A new black Cadillac appeared in Kit's mirror. She sank in the seat. "Jesus, Billy, they're here," she whispered. "They just drove past me."

"Why are you whispering? They can't hear you."

"They're pulling to the curb in front of the gates. . . . Now they're stopping."

Robbie Glanz popped out the driver's door. Kit felt a flutter in her gut at the sight of him. *That little son of a bitch.* She recalled how he had punched her until he was exhausted and neither of them could breathe.

She needed to harness as much hate in her heart as she could muster, to do what she must do.

Robbie walked around the car and opened the back passenger's

door like a chauffeur. He reached a hand inside the Caddy and helped
an old man to the sidewalk.

"Kit? Kit?" Billy shouted in her ear.

"I'm fine," she replied. "My God . . . is *that* Rhubarb Glanz? He's a
broken-down old man."

"He's sixty-nine years old," Billy said. "I checked the database at
the paper."

"Lot of miles on those sixty-nine years."

Robbie brushed dandruff or something from the old man's black
suit jacket, and then reached into the car and withdrew a bundle of
red roses. He handed them to his father as gently as he would have a
baby. Then he walked with Rhubarb. The gates were locked with a
loop of iron chain that allowed them to open about two feet. Robbie
held them apart as his father stepped through. The old mobster gave
his son a self-conscious little wave, and walked into the cemetery.

"Rhubarb is on the move," Kit reported.

"Took me ten minutes to walk here," Billy said.

"It's going to take him longer than that, so I'll wait fifteen minutes to be safe."

Billy cleared his throat. "Kit," he began.

"Don't say it, Billy. I am *well* aware of your concerns." She gave him
her sarcastic, impatient voice. Her adrenaline was already flowing, and
Kit didn't want to waste it on a debate. She would need every drop.

Billy pressed on: "I don't want to beat a dead horse—"

"That horse is glue by now," she interrupted.

"Are you sure you want to do this?"

"I'm fully insured."

"You don't have to do this for me."

"I'm not," she said sharply.

"I know—you're doing it for Gil."

"To hell I am," Kit corrected. "Robbie Glanz beat the shit out of
yours truly. I'm doing this for *me*."

He sighed noisily. She heard the wind whip past him and crackle into his telephone. "Be safe," Billy said gravely.

Kit laughed. "Hardly," she replied. "Just get what we need to know. By any means."

They hung up.

Robbie got back into the Cadillac. He powered down his window six inches, checked his wristwatch, and then relaxed with a newspaper.

Kit waited. Her foot bounced by itself, bleeding off tension. Her windshield soon began to fog from her own wet breath, and she cracked her window an inch.

Fifteen minutes ticked off the clock like 2 percent of eternity.

Finally, the time was right.

Rhubarb Glanz would be at least half a mile into the cemetery. Kit took three deep breaths, then dialed 911 on her cell phone.

"Police," came the answer after one ring. "What's your emergency?"

"I've had an accident," Kit reported, trying to sound ragged. "I had to swerve, uh, oh my . . . to miss a dog."

"Stay calm, miss. What's the address?"

Kit gave the address, and added, "Right in front of the cemetery gates."

"I'm dispatching. Any serious injuries?"

"Hmm, good question," Kit replied. "I guess it's too soon to tell. Please hurry."

She hung up.

Then she checked that her seat belt was clicked. She pulled her ski helmet over her head and buckled the strap under her chin. She took one more deep breath and held it. Then she put the car into gear and rolled toward Robbie's sparkling new Cadillac.

How fast? she wondered. Twenty-five should be fast enough to inflict enough damage to keep them tied up with the police for an hour.

The legal citations for the laws she was breaking rolled through her head. She ignored them.

As she bore down on Robbie Glanz, she eyed him sitting there in those *stupid* sunglasses, under that *goddamn silly* derby hat. Those were the accessories he wore the night he beat her.

What the fuck? Let's do thirty.

The crows warned Billy that Rhubarb Glanz was coming. The birds flew tree to tree, cawing to each other, following Rhubarb's slow progress toward the newer section of the cemetery, where Margery Glanz had been buried for nine years. Her stone was pink marble, very shiny, on a black base. A bouquet of roses at the foot of the stone had shriveled. Rhubarb's stone had already been erected next to his late wife's. His stone was a mirror image: black on a pink base. *His and her tombstones?*

Glanz ambled into view. He wore dark sunglasses and a funeral suit, and carried fresh red roses.

Kit was right, Billy thought, *he looks used up.*

Billy hid among the tombstones. The grizzled crime boss shuffled to his wife's grave. Glanz was bald but for a few odd clumps of white. His skin was lifeless and chalky, except for reddened cheeks. He had once stood more than six feet tall, but a hunch in his back stole at least six inches, and gave him a buzzardlike quality. His shoulders were smaller than his hips, and his huge feet seemed out of proportion, as if he were a child in his father's wingtips.

This was the fearsome mobster who had ordered his goons to bury Billy almost to death?

Glanz stood before the grave, blessed himself with the sign of the cross, and patted the bundle of roses. He heard Billy approach, glanced Billy's way for a moment, then turned back to the stone.

"My son is waiting for me at the gate," Glanz said, in a high, empty voice. "If I am one minute late he will come looking, and you will not leave those gates alive."

"Your boy's busy right now," Billy said.

Glanz coughed, then cleared his throat and spat in the road. "You waste your time taking me out now."

"Not here to take anyone out, Mr. Glanz. My name is Povich. I want justice for Judge Harmony."

The name surprised Glanz. He turned suddenly to Billy. The crows cawed down at them from the trees. Glanz looked up and grinned.

"You have been chasing an interview with me for some time, Mr. Povich," Glanz said. "You think I paid that kid to kill Gil Harmony."

"Didn't you?"

Glanz bent down creakily, grunting and sighing, in painful human origami, and placed one knee on the ground. He laid the roses on his wife's grave. Then he brushed dust from her stone and seemed to forget that Billy was there.

"You threatened the judge," Billy said. "His clerk was there. She heard it. Harmony put your son away for life. You told the judge you'd get even, and you did. You persuaded Rackers to accept June Harmony's diamonds as payment, and then you double-crossed him. You gave Rackers a phony combination for a wall safe that didn't exist. A great investment for you—you got your revenge, and it didn't cost you a penny. Then Rackers was killed trying to get away, which saved your goons the trouble of burying him in a sandpit."

Glanz took a deep breath, put a hand on his knee, and pushed himself unsteadily to his feet. "I told Robbie you were not to be killed," he said. "That you were to be buried feetfirst until you told us what we needed to know."

He smiled at Billy.

"I've been coming to this spot for nine years," Glanz said. "Watch this. . . ." He fished a hand inside his coat pocket, pulled it out, and showed Billy a few kernels of dried yellow corn. He held the kernels to the sky in his open hand, and whistled twice between his teeth.

Then he balanced the kernels on his shoulder. "Don't move," he whispered.

Within a few seconds, a crow swooped down to a nearby head-stone. It hopped from stone to stone, eyeing Glanz, feinting toward him and then backing away. Then suddenly it flapped to his shoulder, landed there, pecked at the corn for a few seconds, and flapped off. Glanz laughed in delight, dug more corn from his pocket, and spread the kernels over the ground. The seed drew a dozen crows that cawed and pecked at each other in competition for the prize.

"Do you know what a group of crows is called?" Glanz asked.

"A murder."

"Ah, very good. It's not a flock, as most people think; it's a murder of crows. Because crows sometimes gang up and kill a dying cow." He sighed and rubbed his hands together. "I did not pay that kid to kill Gil Harmony."

"I don't believe you."

Glanz shrugged. "Who cares?"

"Take off your glasses," Billy ordered.

Glanz hesitated. Then he nodded and pushed the glasses up on his head, and turned pale green eyes to Billy.

"Can you see the truth now in my eyes?" Glanz asked, mocking him. "Can you see what you're looking for? Or do you see only the crimes of a young man, and the regret and the pain of an old one? Can you see my *soul*, Povich?"

Billy turned away. "I see nothing." He dropped to the ground, dejected. "I had expected you wouldn't see me as a threat, and wouldn't care enough to lie. I want the truth, even if it can't stand up in court."

Glanz rubbed his hands together again in the cold. He folded himself down, sat on the thick bluegrass, and leaned back against his own tombstone. After a few moments, he said to Billy, "This is going to be my eternal view. I can see the marsh from here. I like that. The crows will keep me company. Margery has lain here alone for a long time. But not much longer. I'm dying, Povich."

"Dying? Dying how?"

"The cancer in me is as malignant as my nightmares." He smiled sadly at Billy. "Six months, give or take, is the time I have left."

What to say?

I'm sorry didn't fit the moment. Billy had just accused him of ordering a murder. He said nothing.

"I'm about to meet the real Judge face-to-face," Glanz said, casting his eyes skyward, "the one who doesn't need testimony to know everything you've ever done. He has felt every drop of blood I spilt in my life, and will hold those crimes against me. I did not increase my burden, this close to my judgment, by killing Gil Harmony."

"But he put your son away. You threatened him."

Glanz grimaced at a painful thought. He said, "David's sentence is an agony in my heart, second only to Margery's death. My greatest regret is that he took after me, and not his mother. But I can't say the sentence was unjust, and I told Gil Harmony that."

"What you told him," Billy corrected, with anger rising, "is that you'd have your revenge."

"In the restaurant, yes, that's what I said," Glanz conceded. "Gil and I had arranged that encounter over the telephone."

"I don't believe you."

He shrugged and gazed over the marsh. "Who cares?" he said again. But the tone was too soft; it seemed he *did* care if Billy believed him. "I had to make a show of it to avoid looking weak to my *employ-*

ees. I need their loyalty. Forever. The men I employ must take care of Robbie after I'm gone."

"And Gil agreed to go along with this?"

"Gil Harmony was a father. He understood what fathers must do."

What Glanz claimed was *outrageous*, though in a funny way it made sense. Gil told Kit not to report the threat to the police. The judge had not taken it seriously. *All for show*, he had told her. Maybe that wasn't bluster; maybe the judge with the double life had told the truth. All for show.

Glanz stroked his wife's tombstone. "She could have been canonized, this woman."

Billy felt a crack in his hatred of Rhubarb Glanz. The mobster had all but admitted being a murderer in his youth, so why lie about killing the judge? Even if he suspected Billy wore a wire, Glanz would be dead from cancer before a trial.

"You'll see your wife, soon, I guess," Billy offered.

"Naw, not me; I'll not see heaven," he said, sounding matter-of-fact about it. "Not after the life I've lived."

"What about redemption? You've got six months to repent. You're lucky, in a way. Most people have no idea when the end will be."

"It's too late," Glanz said. "To plead for forgiveness now, as cancer eats me from the inside out, would be disrespectful." He shut his eyes for a moment and seemed suddenly exhausted. "I'd be embarrassed to ask. No, Povich, I'll take what's coming. It's what I deserve." A crow hopped near his feet. Glanz drew a few more seeds from his pocket and scattered them on the road.

Then he pulled up his sleeve and checked his wristwatch. "You were truthful about keeping Robbie busy," he said. "Smart on your part—Robbie would shoot you where you sit." His eyes narrowed. "He better damn well be okay."

"We're not murderers, sir."

Glanz looked at him with tight lips, and seemed to accept the explanation. "Don't judge Robbie too harshly," he advised. "What he did to you in that sandpit, he did to protect me. Are you a father, Povich?"

"I have a son."

"Do you know what's the strongest and most complicated bond in the universe, by my experience?"

"Tell me."

"The bond between father and son. No other relationship provokes such intense loyalty and pride. Or disappointment, competition, and even rage."

"Rage?" Billy challenged.

"At a failure or a betrayal—rage, absolutely," Glanz said. He tapped the back of his head against his own tombstone. "These feelings are larger than any individual. They go back a long way, not to our births—but to the birth of mankind. They are complicated feelings. Men don't talk about them; we speak through action." He pointed at Billy. "Would you kill to save your son?"

"Of course," Billy said. He surprised himself by how reflexively he had answered, and added, "If he were threatened."

Glanz smiled. "You didn't even think about it. By instinct you know the relationship may require a moral man to kill."

Billy picked at some grass and tossed the blades away. "My father is trying to kill himself."

Did I just say that out loud?

"How so?"

"He's skipping his blood treatments. He's bored with his life, and with being too old and too sick to chase women in short skirts."

"He's not bored with life," Glanz said. "He is convinced of his own uselessness. Convince him otherwise and he will claw the earth to live."

They sat together a few more minutes, watching the crows pick at the ground.

"I believe you," Billy admitted.

"Who cares?" Glanz said weakly.

"But that leaves me further from the truth. I have no idea who paid Adam Rackers to kill the judge."

"Reassess your assumptions," Glanz advised. "One of them is wrong. When you find out which one, the truth will be obvious."

twenty-seven

The kitchen floor felt tacky under Billy's bare feet. "Somebody spilled something and didn't wipe it up," he complained, though he had no mind to do anything about it at the moment. The cabinet had no clean mugs. Neither did the drying rack in the sink. He poured himself coffee in an old mason jar.

"You slept in," the old man said. He had parked his wheelchair at his traditional place at the table. The newspaper comics lay spread before him.

"I've been awake in bed for a while, thinking about things." Billy slurped ancient coffee and grimaced at the bitterness. At Bo's place on the table, disintegrating cornflakes floated in a bowl of milk.

"Bo at school?"

"I got him out the door, but that don't guarantee he got on the bus."

"Thanks, Pop."

The old man looked up in surprise from the funnies. "You're welcome."

Billy pulled a chair from under the table, and found it occupied by

Mr. Albert Einstein. "Good morning, Al," he said to the doll. "You had an IQ of a hundred eighty-five, but it's not smart to hide where you might get sat on."

"We should talk about the doll," the old man said.

Billy tossed Albert on the table and plopped down. "The way Bo was speaking, I thought we'd never see old Albert again," he said. "I figured the kid had graduated to some new security blanket. Where'd you find Mr. Einstein?"

"Charlie Metts brought him up this morning after Bo left for school."

"Hmm?"

The old man dithered with the newspaper for a few moments. He said, "Uh . . . Metts wanted to know how the twentieth century's greatest scientist wound up inside the casket of a nine-year-old boy who died of leukemia."

"Oh, Jesus, Bo," Billy whispered. He grabbed his own head . . . before it could explode.

"Charlie found the doll tucked shoulder to shoulder with the body, as if little Mr. Einstein here was keeping the dead boy company. Charlie loves Bo—as you know. So he ain't mad. But I'd say he's worried."

This was Mr. Einstein's new mission. Top secret. Keep a dead boy company in a cold, dark grave.

Billy smeared tears on his palm. The kid's gesture was more *giving* to a family obliterated by disease than anything Billy could have done, despite Billy's grown-up mind and grown-up paycheck. He turned away from his father. "When's the funeral?"

"This afternoon."

"Call Metts," Billy directed. "Ask him to put the doll back in the casket, if the family doesn't mind. Tell him Mr. Einstein was a gift, from one lonely little boy to another."

"Fine, Billy."

"I have to meet Martin," Billy said. "I've struck out on this case. I followed a one-way street to a dead end, and now there's no place to go. Rhubarb Glanz didn't pay to kill the judge." He threw his head back, let out a long breath, and wrestled control of his tears. "It's over. Some truths are just unknowable. Harmony was Martin's friend. He won't be happy."

"I'm taking the senior van to the hospital today," the old man said. "Not for treatment—I'm done with that shit."

Billy lacked the spirit to argue.

The old man explained, "But I thought, you know, I should say good-bye to Stu Tracy. I like the kid, and he's had a rough go of it. But he gets the bandages off his eyes in a few days. . . . At least he has a chance to get better and have a normal life, unlike some of us."

The old man was trying to draw Billy into a conversation about speeding his death.

Suicide by inaction and procrastination.

"Not now," Billy said. He left the table, adding ruefully on his way to the shower, "Stu's the one guy in this mess who can't see that I failed. But he's getting better, so even that's about to change."

twenty-eight

The restaurant on the first floor of a triple-decker house in a remote corner of Providence was smaller than the kitchens being installed in the new McMansions all over the southern half of the state. The diner mostly fed people who smelled like hard work and cigarettes. With just a lunch counter and two tables, no more than eight or ten could eat here at one time, yet over his years of sneaking here for long home-cooked lunches, Martin never had to wait for a table. The place sent him back in time to his grandmother's kitchen: he loved the faint odor of cooking gas, the clang of indestructible iron pans seasoned black by a million meals, the lack of any printed menu—you ate what was on the stove; the choice was take it, or leave it—and the fawning service that reminded a nostalgic middle-aged lawyer of love.

"I'm meeting somebody today, Phyllis," Martin told the cook. "He'll probably want coffee."

"I'll make a fresh pot," she said. "Something while you wait?"

"I'll grab myself a soda. There's nothing like sugar-free root beer and the obituaries on a sunny day."

"Help yourself, young man."

Martin smiled. This was the only restaurant in town where Martin could still be called young, though Phyllis was probably no more than ten years older than he. He grabbed a root beer from the cooler and settled into a chrome and vinyl kitchen chair near the window. Billy Povich had sounded distraught on the phone, and it would be up to Martin to absolve him.

Povich arrived ten minutes late, after Martin had already eaten his fried eggplant.

Billy dropped into the chair. "Sorry," he said. "I walked and got lost. Been doing a lot of that lately."

Martin forgave him with a smile and called to Phyllis. "Can my friend have some coffee and some of this terrific eggplant?"

"Mm-hm!"

Phyllis set Billy up with the day's first course. They watched her step back behind the counter and then dip chicken breast in egg batter and bread crumbs. "Thank God," Martin whispered. "She's making meat today. My secret inner carnivore is hungry."

"Nice to see that the vegan Mrs. Smothers doesn't have you as whipped as you seem," Billy joked. "Maybe she should use a *leather* whip, not a substitute made of soybeans and seaweed."

"What she don't know won't kill me."

Billy watched traffic pass slowly outside the window. "I'm dead-ended," he confessed.

"I know that."

"I was sure the trail would lead to Rhubarb Glanz, but he didn't contract for the hit on the judge. Glanz is dying. He's not interested in revenge. He wasn't even put out with me when the ambulance took his kid to the hospital as a precaution."

Martin covered his ears. "I don't want to know any more. I feel guilty enough for bamboozling you into investigating this case. For me, it was personal. And my obsession got you beaten up, and nearly buried alive. Now I learn you sent the son of a mob boss to the hospital?"

"Just for observation."

"You did far more for me than you should have. You still have that reporter's instinct for the truth. . . ." His cell phone buzzed in his coat pocket. He checked the caller ID and said, "It's Carol. Don't you despise people who answer their phones in restaurants?"

"Yes."

Martin answered: "Carol? I'm with Billy Povich, in a meeting, with the scent of sautéed chicken wafting over us."

"I'll keep it short," she said in his ear. "A kayaker scratched his expensive carbon surf ski on the roof of Gary Gleason's car early this morning."

Martin pulled his fountain pen from his pocket, checked for leaks on his shirt, and then jotted notes on the paper placemat, repeating as he wrote: "On the roof of Gary Gleason's car? How'd he pull that trick?"

"You talking about Scratch?" Billy asked.

Martin nodded and held up the pen to ask for patience.

"The car was off the coast of Portsmouth, underwater at the end of an old industrial pier," she continued.

"Wow. Did he drive into the bay?"

"Excuse me?" Povich said.

"Not unless he steered it from the trunk," said Carol.

"Holy mother of . . . when did they find him?"

"Damn it, Marty, what's going on?" Povich demanded.

Carol reported, "Twenty minutes ago. It's on the news now, with no details, just video of the winch pulling out the car. My source on the police dive team says he was strangled. I'll call when I get more."

"Do it."

They hung up.

Martin paused a second, downed a sip of root beer without tasting it, then summed up for Povich: "Scratch is dead. Murdered. Fuck."

Billy banged a fist on the table and splashed coffee from his mug. Through gritted teeth he growled, "He was our last connection to Adam Rackers."

"Whoever paid Rackers to kill the judge is cutting the links to him," Martin agreed. He thought for a second and added, "Or to her."

A feverish sweat gathered on Billy's forehead. "This means I was close," he said. "I was going the wrong goddamn way, but I passed close to the truth." He rubbed two days' worth of whiskers on his chin and gazed out the window again. "Why didn't I recognize it? What did I miss?"

"I think you were thorough," Martin said, but Povich wasn't listening.

Billy stared at a column of traffic at a standstill. His expressive brown eyes slowly shrank; his thumb turned absentminded little circles in the stubble on his neck. Only at the very point of his chin did Billy's whiskers show any gray. His lips parted, and then shaped silent words, like the physical echo of his thoughts. Martin followed Billy's eyes. What was he staring at? Outside the window, a blue-eyed man with spiked hair, stuck in traffic in a gray Saab convertible, spoke into a cell phone.

Billy's silent thoughts had become a whisper; *"Challenge your assumptions. . . ."* His head cocked and he looked away a moment. He gestured at the man in the Saab. "His lips move but we can't hear what he says."

"Right . . . the window is closed."

Then Billy's eyes passed over the table with a look of detached terror, and a creepy smile broke across his face. He clamped his hand over his mouth. "What was our biggest assumption? So fucking big it could not be challenged?"

"Wha—?"

"That Rackers shot the judge, right?"

Billy slipped from his chair and nearly fell to the floor. He caught himself on the rickety table. His mug toppled and cast a wave of coffee over the place mats. Martin jumped from his chair to grab Billy by the arm. "Are you taking a heart?"

"I'm not having a coronary, Marty. Jesus Christ, he never said a word. . . ."

"Who? Billy!"

"In the hospital, we never heard him speak! Holy shit, Martin, *nobody* paid Rackers to shoot the judge. He just took the fall!"

twenty-nine

The hospital reminded him of a submarine, with its narrow, windowless halls cluttered with exposed pipes that carried steam to the ancient heating system ringing with clangs and pings.

Ugh, would a submarine stink like this?

He hit the button for the elevator, then changed his mind and decided to walk up the fire stairs. He did not want to run into someone he recognized.

This is it. The last one.

With Scratch Gleason dead, this was the last link between him and Adam Rackers.

Once the link was severed, he would be free.

He thought of Scratch, dead in his car, underwater. Some sick part of him—not the pragmatic part that had no choice but to kill in self-defense, to protect himself from being discovered, but some twisted sliver of himself deep inside—pushed a little tune into his head to the music of Otis Redding's "Dock of the Bay."

Dead in my trunk in the bay . . .
Feeling the tide roll my way . . .
Dead in my trunk in the bay, cov'red in slime.

The words repeated in his head. His feet knocked the stairs in time with the music. He began to whistle. There was something grotesquely funny about the little tune, though he felt guilt over the pleasure it brought him.

But what could he have done? He could not have let Scratch live. That little thief was too dangerous. Who knew what Rackers had told him about the plan?

The final threat, to be eliminated in this hospital, was infinitely more dangerous than Scratch Gleason. He put a hand to the knife in his waistband, under his shirt.

He left the stairwell at the trauma recovery unit, put his head down, and marched the halls.

At the door, he hesitated. What if somebody he knew was inside? He made sure the hall was clear, then placed an ear to the door. Nothing but the hum of machines. *He's more machine than man right now. He's not even a human being.*

The door closed behind him.

"Hello?" said Stu Tracy from the bed.

A ghastly bruise, like a purple wave, had spread across Tracy's neck since the last time he had seen him.

He chuckled in reply without opening his mouth.

"Are you on the staff?"

"Mm-hm." He stepped toward him. From his jacket he pulled a black ski mask. No plastic bag this time. This was the mask he wore when he helped Scratch's car into the drink. When he had finished with this task, he would burn the mask and get back to his life. What he had done would fade from his memory—maybe not completely, but he was confident that the events of the past several weeks would soon seem like the color-washed recollections of a childhood nightmare.

"You a nurse?"

"Mm-hm." He pulled on the mask.

"You have leather-soled shoes," said Stu Tracy. "The nurses on the day staff wear rubber soles because they're on their feet so much."

At the bedside, he discreetly shoved the emergency call button aside. He felt the knife and looked at the shield of bandages and tubes over Stu Tracy. No, he decided, the knife might be noisy.

"Why won't you say anything to me? Are you really a nurse?"

"Yes," he said. He pulled a pillow from under Stu Tracy's head. "Let me fluff this for you."

"That voice," Stu said.

"Yeah, it's me."

Stu stammered and tried to sit up. "That's not . . . not possible! You're *dead*!" He grabbed blindly for the alarm.

When he inhaled to scream, the pillow came down over his face.

Stu Tracy writhed weakly under him. He held the pillow in his fists and pressed down with his forearms, channeling all his weight into the task. One of Tracy's arms slapped pathetically against him.

Just three minutes and it's over.

He thought ahead, three minutes into the future. He would toss the pillow in the closet, smooth the sheets, and put everything back as he had found it. Stu Tracy was already so mangled . . . might take them hours to figure out he was dead.

He never heard the door open. He thought he imagined the sound of an electric wheelchair, and then he howled in shock and pain when something crashed into his legs.

thirty

Billy found his father on the hospital floor in a puddle of his own bad blood.

"Pop!"

He bulled past the overturned wheelchair and threw himself to the floor. He stopped suddenly as he was about to grab him; an old first-aid postulate screamed in his mind: Don't move an injured person! The old man grimaced and held a hand over a bloody gash on his chest, near the armpit on the left side. Billy pulled off his sweatshirt and pressed it to the wound.

His father turned sad blue eyes on him. "He was trying to smother Stu," he said, in a whispery voice, like a draft through an old mine shaft. "You just missed him. Not five minutes ago."

Stu Tracy lay limp in the bed; his breathing sounded ragged. "Billy," he wheezed. "It was *him*—Adam Rackers. He's alive!"

"Not exactly, Stu."

Billy ran to the door and screamed down the hall, "Help us! Help! Help!" His tone was not to be questioned; people in white came running.

Billy dashed back to his father and laid a hand on his chest. "Easy now, Pa," he said. He chuckled against the tension. "If you're going to get hurt, it might as well be in a hospital."

"He's got a knife, son. I tried to grab him but he cut me. I couldn't hang on. He's wearing a mask."

"I know who it is, Pop."

"Which one of your assumptions was wrong?"

"All of 'em. The truth was in my face the whole time. Breathe easy."

The old man closed his eyes and shivered against a tremor of pain. His face blurred in Billy's tears.

Billy informed him, "If you fucking die before we have our talk, I swear to Christ that Charlie Metts will lay you ass-up for the wake."

"He's gonna kill somebody," the old man said, nodding in agreement with himself. "I saw it in his eyes."

White shirts and voices flooded the room.

"Go stop him," the old man said. "Don't let him hurt nobody else." He pushed Billy gently away. "Do it."

Twenty yards from the hospital's exit, a hand clapped him over the shoulder.

"Hey, nice to see you! What's the rush?"

He whirled. There stood Martin Smothers, a dopey smile on his face. His beard was tied with two rubber bands into twin ponytails. He looked like the world's wimpiest Viking.

"Hiya, Martin," he said, and stuck out a hand to shake the lawyer's sweaty palm. His other hand discreetly patted the knife under his shirt, in his waistband. His knee throbbed where that son of a bitch had rammed him with the wheelchair. He was desperate to run, but reason overruled those instincts. After ditching the mask and stumbling down the stairs on a bad knee, he was *this close* to getting away. And then, of all the luck, to run into Martin Smothers in the hospital lobby? Like a cosmic practical joke.

Be calm. I can act my way out of anything.

He seized control of the conversation before Martin could question him. "I came here to visit a buddy who had back surgery," he said with a broad smile.

"How's he doing?" asked Martin. "If he needs visitors, maybe I'll drop in and say hello."

"He's not here, actually. I guess they sent him home a day early." He shrugged. "So I thought I made a trip for nothing, until I had the good fortune to run into you."

Martin stood back, put his hands on his hips, and beamed. "I can't remember the last time I've seen you so chipper."

"Well, circumstances haven't been the best recently—"

Martin looked past him and waved down the hall. "Hey, Billy!" he called. "Look who I ran into."

Great. There's Billy Povich. Was there a convention here I didn't know about?

He tightened the smile, adjusted the facade, turned to face him. "How are you, Billy?" he said. He extended a hand as Povich walked up.

"I'm great, Brock, just fuckin' dandy. And you?"

Without breaking stride, Povich cocked back a fist and drove it so hard into Brock's chin, he heard his jawbone crack before he hit the floor.

Barely conscious, he felt Povich's hands tighten around his throat. Povich screamed hoarse into his ear:

"Rackers didn't take *you* hostage, you took *him* hostage! *You* carjacked Stu Tracy, Brock! And if you've killed my father like you killed your own . . ."

He squeezed tighter.

"No, Billy, no!" Smothers shouted. Unseen voices screamed and hollered for the police.

The world grew dark around the edges, and then Brock blacked out.

thirty-one

The old man struggled with the details. "So nobody paid Adam Rackers to kill the judge?" he said.

Billy pulled the hospital blanket higher and tucked it under his father's chin. He checked the IV drip running into his father's arm. "Judge Harmony was dead before Rackers even broke into the house," he explained. "Brock had already killed him."

The old man let out a low whistle. "What could drive a boy to do that?"

"The police who interrogated him say Brock doesn't really have a good answer. He found out that his dad, who acted like Mr. Perfect, had a second family, and another son. Gil was leaving June and Brock, and moving to New York—that's a potent betrayal. Gil was taking most of his money with him too. You looking for a motive? Greed, or revenge?"

"Name your poison."

"Rackers was the key to the murder plan, but he didn't know it," Billy said. "Two weeks before the killing, Brock got the drop on Rackers when the little thief broke into the judge's town house in

Providence. Brock pulled a gun on him. But instead of calling the police, he hired Rackers to rob the Charlestown house and steal June's diamonds, supposedly as part of an insurance scam.

"We bought Brock's story from the beginning—that Adam Rackers broke in and then took him hostage. The first part was true—Rackers did break in, as they had planned—but then he fell right into Brock's trap. The rest of Brock's story was a lie. It was Brock who marched Rackers through the woods at gunpoint. Then Brock carjacked Stu Tracy, and forced Rackers to drive the car."

"Probably was going to kill them both later," the old man offered. His quivering hand pressed the oxygen tube under his nose. "So he could make it look like he had escaped from his kidnapper."

"Brock's plan went off the road, literally, when Adam Rackers panicked at the wheel and drove into a tree," Billy said. "But Rackers was killed, and Stu was incapacitated, so he couldn't contradict Brock's story. They never used their names in the car, so Stu didn't know which guy was which. That's why Brock faked a crying jag in Stu's hospital room before he had said a word. He couldn't have Stu recognizing his voice."

"And that's why Brock couldn't let Stu live long enough to get back his sight," the old man said. "Boy, he had everybody fooled."

"Brock was a great drama student—his school said he was the best actor they had ever seen. Could have had a career. And so could Martin Smothers, I think. Martin staked out the lobby while I went up to check on Stu Tracy. He was clever enough to hold Brock there until I came back."

The old man licked his lips and turned approving eyes on Billy. "Being an investigator suits you," he said.

"I nearly got buried alive."

"You haven't been to the dog track once since this case began."

Billy thought back. "You're right," he said, surprised that he hadn't noticed. He shrugged. "I haven't felt the impulse. . . . Maybe I finally caught the rabbit."

The old man smiled. When the grin faded, he asked, "How's Stu?"

"You saved his life. And risked your own to do it."

"Eh, not much to risk."

"In a few days, we'll get you transferred to a better room. Something with a view of the highway, so you can feel better about not being stuck in traffic. In two weeks, you'll be home. Bo's painting some get-well pictures for the walls."

The old man looked away. His blue eyes scanned the ceiling. "Might have been a better way to go, you think? Bleeding out after trying to help a friend." He turned suddenly to Billy and barked with surprising strength, "I'm jealous of you and Bo, and I'm sick of hiding it."

Billy fiddled again with the blanket. "I've seen the jealousy in your eyes. Though I don't know why. Bo loves his grandpa."

The old man frowned and grew impatient. "Not jealous that way. Are you really as *thick* as that?" He huffed and seemed about to cry. He confessed, "I'm jealous of *you*, Billy, because you have a son who adores you . . . and I don't."

For the rest of his life, Billy Povich would marvel at how suddenly forgiveness had filled him, that moment beside his father's hospital bed. The old man's cheating, his selfishness, the way he had dropped his family like a day-old newspaper—those wounds vanished that instant, as if they had never been, a weight he had dragged three decades, suddenly cut free.

He laid his ear on the old man's stomach and quietly cried. Trembling hands cradled his head.

"I finished your obituary last night," Billy said, finally. "My best work. I have a copy, if you'd like to read it."

The old man sputtered, "Don't have my glasses."

"I could read it to you, *Father*."

The old man grinned and playfully pushed his son away. "Not yet. I want to make it a little longer, before it goes in the paper."